CHAPTER ONE

T he bell rang for the end of school. Moments later, floods of students poured out of their classrooms, eager to escape and start their weekends.

Ella flowed with the rushing sea of people until she finally spilled outside, where the warm September sun greeted her like an old friend. She paused at the entrance, letting the stream of bodies bump and brush past her. Only after taking a deep, calming breath that filled her lungs did she bounce down the steps toward her waiting bicycle. As she bent down to unlock the security chain, a loud noise cut through the air.

"WOOOHOOO!"

Instantly, Ella knew it was her best friend. She turned toward the sound and saw Rhi racing down the steps, arms outstretched, with an enormous, toothy grin on her face.

"I'm so glad that day is over," Rhi said, tilting her face up toward the sun as if in worship.

"Right?" Ella agreed as she clipped on her helmet. "My

last class dragged on like time was moving in reverse. I'm not sure how Mr. Edwards manages to make maths so soul-shatteringly boring."

Rhi scrunched up her nose as if she had just smelled something rotten. "Well, I'll tell you how—and it's simple, really—*because maths is boring!*"

Both girls giggled as they climbed onto their bikes and rode off, neither having any inkling that their friendship had only a few hours left.

The hazy pollen that filled the air with sweet scents as they quietly peddled down the small roads of their sleepy village seemed to lift both Ella's and Rhi's spirits. Ella's long, wavy brown hair tumbled and tangled behind her as they twisted and turned through the lanes. She was never one to fuss with her hair, so it always had a slightly messy look. On the other hand, Rhi's dark brown hair flowed gracefully, like a silk wedding veil, glossy and smooth. Rhi came from a very different background than Ella and was always slightly more... put together.

Ahead of them, their destination briefly but proudly revealed itself before being blocked again by the towering hedges on either side of the road.

Their final turn took them down a bumpy dirt track, where tall trees loomed over the hedges. Thick, bushy branches, still full of summer leaves, stretched across the track as if they were trying to hold hands. This always made Ella smile—the thought of trees purposely touching.

The girls hadn't spoken since they left school, each choosing to ponder, wonder, and mentally drift as they cycled through the chirping, rustling countryside. But just

Twins of Fire

The World below Book 1

Katie Butterworth

Twins Of Fire

By Katie Butterworth

Cover Design: Katarina @nskvsky

Printed in United Kingdom

First Edition: 2024

For Bertie and Pixie

xx

over two-thirds of the way through their journey, Ella broke the comfortable silence. "Are you coming to mine for dinner?"

Rhi spent as much time as she could at Ella's house. She didn't get along with her own parents, and most of the time, they didn't even notice she wasn't home. Without any siblings, Rhi had grown as close to Ella's family as if they were her own. In fact, Rhi even kept a toothbrush and pyjamas at Ella's house.

When they reached the field, they hid their bikes behind the farm hedge and set off through the tall rows of corn toward the tree standing regally at the centre of the crop, as if it were guarding the entire surrounding farmland. The massive Tulip tree had been a constant in their friendship, almost like a third companion. They always made sure to sit beneath—or sometimes climb into—this giant of nature at least once a week, though neither girl ever thought to question why.

"I wish I could, but Mum wants to have a *chat* with me," Rhi said, looking uneasy as she raised an eyebrow in suspicion. "I mean, what does she even want to chat about? In fact, I'm not sure she's ever wanted to *chat* with me before!"

Ella didn't know how to respond. As far as she knew, Rhi's mum, Mrs. Byrne, wasn't the most maternal woman and sometimes seemed to even dislike her daughter.

"Maybe she wants to talk about your birthday?" Ella suggested encouragingly.

"I doubt it. She's probably forgotten, like most years."

Ella thought for a moment as her lungs filled with the steadily cooling air. Then, with a panicked tone that raced out of her mouth, she blurted, "You don't think it's because you're moving, do you?"

"No way!" Rhi laughed, but Ella noticed that the laughter was tinged with a very specific kind of sadness—the kind that only comes from truth.

"You actually think my parents would talk to me about something that big?

Ha – no!"

Rhi was being blasé about her relationship with her parents again, but Ella saw through it, as usual. She could feel the hurt Rhi felt from the persistent lack of parental love.

When the girls were younger, Rhi would often talk about wanting a brother or sister, someone else in the house to help warm the coldness, someone she could love and be loved by. She had always felt a little jealous that Ella had Kal, her twin brother. But as Rhi grew older, she realised that Ella was the only sister she'd ever have or need, in every way but blood.

After five minutes of walking, the girls reached their tree and pulled themselves up onto its lowest branch, which was wide and long enough for them both to sit comfortably. There, they sat, swinging their legs like they were ten years old again.

Ella wanted to change the subject and move on to more exciting topics—specifically, what they were going to do for Rhi's sixteenth birthday the next day. But before she could, Rhi said thoughtfully, "Do you remember when you first brought me here?"

Ella smiled at the nostalgic memory as Rhi gazed out

over the field in front of them. "It was after my second day at school, in our last year of primary."

"Yeah, I remember," Ella replied, "I was so excited to have a friend!" She suddenly felt embarrassed and laughed. "It sounds so sad when I say it like that!" Ella blushed and put her head in her hands.

Rhi grabbed Ella's arm with a force that could have been mistaken for anger, unbalancing them both. As their arms spun in erratic circles to avoid falling, they exchanged matching expressions of mock fear. Finally, they half fell, half jumped down from the branch, collapsing in a fit of laughter into each other's arms. Once they composed themselves, Rhi took Ella's arm again, this time more gently but still with intent.

"Ella, it wasn't sad that you were excited to have a friend..."

Ella opened her mouth to talk but Rhi carried on.

"It was hard for me, starting a new school halfway through the last year, and having you there, willing to be my friend, meant more to me than you'll ever know."

Ella hugged Rhi, feeling more than ever that she had never felt so close to anyone except her twin brother, Kal—though he also annoyed her far more. "Alright, 'Miss Sentimental,' let's think of some wildly ambitious birthday plans."

Rhi smiled sheepishly and perked up. "To be honest, El, I'd be happy with bowling and your mum's homemade '4 Cheese & Extra Chilli Oil Pizza,'" she said, announcing the pizza's name as if she were voicing an advertisement.

Ella smiled. She had expected this response, knowing

that Rhi was never one for making a big fuss, always preferring simple creature comforts over excess and drama. "Bowling and pizza it is then."

The air had cooled even more, and where the warm September sun had been moments earlier, there was now a black, sprawling, and low-hanging cloud that seemed ready to envelop them.

"I'd better get going before Mum gets annoyed that I'm late for our *CHAT*!" Rhi said, rolling her eyes and emphasising "chat".

"Yeah, I don't fancy getting caught in that rain either," Ella said, nodding toward the approaching cloud, which was bulldozing across the sky as it started to empty itself over the land below.

The girls raced back through the field toward their bikes, heading directly into the path of the dark cloud. The first wisps of rain gently brushed their faces as they ran, but by the time they reached the hedge, the full force of the downpour was upon them.

The girls hugged goodbye, and as Ella pulled away, she noticed something strange in Rhi's eyes. Instead of their usual dark brown eyes, that could almost be mistaken as black, she was certain there was a hint of green. Before Ella could say anything, the moment vanished as Rhi turned and climbed onto her bike.

The rain became so heavy that Ella had to shout to be heard.

"CALL ME LATER IF YOU WANT TO CHAT, AND GOOD LUCK WITH YOUR MUM!"

"THANKS, WILL DO!" Rhi shouted back, though Ella only understood by reading her lips.

Ella watched as her best friend cycled away. She wasn't sure why she was just standing there, watching her, but it felt necessary for some reason. She studied Rhi's back, her drenched hair, and her peddling legs, noticing they looked strangely unfamiliar, as if she were seeing them for the first time.

Ella snapped out of her reverie when a trickle of rain ran down her spine, making her shiver with sudden cold.

On the ride home, Ella kept thinking about the colour of Rhi's eyes. It must have been the twilight or perhaps the storm reflecting, she thought. She peddled as fast as she could until she reached the small turn onto the lane where she lived, taking the corner without braking, almost skidding on the mud draining from the neighbouring fields. She could see her house and its welcoming lights, which seemed to grow brighter as she got closer.

Their windmill stood tall and proud behind the house, intermittently cutting off the light from the rising moon as it ignored the rain and went about its endless business of gently turning. The earthy smell from the wood burner chimney filled Ella's lungs, and the familiar soft patter of rain on the thatched roof welcomed her as she hurriedly jumped off her bike, letting it fall to the ground.

Ella raced through the low front door to escape the wet and cold, though by that point, she couldn't have gotten any wetter if she'd jumped fully clothed into a river.

The soothing warmth and inviting smells hit her like a

soft cloud the moment she stumbled through the doorway instantly relaxed her.

"Oh, Ella, look at you!" her mum, Diana, chuckled. Glancing behind her sodden daughter, she asked, "No Rhi tonight then?"

"No, not tonight. Her mum wants to *chat* to her. It's kind of weird, honestly, and Rhi's not really looking forward to it. But she'll be here tomorrow." Ella hopped from one rug to the next, trying not to drip water all over the flagstone floor as she made her way to her bedroom, which branched off from the back of the kitchen.

"Some conversations have to be had, whether we like them or not," Diana muttered, her voice so low it was almost drowned out by the sound of the boiling pot.

"WHAT DOES THAT MEAN?" Ella shouted from her room.

Diana winced, caught off guard. "Uh," she hesitated, stirring the pot with a little more force than necessary, "I just mean, I'm sure there's a good reason for it."

Ella didn't answer, shutting her bedroom door as she started changing into dry clothes.

Diana let out a quiet sigh of relief, glad she'd gotten away with her slip of the tongue.

Ella began drying her hair as she sat at her desk, her eyes drifting to the photos pinned around her room of her and Rhi over the years. Smiling at the funny memories staring back at her, she suddenly felt a deep ache inside, a sadness that started in the pit of her stomach and slowly spread through every cell. Her mum's voice interrupted her thoughts, calling her to dinner.

As she walked into the kitchen, the feelings of sadness faded into the background. Over the years, her mum had created such a haven of warmth and love in their home, especially in the kitchen, that Ella found it almost impossible to stay sad or upset while there.

Diana, a devoted vet with a passion for herbalism, had transformed the kitchen into a sanctuary of both science and nature. The air was often full of the calming scent of lavender and chamomile, with bundles hanging in rows above the large, cast-iron stove.

At the heart of the room stood a large, round wooden dining table, that was forever adorned with numerous bowls overflowing with both local and exotic fruits and a vase of wildflowers always sat proudly in the centre.

The twins' bedrooms branched off the kitchen's back wall, opposite the front door. Between their doors sat a massive bookcase, overflowing with science papers, veterinary volumes with cracked spines, thick herbalism encyclopaedias, and history books that explored cultures and countries far and wide.

Above the sink was a long shelf lined with glass jars of various sizes, each filled with different herbs, spices, and teas. Diana regularly used them to make tinctures for her family and friends, whether they were dealing with physical ailments or emotional struggles. Ella and her brother Kal often teased their mum, calling her a "hocus-pocus witch doctor," but they couldn't deny that they were almost never sick.

As Ella and her mum sat at the table, waiting for Kal and Ella's dad to arrive, Diana looked at her daughter questioningly, her voice soft and comforting, as if it could carry Ella to a place where no pain could reach.

"Is everything okay, darling?"

Ella's voice broke slightly as she began to speak.

"I'm okay, I think. I'm just feeling a little off, but I'm not sure why."

Before Diana could respond, Kal came bounding out of his bedroom, his long legs carrying him into the kitchen in half the time it took Ella. He brushed aside his floppy blond hair, which was always falling into his eyes, and greeted his mom with playful flattery.

"Mother, you've outdone yourself yet again! This smells even better than last night's dinner."

Ella smiled at her brother's chivalrous gesture toward their mum. Kal sat down next to her as Diana waved him off with a laugh.

"Mum, is Dad home for dinner?" he asked. "I'm struggling with designs for my school project."

Kal was—quite unashamedly—a geek, but the kind who managed to transcend social groups at school to the point where almost everyone liked him. One of the main reasons for this was his constant upbeat attitude. Nothing ever seemed to dampen his excitement for a new activity or project. No failure left him disappointed, and he tackled everything with contagious enthusiasm. He was part of the chess club, science club, and computer club, excelling in all of them—and everyone was genuinely happy for him. No one resented his successes because he never boasted or made others feel lesser.

Despite all of this, and perhaps because of it, Ella sometimes felt a twinge of jealousy. While she was mostly happy for her brother, she couldn't help but feel envious of his natural abilities—qualities that seemed to have completely skipped over her DNA. She tended to feel socially awkward and struggled academically.

Diana ladled steaming soup into Ella and Kal's bowls as the aroma of freshly baked bread teased their senses. The front door creaked open, and their dad, Rowan, bustled in, wet and cold from the rain, despite only walking the 30 feet from the car to the house.

"Ahh, it's so good to be home. I've had the worst day, but this…" He gestured to his family. "…has made it the best day."

Ella half-smiled, then rolled her eyes in mild annoyance. "Maybe you should find a new job. You might actually enjoy going to work then."

Ella had never understood why her dad worked for GEI, as it went against everything that he and her mum believed in.

GEI, or Global Energy Incorporated, was a massive corporation that designed machinery capable of drilling the largest fracking holes to extract the maximum amount of natural gas for their customers. They also owned most of the world's uranium mines and built colossal nuclear power stations, producing more plutonium than ever before—though this wasn't common knowledge. Ella's dad spoke openly with his family about his work, because—so he said —he wanted his children to know the truth about the world, the people who controlled it, and the importance of protecting it.

Ella frequently had heated conversations with her dad, questioning how he could work for a company that seemed to have no interest in preserving the health of the planet, only in extracting as much as possible from it.

Another reason for Ella's strong dislike of GEI was that Rhi's dad was the CEO. From what she had heard from both her dad and Rhi, he wasn't exactly a kind-hearted man. He seemed disconnected from the outside world—'grey on the outside, black on the inside,' as Rowan had once described him.

But that night, Ella decided not to pick a fight with her dad, knowing it never ended well, and she was already feeling a bit emotional.

Kal spoke up almost as soon as his dad sat down.

"Dad, could you help me with my design project after dinner? I'm having some trouble finding the right equations."

Kal had always gotten along a little better with their dad, as they were so alike—both loveable and geeky in equal measure.

Rowan's eyes lit up as he tucked into his bowl of steaming soup. He always enjoyed helping the twins with their homework and projects. Diana often joked that Rowan loved school so much, he'd gladly go back if he could.

"Of course, let's finish up here, and we'll dive right in."

Diana quickly interjected, "Before you boys get lost in homework and we don't see you for the rest of the evening —it's Rhi's birthday tomorrow. Does anyone have any thoughts on what we should do?"

Ella glanced at her mum with gratitude. Diana really did treat Rhi like a daughter.

"Sorry, Mum, I forgot to tell you. Rhi just wants to go bowling and then come back here for homemade pizza. Is that okay?"

"Oh, that sounds lovely—of course! That's..." Diana began, but she was abruptly cut off.

"DIANA!" Rowan suddenly snapped, startling everyone. They all turned to look at him, wide-eyed and shocked. He stood up, his face inexplicably pale, and some of his soup had spilled across the table.

"Dad, are you okay?" Kal stood up too and touched his dad's shoulder.

"Yes, yes, I'm fine. I just... uh... Sorry, I um... I forgot we have something on tomorrow."

Diana's eyes searched Rowan's face for clues to his sudden outburst, but she found none.

Ella's already fragile mood quickly darkened. With a deepening frown and stinging eyes, she ran to her bedroom and slammed the door.

Kal gritted his teeth, smiling sarcastically. "Good luck with that one. You guys can be so weird sometimes."

Ella threw herself onto her bed, crying, though she didn't quite know why. Something just didn't feel right—that's all she knew.

Suddenly, she grabbed her phone and dialled Rhi, but it went straight to voicemail without ringing.

"Hey, Rhi, just wanted to chat and see how things went with your mum. My parents have been super weird tonight too; it must be a full moon or something." Ella gave an almost convincing laugh, but sarcasm was hard to pull off when she was holding back tears. She ended with a quick "Call me back," before hanging up.

Ella sat up, glancing into the long mirror opposite her bed, staring at her own worried expression. She tried to shake off the uneasy feeling and immediately called Rhi again, convinced that if she could just talk to her, she'd feel better. But again, Rhi didn't answer.

In frustration, Ella decided to ring the landline—something Rhi had always told her not to do, embarrassed by how rude her parents could be.

"Hello, Mrs. Byrne speaking," her voice was slow and devoid of any warmth, each word unnecessarily over-pronounced.

"Oh, hello, Mrs. Byrne, it's Ella—Rhi's... ah, Rhiannon's friend. I was wondering if she was available to speak, please?" Ella tried to sound as polite as possible.

"I'm afraid Rhiannon can't come to the phone. Goodbye."

The line went dead before Ella could respond, leaving her even more confused. She knew Rhi's parents didn't like her, even though they'd never actually met her in the six years she and Rhi had been best friends, but this level of rudeness felt unnecessary.

Ella, exhausted by her swirling emotions, decided to go to bed and sleep off whatever bad mood had taken hold of her. Although her mind buzzed with thoughts and worries, sleep eventually claimed her.

The next morning, Ella woke feeling better—maybe even a little excited about Rhi's birthday. As she lazily stretched in her bed, her phone rang. She glanced down and saw the grinning face of her best friend, Rhi, smiling back at her from the screen.

Breathing a huge sigh of relief, Ella picked up her phone. "Morning, birthday girl! Hey, what was up last night? Did you get my message? My parents were acting so weird."

Ella paused, but there was no reply.

"I even called your landline; sorry if you got in trouble. Your mum didn't seem too happy to hear my voice."

This time, the silence stretched longer. Ella quickly checked her phone to make sure she hadn't accidentally hung up or muted the call, but everything was fine.

"Ella, I won't be able to see you today." Rhi's voice was flat, almost unrecognisable. Was there a tinge of sadness? "I'm actually busy all weekend. Bye."

And just like with the call to Rhi's mum, the line went dead before Ella could say anything.

For a moment, there was nothing—no questions, no hurt —just disbelief. Then a wave of prickling heat surged through her, burning and numbing her body. It hit her stomach, making Ella feel like she might vomit.

She didn't hear the knock on the door or notice that Kal had come in and was now standing in front of her.

"Sooooo, who's ready to get beaten in bowling toda—" Kal stopped mid-sentence as he saw the look on his sister's face and the silent tears rolling down her flushed cheeks. "El, what's happened?"

Ella didn't speak at first, then softly replied, "Honestly... I don't really know." She stared blankly into space. "Rhi just called to say she couldn't see me today or the rest of the weekend, then hung up with no explanation."

"That's a bit weird," Kal said, scrunching up his nose.

That simple comment pushed Ella over the edge. "A *bit* weird?" she snapped. "It's like she's not even herself! She would never do this! Something must've happened."

Ella picked up her phone and tried calling Rhi again. It rang and rang, but this time there wasn't even an option to leave a message.

"Okay, I'm calling her parents house," Ella said, her expression wild, nostrils flaring.

Shocked by his sister's reaction, Kal sat next to her on the bed. "Ella, calm down or you'll end up saying something you'll regret."

But Ella had already dialled the number. Kal could hear the ringtone stop as a voice came through on the other end.

"Hello, Mrs. Byr—"

Ella didn't let her finish. Her tone came across as aggressive and desperate.

"Where is Rhi? What have you done to her?"

"Rhiannon doesn't want to speak to you. Please leave her be." Once again, the line went dead, leaving Ella more confused than before.

Kal rolled his eyes. "You handled that really well—interrupting and shouting at your best friend's mum," he said sarcastically. The half-grin that had started to form on his face quickly vanished.

Ella looked up at Kal.

"I don't get it. Why is this happening? It makes no sense."

"Are you sure nothing's happened? Maybe there's a guy you both like, or..." Kal didn't need her to speak—he could tell from her expression that it was a silly question.

Wiping her running nose on her sleeve, Ella stood up and tried to smile at her brother.

"Could you leave me alone for a bit, Kal? And please don't say anything to Mum. I just need..."

Kal was already turning toward the door. "Sure." He turned back and ruffled her hair on his way out, trying to lighten the moment. He got a half-hearted, forced smile in return.

"Thank you," was all she could muster in reply.

As Kal left his sister's room, he found their mum standing in the middle of the kitchen, looking smaller than usual in the space.

"Is everything okay in there?" Diana mouthed worriedly.

Kal knew from the look on her face that she suspected everything was *not* okay. He was a terrible liar, and he knew it.

"Ella's had some bad news... ruddy strange too, if you ask me."

Diana stood still, staring at her daughter's door, her eyes prickling with tears and her breathing heavy. This was the beginning of what she had been dreading for the last sixteen years, and she felt utterly unprepared.

CHAPTER TWO

Diana sat restlessly in front of the fire, feeding logs into the flames since hearing about Rhi's behaviour an hour ago. She stared blankly as the fire devoured the wood, flaring up bright and fierce before shrinking back down, needing more fuel. She already knew why Rhi had acted the way she did—not because anyone had told her, but because Rhi had just turned sixteen, meaning she now knew the truth about who she was. Ella and Kal still had a week before their birthday, and with it, the revelation of the truth about themselves.

She glanced at Rowan- who was nestled in his usual spot on the sofa, calmly reading his book- to see if he seemed at all affected by the tense, claustrophobic energy that had been swirling through the house since dinner.

"I feel awful about how hurt Ella is. Surely telling the kids a week early won't make a difference?" she asked, turning to him, leaning forward, and holding his hand. She looked into his eyes, willing the answer to be different to the one she knew it would be.

"Di, you know we can't. It's against The Council's laws. We don't want to do anything that will draw attention to them. It's going to be hard enough that they're twins. We can't risk messing this up and leaving them vulnerable when their Shift happens, because as soon as it does, the Byrnes will find out who we are, and the kids will no longer be safe."

Diana's shoulders dropped in disappointment. She closed her eyes and took a deep breath, trying to compose herself. "I know you're right. It just feels so unfair."

Rowan sighed, gently tucking her stray grey hairs behind her ears. Touching his forehead to hers, he whispered so softly it could have been mistaken for a breath, "We have to trust they're strong enough to handle it, and be grateful they have each other."

Sunday evening arrived after an eerily quiet weekend. Kal knocked on Ella's bedroom door and poked his head around the corner, finding his sister standing at the window, gazing out over the dark green fields that stretched out behind their house.

"How are you feeling about going to school tomorrow?" Kal asked, trying to sound relaxed, though he was anything but.

"Yeah, okay. She'll have to talk to me there. Surely, she can't keep hiding, and hopefully, we can get this all sorted."

Kal attempted to stay positive. "Let's hope so, because I'm not sure I can handle this mood of yours much longer." He winked to make sure Ella knew he was joking.

"Thanks!" Ella responded sarcastically, though she appreciated her brother not pandering to her like their mum had.

The next morning, Kal waited for Ella so they could walk to school together. Usually, he would meet up with his best friends, Alex and Ben, to discuss the pros and cons of their ever-evolving concept designs from the night before.

After a mostly silent walk, they arrived at the school entrance. Standing in front of the large double doors, they let the steady stream of students flow past. Ella nervously glanced around, half-expecting everyone to be staring at her or whispering rumours. Over the next ten minutes, the crowd of students swelled, then gradually thinned as the latecomers jogged past the twins on their way to class.

Ella's worry deepened. "Kal, I can't see Rhi, and the bell's about to ring any minute."

Kal scanned the remaining students, then placed a reassuring hand on Ella's shoulder. He looked her in the eyes and said, "Meet me by the water fountain at the main doors after first period and let me know how it's going."

"I'm sure it'll be fine." Kal nodded, as if the gesture alone could make it true, before turning and jogging through the entrance doors to his first class.

Ella was now alone in front of the school, where moments ago students rushed in to avoid being late. Now, they were all seated at their desks, retrieving books from their bags, while she stood at the entrance, feeling oddly out of place. Taking a deep breath, she pushed the doors open and walked down the corridor toward her History classroom. Her footsteps echoed in the empty hall, amplifying her growing anxiety.

As she pulled open the heavy door, time seemed to slow down. She stepped into the room, her heart pounding in her chest, and immediately looked toward the window where she and Rhi always sat. But the seat was empty.

Her stomach clenched as she moved through the classroom, only to realise Rhi was there—sitting at a different desk next to people she didn't even like. Ella's heart sank.

She sat down at her usual spot, unpacking her books, trying to push down the rising panic. Her throat tightened, but she fought back the tears that threatened to spill. Throughout the lesson, Rhi didn't look her way once. It was as if Ella didn't exist.

When the bell finally rang, Ella bolted out of her seat and raced for the door, she needed to find Kal. Without looking back, she fled the classroom, seeking the comfort of her brother.

As Ella approached the water fountain, she saw her brother scanning the crowd for her. When he spotted her, he could immediately tell things hadn't gone as they'd hoped, but he tried to stay optimistic.

"Hey, so how'd it go?"

Ella, still holding back tears, not wanting anyone to see her cry, replied, "It went about as bad as it could."

Kal hoped Ella was being overly sensitive and that he could find a way to spin the situation positively. "It can't have been that bad. What did she say to you?"

"That's just it. She didn't say anything to me. She didn't

even look at me. She sat on the other side of the class, nowhere near our usual seats."

Kal looked at her, realising the situation was worse than he'd thought. Without saying a word, he pulled Ella in for a hug. Kissing her on the top of the head, he whispered, "We'll sort this out, sis, I promise."

Ella pulled away, wiping the tears that had escaped despite her best efforts. She straightened up, trying to regain her composure, but the strength didn't last long. Her eyes welled up again. "I think I'm going to go home. I can't concentrate here. Will you cover for me?"

"Of course I will. Call me if you need anything."

Kal watched as his sister walked away, her posture heavy with what seemed like a broken heart.

Kal muttered to himself once his sister was far enough away, "Right, Rhi, I think we need to have a little talk!" Then the bell rang, and he rushed off to sports class.

Kal knocked on the sports office door. It always felt strange being so formal with his uncle, who had been teaching at the school since the twins started.

"Kalan, what can I do for you?"

Their uncle, Warren, had always been especially strict with them making them work twice as hard as everyone else. While he didn't show much affection toward Kal and Ella, he was fiercely protective of them.

"Just letting you know, Ella went home sick, so she won't be in class today."

There was a pause, longer than Kal expected, as his uncle's eyes darted about, as if a hundred thoughts had rushed through his mind. Then Warren snapped out of it, his expression returning to the vague ambivalence of a schoolteacher.

"I hope she's okay. I'll call around after school to check on her. Thanks for letting me know. Now go get yourself ready for hockey," he said, waving Kal off like any other student before returning to his paperwork.

Ella had taken her time walking home, enjoying the scent of freshly cut grass and the warmth of the late summer sun. When she finally arrived, she quietly crept through the front door and tiptoed through the kitchen toward her bedroom, hoping to avoid a conversation with her mum about skipping school. Just as she reached her bedroom door, her mum appeared around the corner holding a basket of washing, they both stopped abruptly. " Oh, Ella! You scared me. Are you okay, darling? What are you doing home?" Diana asked, her voice full of concern. Ella turned to face her, her eyes red, puffy, and filling with tears once again.

"Mum, I don't know what to do. Rhi won't even look at me!"

Diana immediately dropped the basket and pulled Ella into her arms, holding her tightly and letting her emotions flow freely. For the rest of the day, they quietly gardened together, sharing each other's company in silence. Very few words were exchanged, but in that peaceful quiet, Ella felt deeply loved and cherished.

Back at school, Kal spent every break between lessons hunting for Rhi, determined to talk to her before the day ended.

"Kal, come on, why are you so desperate to find Rhi

anyway?" asked Alex, one of Kal's best friends and a fellow geek.

The bell rang for their next class. Alex glanced nervously at Kal, not wanting to be late. "We're going to be late for physics if we don't get going." He hefted his heavy, book-filled bag onto his back. "I don't want to miss the start, so I'll meet you there, okay?"

"Yeah, you go ahead. I just want to check one more place. I won't be long."

On his way over to the old english block which was on the other side of the school, Kal realised he didn't actually know what he would say to Rhi if he found her; he just knew he had to say something. As he mulled over different ways to start the conversation, he almost didn't notice Rhi emerging from the toilet block until they nearly bumped into each other.

They both froze, stunned, neither of them saying a word at first. Kal looked directly into her eyes and felt something was different about her, though he couldn't quite figure out what.

"Rhi," he said, though it came out more submissively than he'd intended, "I've been wanting to chat with you."

"Kal, I can't be talking to you. Please, I need to get to class," Rhi responded, her tone clipped and hurried.

Kal was taken aback by her choice of words, and for a moment, he was too confused to react. Rhi started walking away, but Kal quickly gathered himself, jogging to catch up. He turned to face her, walking backward as he tried to slow her down. "But I don't understand! You can't just drop Ella like that. She's devastated!" He thought he saw a flicker of remorse cross her face, but it was quickly replaced by a steely determination he'd never seen in her before.

"Look, Kal," she said coldly, "it was fun being friends with Ella for a while, but that time is over. I don't need to spend time with her or your family anymore, so please, just leave me alone."

Kal's frown deepened until his forehead ached. Her words angered him so much that he blurted out, "I have no idea who you are anymore. And Ella's better off without a poison like you in her life."

Rhi stopped dead in her tracks, her eyes flashing with an intensity that made Kal's stomach twist with unease.

"Exactly—you have absolutely no idea who I am!" she spat, before turning and running off to class, leaving Kal standing there in shocked silence.

Annoyed at himself for mishandling what could have been his one chance to resolve his sister's troubles, he muttered to himself, "Great job, Kal. You really showed her."

After school, Kal decided to take the long way home, walking through the fields to give himself time to think. He played over the conversation in his head, wrestling with whether he should tell Ella the truth about what Rhi had said, in the end he decided it would hurt her too much.

As soon as he walked through the front door, Ella rushed up to him. "Did you see Rhi? Did you talk to her?"

In the kitchen, Diana was peeling carrots feverishly at the table, as she waited to hear Kal's response.

"Um, yeah," Kal started, hesitating. "I saw her, but I didn't get the chance to talk to her. She saw me, then changed direction and walked off. The bell rang for class after that. Sorry, sis."

Ella's face fell, though she didn't seem surprised by Rhi's reaction. Shoulders slumped, she sank into a chair at the kitchen table, resting her chin in her hands, looking completely deflated.

Kal sat down beside her, unsure of what to say. He was about to reach out when he remembered something. "Mum, Uncle Warren said he'd come by later to check on Ella. I told him she wasn't feeling well."

Diana, still busy preparing the vegetables for dinner, nodded. "Yes, he already called. He said he'll come after dinner. Thanks, darling." She finished chopping, then moved to the stove, setting a kettle on for tea. The sound of the water boiling was the only noise that filled the silence between them.

"I've got quite a bit of homework to do, so I'm going to get on with that," Kal said, hating the lie as it left his mouth. He headed to his room, intending to keep as much distance from his sister as possible.

Ella, feeling emotionally drained, also retreated to her room, telling her mum she didn't want dinner and just wanted to be alone. Diana watched as her daughter quietly closed the door, then turned back to stir the vegetables in the pan, her movements slow and mournful.

From her room, Ella could hear the normal sounds of dinnertime: Kal skidding across the floor, followed by their mum's playful scolding. It annoyed her that life seemed to carry on as usual for them while she was trapped in the middle of a storm of bad emotions. Eventually, the noises quieted as Kal returned to his room and shut the door, allowing Ella to slip back into her sadness without fear of interruption.

A few minutes later, she heard hushed voices coming from the kitchen. She knew it wasn't Kal—his door was near hers, and it always scraped loudly across the rug when opened, something that never failed to annoy her. Her dad hadn't come home yet either, as he was usually quite loud about his return from work.

Curiosity finally got the better of her. She went to her door and cracked it open just enough to hear what was being said.

"Di, you are not to tell Ella before it's time. It's forbidden, and you know this!"

Ella recognised her uncle's voice, sounding uncharacteristically stern towards her mum. Words like "forbidden" didn't seem like something he'd ever say to her. She was about to step out and confront them, but decided to wait a moment longer, hoping to learn more from their semi-secret conversation.

Ella heard her mum pleading, something she had never heard before.

"Please, Warren, I can't bear seeing her like this. It's so unfair, especially when there's something we can do to help."

"You think Ella knowing the truth is going to help?"

Warren sounded genuinely shocked. "When Ella and Kal find out who they are, it isn't going to make things better. There'll be so many questions, and Ella will eventually realise this was always going to happen."

Ella couldn't listen anymore; she felt sick inside. What were her mum and uncle talking about? As her door swung open, the conversation quickly shifted.

"...and I had to push that damned car all the way back to —" Warren began in his best storytelling voice, pretending not to notice Ella entering the room. He threw his arms wide when he saw her. "Ella, my love, how are you feeling?" he asked, walking over to pat her shoulder. He had never been an affectionate man, and under the current circumstances, the gesture felt even more awkward than usual.

"Fine, thanks," Ella replied frowning, her tone colder than she had intended. She picked up a glass and filled it with water from the tap, the silence hanging thick between them. None of them knew how to break the tension. Once she was done, she glanced pointedly at her mum and uncle before turning and heading back to her room.

Diana winced. "She knows something isn't right. She's not stupid."

"I know she's not," Warren replied, his voice firm and final. "But you have to hold out just a few more days." His tone left no room for argument, and Diana didn't push the matter further.

The next day, Ella returned to school but kept mostly to herself. She went through the motions in class, doing what was required, and rushed home as soon as the bell rang. Over the following days, she occasionally saw Rhi in school and in the classes they shared, but Rhi always sat far away, as though they had never spoken before—let alone been best friends.

At first, Ella thought she could catch glimpses of guilt and sadness in Rhi's expression, but after a few days, even those seemed to disappear. By Thursday lunchtime, Ella had grown tired of the coldness from Rhi and met up with Kal by the benches near the Astroturf.

"Do you feel like going home early?" she asked, desperate for the long weekend to begin. The next day was their 16th birthday, and their parents were taking the day off work and keeping them home from school—a first for their family. Ella felt she had been sulking long enough and needed some fun back in her life.

"Yeah, why not?" Kal replied, sensing his sister needed a break. He didn't like the idea of skipping school, as he genuinely enjoyed his classes, but Ella's mood clearly called for some time together. "Let me find Alex and Ben so they can take notes and grab anything I need for homework. Meet you by the bikes in ten." Kal jogged off toward his next class to track down his best friends.

Ten minutes later, Kal was bounding down the school steps, a nervous grin on his face. "Come on quick!" he called out, gesturing toward the school gates, hoping no one would see them. "Let's get home and eat as many biscuits as we can before Mum gets back." He knew how much Ella loved biscuits and hoped it would lift her spirits, at least temporarily.

On the ride home, Kal asked with a mischievous tone, "What do you think Mum and Dad got us for our birthday?"

Ella looked up at the bright blue sky, smiling slightly at the meaningless chitchat. It was exactly what she needed.

"Hmm, I have no clue this year. Normally, Mum's fishing for ideas, but she hasn't been at all this time."

Kal's eyes lit up with excitement, suddenly looking like a little kid at Christmas. "Maybe they're throwing us a massive, surprise fancy-dress party!" He could barely contain his excitement at the thought.

"I wouldn't get your hopes up," Ella said glumly. "Besides, it wouldn't be fair since I have literally no friends right now, and you're friends with everyone in school."

Kal rolled his eyes at her. "Well, that's a great way to look on the bright side of things."

"Kal..." Ella's tone changed, causing Kal to slow down and glance over at her.

"Have you noticed anything strange going on with Mum and Uncle Warren lately?"

"No... what kind of strange are you talking about?" Kal asked, curious but a little wary. Ella hesitated, not wanting to mention the conversation she'd overheard. She knew he'd think she was being paranoid.

"Come on, El, you can't say something like that and then leave me hanging."

"I don't know," Ella muttered. "I've just had a funny feeling about them lately."

Kal rolled his eyes again and, with a slight wince, said, "Well, you haven't exactly been the easiest person to live with these past two weeks."

Ella knew he was right and felt a pang of guilt for what her family had been dealing with because of her mood. The rest of the ride home was quiet. Ella's mind was consumed by what she'd overheard between her mum and uncle, while Kal was thinking about whether he'd get in trouble for skipping class and hoping Ben would take enough notes for him.

Once they got home, Ella immediately tried to make amends. "Fancy watching a film?" she asked, though she knew she didn't need to. Movies were how they bonded. They loved watching all kinds of films, and after, they'd sit with cups of tea, dissecting the story, characters, plot holes —sometimes even the costumes and sets. It wasn't unusual for them to spend hours analysing, discussing, and arguing over the film.

Diana drove her old car down the winding road toward home, her hands instinctively flicking the indicator left as she turned into the driveway. The brakes gave a gentle squeal as she pulled up in front of the house. She had taken a half-day from work to prepare for the twins' birthday the next day. As she climbed out of the car, she noticed Kal and Ella's bikes propped up against the wall. Her first reaction was concern—it wasn't like Kal to skip school without a reason.

Quickly gathering her bag and coat, she rushed inside. "Kal! Ella!" she called out, dumping her things onto the kitchen table. There was no answer.

"Kal, are you home? Ella! Ella!"

She heard laughter from the TV room at the back of the house and hurried down the low ceilinged hallway. Relief washed over her when she found them both sprawled on the couch, mouths full of food, eyes glued to the screen, completely absorbed in whatever they were watching.

Diana opened her mouth to say something, but paused. She could see how relaxed they both were, enjoying their time together. Perhaps they needed this moment of peace before the whirlwind of tomorrow—the day their lives would change forever. With a soft sigh, she stepped back quietly, deciding to leave them be.

CHAPTER THREE

Ella pressed pause on the TV remote and announced, "We're out of popcorn," before leaving the lounge. When she walked into the kitchen, she nearly dropped the bowl she was carrying and half-shouted, half-asked, "Mum!?" She stopped dead, trying desperately not to look guilty as she blurted, "Kal and I... we had, um, we're not... at... school." She fumbled for an excuse but couldn't think of one. To her surprise, her mum didn't seem angry at all. If anything, she seemed pleased.

"Well, it *is* your birthday weekend—it's a good idea to make it an extra long one. I'm making your birthday cake now. What flavour would you like?"

Ella stood there, stunned, unsure of what to say. She ended up saying nothing at all.

Her mum started getting cake ingredients out from the cupboards. Over her shoulder, she asked again, "So, what do you fancy?"

"Um, I guess chocolate."

Ella and Kal weren't the kind of kids to skip school. Their parents had always emphasised the importance of discipline and getting a good education. They'd drilled into them the idea that knowledge and hard work were the foundation for building the life you want—even if that life was a simple one. So why was her mum being so casual about them ditching school to watch movies?

Diana became absorbed in her baking, and Ella quietly turned to head back to the TV room. Something didn't feel right.

"Kal!" she whispered loudly. "Mum's here!"

Kal shot up from his lazy sprawl on the sofa.

"What? When? I didn't even hear her come in," he said, his face quickly filling with panic.

"She's in the kitchen right now. Making our birthday cake."

Kal frowned, confused. "So, she knows we're here?"

"Yeah, but she didn't seem bothered at all. In fact, she acted like it was a good thing." Ella looked to her brother for validation, hoping he'd recognise how strange the situation was, but Kal's initial confusion faded, and he relaxed back into his seat.

"Phew, I guess we dodged that one," he said, grinning.

Now it was Ella's turn to look confused. "Kal, do you walk around with your eyes closed? Haven't you noticed how weird things have been lately? This isn't an exception."

"El, you're just being too sensitive right now. Maybe you're reading into things that aren't really there."

Ella clenched her jaw, trying to hide her frustration. She felt a knot of anger and disappointment forming in her chest. "I'm going to read in my room. Thanks for the fun movie afternoon," she said flatly, turning to leave.

As she left, she caught a glimpse of Kal's half-hearted smile, a sign that he wasn't taking her seriously. She wondered if she'd really become so paranoid that even her twin brother—who normally understood her better than anyone—had no idea what she was talking about.

As she lay on her bed, Ella looked around at her now-bare walls. Just days ago, they had been covered with photos of her and Rhi, posters of bands they both loved, and sentimental things like a four-leaf clover they'd found next to their Tulip tree.

A soft knock interrupted her thoughts, and her dad poked his head in, she hadn't heard him come home early either, he spoke gently. "Ella, can I come in?" Though she didn't respond, he slowly opened the door and peered around to find her curled up on the bed, staring at the walls.

Ella remained silent but didn't ask him to leave. She didn't know what to say, especially when she felt so uncomfortable in her own home.

Her dad walked in and sat beside her on the bed. "Hey, what's going on?" His voice was calm and reassuring.

"I don't know, Dad. Maybe I'm paranoid, but things just don't feel right anymore. I can't explain it, and you'd probably think I'm being weird, like Kal does."

Rowan gently brushed the hair out of her eyes, a look of concern on his face. "Life takes us in some pretty difficult directions," he said quietly, "and sometimes recognising when those moments are happening is the hardest part."

Ella had never heard her dad talk like that before. It was

usually her mum who talked about *life's path* and *forks in the road*, but hearing it from him brought her a sense of comfort.

"Thanks, Dad. I'll try to cheer up by tomorrow—no one wants to be sad on their birthday!"

He kissed her on the head and quietly left her room. Once her dad was gone, Ella sat up, feeling a renewed sense of determination. She needed to start fresh, and the first step was to apologise to Kal.

Kal was at his desk, focused on his school project.

"Knock, knock," Ella said softly from the doorway. The door was already open, but she didn't want to barge in unannounced.

When Kal looked up and saw her standing there, a smile spread across his face.

"Kal, I'm sorry I've been such a pain to live with. I think this whole Rhi thing has gotten to me more than I realised."

"Hey, it's fine," he fibbed. Kal was easygoing and rarely let things bother him, but seeing his sister upset had been tough. "Let's just put all of this behind us and focus on birthday fun tomorrow, yeah?"

Kal had always been way more excited about birthdays than Ella, but his enthusiasm was infectious and made the day more fun for her too.

That night, Ella tried her best to put the last few weeks out of her mind and forget the conversation she'd overheard between her mum and Uncle Warren. In the warm, cozy living room—its deep red walls giving it a womb-like feel—the family sat together, reading their own books. Ella couldn't help but notice her parents exchanging glances, full of pride and excitement. She chalked it up to her and Kal turning 16 the next day. It was sweet to see her parents still so emotionally affectionate toward each other, even after all these years.

After a while, both Ella and Kal stood up to say goodnight, but before they could leave, Diana stood and gently cupped Ella's face, pressing their foreheads together with her eyes closed.

"I love you, Ella. Sweet dreams." She then did the same with Kal, before their dad wrapped them both in a tight hug.

"Night, Mum. Night, Dad," Ella said as she and Kal turned toward their bedrooms.

As they walked down the hallway, Kal glanced at her with a raised eyebrow. "Okay, I'll give you that one. That was pretty weird, right?"

Ella, not wanting to stir up her emotions again, simply replied, "Mmm. Goodnight, Kal."

As Ella lay in bed, she thought it would take a while to fall asleep with everything that had been happening, but her chaotic thoughts soon blurred into even more chaotic dreams.

Early the next morning, just as the first light of dawn crept over the horizon, both Ella and Kal woke up at the exact same time, though neither of them realised it. Almost immediately after waking, Ella was struck by a strange and unfamiliar symphony of birdcalls coming from her open window. The sounds were unlike anything she'd ever heard before.

For a moment, she lay there, debating whether to drift back to sleep. But before she could decide, something seemed to pulled her from the bed, almost as if guided by instinct. She walked over to the window and drew back the curtains.

A slow, deep breath filled Ella's lungs as her eyes widened, mesmerised by the sight before her.

The sunrise was unlike any she had ever witnessed. It wasn't just the usual reds, oranges, and pinks. No, this was something else entirely. Greens, purples, pale blues, and sparkling copper swirled together in a vibrant, rising rainbow, with an enormous, churning ball of golden fire at its centre. It was as if the sky itself was alive, shifting and pulsing with radiant energy.

Ella felt herself growing lightheaded and realised she had been holding her breath, completely in awe of the sight. She inhaled deeply, steadying herself. Still unable to tear her gaze from the breathtaking sky, she pulled the blanket off her bed, draped it round her shoulder and curled up in her chair by the window.

She stayed there, transfixed, watching the celestial display until a quiet knock sounded at her door, pulling her back to reality.

"Hey, El, you awake?" Kal whispered, poking his head around the door. He spotted his sister sitting by the window, mesmerised by the kaleidoscope of colours in the sky, and smiled.

In a louder voice, he said, "You've seen it too, then?" as he stepped into the room.

Ella turned to look at her brother. He hadn't seen her this relaxed and peaceful in a long time. Her voice came out soft and dreamlike. "It's the most amazing thing I've ever seen. I didn't even know these colours were possible in a sunrise."

"I didn't either," Kal replied, kneeling next to her chair. "But if it puts that kind of smile on your face, I'd say it's the best way to start our birthday."

Together, they sat in silence, watching the sky, enjoying the tranquil moment together.

It didn't take long before a thick, sweet, and spicy aroma began to waft into Ella's bedroom.

"Mum's up!" Kal said excitedly.

"Smells amazing, whatever it is!" Ella breathed deeply through her nose, her mouth watering instantly. She could make out the scents of cinnamon, nutmeg, raisins, walnuts... Was that almond? No, marzipan! Realising how hungry she was, she turned to Kal, but he had already bolted out the door, shouting, "Race ya!"

Both Kal and Ella tumbled out of her room, laughing as they made their way into the kitchen.

"Well, this is a lovely way to start your special day!" Diana said, beaming at them as she stood by the stove. Seeing the twins so happy lifted her spirits and eased some of the anxiety she'd been feeling about the day ahead.

"What are you making, Mum?" Kal asked, peeking over her shoulder.

"Cinnamon pancakes, but they're too hot right now, so hands off!" Diana playfully slapped Kal's hand away as he tried to sneak one off the pile.

Ella's stomach ached with hunger; these were her favourite pancakes, and the smell was making her even more impatient.

"Sit at the table, and I'll bring them over," Diana said, as eager as a mother bird feeding her family.

The twins sat down, their eyes wide with anticipation. As Diana set down a plate piled high with the most incredible-smelling pancakes, Ella and Kal licked their lips before diving in.

With his mouth full, Kal mumbled, "Is this a new recipe, Mum? These are seriously good!"

Smiling to herself, Diana replied, "No no, same as always."

Ella couldn't even join the conversation—she was lost in her own little pancake heaven.

Rowan walked into the kitchen with an enormous smile on his face, his voice filled with excitement. "HAPPY, HAPPY BIRTHDAY, GUYS!"

"Come sit down, Rowan, before the kids eat all the pancakes," Diana said as she joined the twins at the table, tucking into the family breakfast. Rowan followed, grinning eagerly.

The four of them enjoyed a breakfast like no other, with blissful sounds coming from both Ella and Kal as they devoured their pancakes. In contrast, their parents sat more quietly, nibbling at their food while watching the twins enjoy themselves. Diana and Rowan exchanged amused glances, a mixture of pride and excitement sparkling in their eyes.

Once the pancakes, orange juice, and coffee were finished, Rowan suddenly stood up, his voice louder than necessary, "Shall we move to the living room for your presents?"

Diana nearly choked on the last of her coffee. "Right now? Can't we wait a bit? I'm worried it mi—"

Rowan cut his wife off with a casual wave of his arm, trying not to alarm the twins. In a more normal tone, he reassured, "It's all fine. It *will* be fine." He squeezed Diana's hand, his eyes urging her to stay strong.

Diana straightened up, took a deep breath, and said, "Okay, you two, are you ready for your surprise?"

Ella and Kal exchanged eager glances. Slowly, they stood and followed their parents into the living room. The atmosphere had taken on a strange seriousness. Kal leaned over and whispered to Ella, "I bet they got us a car!"

"Don't be ridiculous," Ella whispered back, rolling her eyes. "We can't even drive yet!" She watched her brother's mind race through all the possible gifts, but she couldn't shake the odd feeling building inside her.

Sitting down on the edge of the sofa, Ella suddenly felt a wave of nausea. The once cozy, deep red walls of the room now felt suffocating and cramped. She slipped off her dressing gown, trying to relax, but the seconds seemed to stretch into what felt like hours. It was as if time itself had slowed to a crawl.

Ella could feel the pulse in her temples intensify, the throbbing pain spreading into her eyes. She glanced at Kal, trying to read whether he was feeling the same. His face showed a mixture of uncertainty and eagerness, and she guessed he was wrestling with his own kind of panic.

Their dad finally broke the silence, reaching behind the sofa and lifting two large, oddly shaped items. They certainly weren't car keys, that much was obvious. Ella's pulse quickened as she stared at the objects in front of them. Both were about half her height, though each had a different shape. They didn't seem heavy, judging by how easily their dad held them.

"Now today..." their dad began, his voice unusually serious, "...isn't just your 16th birthday. It's the day that changes your lives forever." He glanced at Diana, who was nervously shifting her gaze between Kal and Ella.

Ella felt a sudden, icy grip tighten around her throat. The warmth she had been feeling vanished, replaced by a cold that chilled her to the bone.

Her dad continued, "Today is the day you find out who you truly are."

"Is this where you tell us we're adopted?" Kal tried to joke, but Ella could hear the slight tremor in his voice. He was just as anxious as she was.

Diana quickly flustered. "Oh no, no, it's nothing like that."

"Well, what is it then?" Kal demanded impatiently, glancing at Ella. Did he sense how nervous she was?

Diana leaned forward, her voice softer. "Rowan, I think you should give them their gifts first. Then we can explain."

Rowan nodded and handed Kal his present, wrapped in an old, musty-smelling green cloth. Kal's eyes widened as he took it, his disappointment barely concealed. Then, Ella was handed hers—a long, thin box wrapped in a similar cloth. The air in the room seemed to thicken, the twins glanced over at each other. There was a moment of complete stillness, like a calm before a storm, which unbeknown to them was the end of their lives as they knew them.

Kal began to feel his present, as he always did. Ella watched him, realising that this was his habit—he explored new things by touch before anything else. His hand slipped beneath the cloth, fingers tracing over curved shapes and intricate grooves along a long arch.

Ella, on the other hand, felt reluctant to even touch her present. All she could gather was that it was long, thin, and light.

Without looking at each other, they both unveiled their gifts at the same time. To their surprise, they found themselves holding what appeared to be very real and beautifully crafted weapons—Ella with a sword, and Kal with a bow and arrows.

Kal half-laughed, glancing over at Ella, who was frozen in place, staring down at the sword. When he looked back at their parents, expecting them to laugh along, he was met with something entirely different—a mix of fear and pride in their expressions.

"Okay, Mum, Dad, I think it's time you start talking," Kal said, still hoping this was some elaborate joke. He nudged Ella with his elbow for support, but she remained transfixed by the weapon in her hands.

Desperate to fill the silence, Kal tried to make sense of it. "I'm really hoping these are for an amazing fancy dress party you're throwing us?" He looked at his parents with a glimmer of hope, but deep down, he knew this was no joke.

Ella slowly emerged from her frozen state, her eyes drawn to the intricate details around the handle of the sword. Light green crystals seemed to have grown naturally from the metal, as though they were part of the sword itself rather than being set into it. The blade was long, its power apparent despite its surprising lightness. Ella reached out to touch it, but her mum quickly grabbed her hand before she could.

"You need to learn about her before you bleed by her," Diana said, her voice firm.

Ella's eyes widened as she looked up at her mum. "Mum, what's going on? You're really scaring me." Her voice trembled with worry and a hint of anger.

Kal, meanwhile, examined the dark wooden bow and ebony arrows in his hands. The detail was incredible, almost as if the bow had grown naturally into its elegant form. The arrows felt like steel, but he didn't dare touch the points after hearing what their mum had said about Ella's sword.

Diana glanced at Rowan, silently urging him to begin the conversation they had waited 16 years to have.

CHAPTER FOUR

Rowan cleared his throat and leaned forward in his chair. There was no turning back now; the moment they had prepared for over so many years had finally come. But now that it was here, the air in the room felt thick and heavy with silence.

"Kal, Ella," he began, "this is going to be difficult to understand, maybe even impossible to believe... but now that you've both turned 16, it's time to tell you the truth about who you are. In every Fae's life, this is the age when they learn the truth."

"Hang on—what do you mean, Fae?" Kal interrupted, barely daring to look up. He didn't want to see how serious his dad's expression might be.

Rowan straightened, his voice steady as he recited what he'd been practicing in the days leading up to this. "Fae is the collective term for our folk—Faeries, Elves, Goblins, Dwarves, Pixies, and others. And we... we are Faeries."

Kal burst out laughing but looked like he might vomit at

the same time. Ella remained silent, her eyes still fixed on the sword in her hands as the icy grip around her throat tightened.

Kal's laughter quickly faded, replaced by disbelief, and within moments, his expression settled into anger.

"So, you mean to tell me that I'm actually a Faerie? You really expect me to believe this?" Kal's voice was laced with disbelief.

Ella suddenly stood up, the sword dropping from her hands with a heavy thud onto the floor. Without a word, she walked over to the window, needing space to think, to breathe. As she stared out at the morning sun, she felt the icy grip that had silenced her beginning to loosen.

She closed her eyes and took a deep breath through her nose. A strange but familiar scent filled her senses. It was the smell of lightning—not of a storm, but of pure, electrical energy. Though the skies were clear, Ella couldn't shake the unmistakable scent.

"You can smell that, can't you?" Diana's gentle voice came from behind, and she placed a reassuring hand on Ella's shoulder.

Ella jumped, startled not only by the touch but by her mother's knowledge of the scent she was smelling. She turned to look into her mother's eyes, her voice barely a whisper. "Yes."

Diana wanted to hug her, but held back, knowing how important it was for Ella to hear the rest of the truth.

The silence was broken by Kal's soft voice. "Ella... can I look at your sword?"

The simple question shattered the stillness, pulling Ella

back to the moment. She returned to sit next to Kal, picking up her sword. She managed a small smile, giving Kal the silent permission he sought.

Diana opened her mouth to speak, but Kal had already reached for the sword. His arms extended, as if he were about to cradle a baby. As Ella carefully let the cold, light blade slip from her hands, it suddenly dropped, its surprising weight pulling Kal down with it.

"Aww!" Kal groaned, his hands trapped under the weight of the sword. He tried to lift it again, but couldn't budge it. The ridiculousness of the situation made Ella smile, and soon she spat out a giggle.

At first, she thought Kal was trying to make her laugh, as he always did when she was upset. But then it dawned on her—he actually couldn't lift it. His fingers were turning purple beneath the blade, and he still couldn't move it.

Both twins turned to their parents with questioning looks. Diana, smiling in her usual warm and nurturing way, began to explain.

"Weapons belong only to their master," she said calmly. "Once they've connected with you for the first time, no one else can hold them or fight with them."

The words felt strange and otherworldly, leaving Ella and Kal in stunned silence. Seeing that she had their full attention, Diana continued, her tone more serious.

"Each weapon has the ability to change into five different forms, one of which is an animal Bonded to you alone. This animal will protect you and fight for you when needed. It takes a lot of training to reach that point, and sometimes it can take years to awaken the other forms." She paused, giving them a moment to absorb the information, waiting to see if they had any questions.

Kal shot Ella a silent, pleading look—'*Can you take this off me?*' Ella quickly lifted the sword from his fingers and set it on her lap. Kal spent the next few moments massaging the pins and needles as they flushed through his purple-tinted fingers.

Rowan glanced at Diana, placing a reassuring hand on her knee, signalling that he would continue.

"Fae can only have one child in their lifetime," he began. "Not because that's all we're allowed, but because that's how our biology works."

Ella and Kal immediately frowned, and Rowan pressed on.

"However, there have been rare cases of twin births throughout the history of the Fae. These are incredibly rare —and highly dangerous."

The twins' frowns deepened.

"Why dangerous?" Ella asked, her curiosity edging through her disbelief.

Diana's heart lifted slightly, hoping this question was a sign Ella was beginning to accept what she was hearing.

"Twin Fae are incredibly powerful," Rowan explained. "They are usually born into warrior families. It can be hundreds of thousands of years between sets of twins, and in fact, you two are the first twins to be born in the last 500,000 years." Pride laced Rowan's voice, genuine and honest.

Kal rubbed his head, trying to process everything. "OK,

OK—wait. This all seems... You can't be serious? How have we not heard of any of this before now?"

Rowan raised a calming hand, his voice steady. "Kal, I know this is a lot to take in, and it's unexpected. But if you let me finish, things will start to make sense."

Kal took a deep breath raising an eyebrow with a slight shake of his head "OK, fine. Let's see where this leads. So, how does being a twin make us more powerful?"

Rowan continued, "All Fae have an element of magic—some more than others—and that magic tends to influence or, rather, guide the kind of work you'll do as you get older. But twin magic is different. It's connected, and when used properly, it's incredibly powerful against any enemy."

"Wait, what do you mean, 'enemy'?" Kal's eyes widened, the shock clear on his face.

"The Fae live in what we call the *World Below*, and it's very different from what you're used to above ground. There is so much for you both to learn, but we have time—there's no rush," Rowan said gently.

Ella felt a wave of mixed emotions. She was upset with her parents for keeping so much from them, but she also had so many questions that she didn't even know where to start.

"Okay, can I ask why it's taken you sixteen years to tell us? And if we're Fae, why don't we live in this *World Below*?" Her tone became more argumentative as she swung between belief and disbelief. She half-expected this to be the point where their story would unravel.

Rowan, still calm, responded, "That's a good place to start." His matter-of-fact tone made it hard for Ella to believe he was lying, though she didn't want to admit that just yet.

"When a Faerie couple is expecting a child, they move to the World Above—the realm we're in now. This is done to give Faerie children a life without magic or responsibilities, until they turn sixteen and are old enough to understand the importance of being Fae."

Ella had sunk back into the sofa, unconsciously clinging to Kal's arm. She could sense his uncertainty, mirroring her own. Rowan continued, careful yet determined to push the conversation forward.

"If a Faerie child is born a warrior, the *Birth Seer* feels their essence and transfers it into the mind of a *Forger*. Forgers are Fae who have been trained since the age of sixteen to craft and evolve the warrior's weapon from that essence. Forging is a skill that can take a lifetime to perfect. Some Forgers may only craft one or two weapons before they pass on, but there's no higher honour in our clan.

Kal didn't know what to think. He could tell his parents weren't joking, but believing them seemed impossible.

Ella felt the same, deciding to ask as many questions as possible to piece together some kind of sense from all of this. "Okay, so what exactly is a Birth Seer? It sounds kind of gross!"

Diana smiled, knowing one of them would eventually ask—though she had expected it to be Kal.

"No, nothing like that. A Birth Seer is connected to every essence born into the Fae Clan they serve. When a warrior child is born, part of their essence—their being—is drawn to the Seer. They then duplicate that essence and pass it on to the Forgers. They can only sense a warrior's essence, though; everyone else must find their own path."

"You do realise how crazy this all sounds, don't you?" Kal asked, with a slight laugh, as though he were trying to convince himself as much as his parents.

Diana half reached out to place a comforting hand on Kal's leg but pulled back. "Of course, we do! We've both been in your position—on our 16th birthdays. Honestly, you're taking it better than I did. I locked myself in my room for two days and refused to talk to anyone."

Diana hoped they would soon understand that she and Rowan had gone through the same emotions and that they knew exactly how the twins were feeling.

Rowan gently put his arm around Diana and leaned his head toward hers. "I think it might be a good idea to let the kids process what we've told them together, we'll be in the kitchen when you're ready."

Diana and Rowan rose from their seats and left the living room, leaving Ella and Kal in a dazed silence.

In the kitchen, Diana began making tea, casting a helpless look at Rowan. "I know we have to do this, but part of me wishes we could stay up here and live this life."

Rowan saw the conflict in her eyes and agreed, to some extent. But he knew Kal and Ella would never be ordinary teenagers—not even ordinary Fae. Their calling was far greater than they realised. He wrapped his arm around Diana and kissed her cheek.

"Let's make a big pot of lavender and chamomile tea. You know that always relaxes you." Rowan's eyes twinkled, and Diana, smiling, mirrored the warmth in her mossy green eyes.

Back in the living room, Kal turned to Ella. He was silent, but she could feel his energy buzzing with unease. Looking down at the sword in her lap, Ella spoke softly, her voice almost broken.

"I know, I can't wrap my head around it either. But... as crazy as it sounds, something about it feels... right."

Kal wasn't shocked by her words, which, in itself, he found strange. "I don't even know which is worse—being told we're adopted or that we're Faeries!"

A small smile tugged at the corners of Ella's mouth. Kal had a way of making light of any situation, even in the midst of confusion.

Kal's tone grew more serious as he looked at his sister, trying to read her thoughts but only finding his own frustration reflected back. He asked quietly, as though afraid of the answer, "So... do you believe any of this?"

Ella hesitated. "I feel like I need to know more. I can't believe Mum and Dad are joking at this point, but... what does it all mean?"

"I need to know more too," Kal said, more firmly this time. "It feels like we're stuck on a mind-bending cliffhanger."

They both got up and headed through the low ceilinged hallway to the kitchen, where they found their parents talking softly over tea.

Kal spoke first. "Mum, Dad, we realise you're not joking. But believing you still feels ridiculous. Can you tell us more?"

"Of course!" Rowan's excitement slipped through his voice.

Ella sat down across from Diana and forced herself to look her mum in the eyes. "What did you guys do in the World Below? I can't imagine you as warriors."

Blushing slightly, Diana cleared her throat. "Well, we're not warriors. That's what makes this situation even more interesting—warriors usually come from warrior families."

Kal muttered under his breath, just loud enough for Ella to hear, "So if the Seer sensed our essence, does that mean we're warriors?" Realising he was mumbling, he asked more directly, "Has the Seer ever been wrong?"

Rowan's voice took on a serious tone. "I'm afraid not. The Seer has been around for many generations. There is only one Seer for the entire Fae Clan, which is vast. A new Seer is appointed only when the current Seer passes. In the entire history of the Fae, no essence has ever been misread."

"Right, okay... guess that answers that," Kal said, sounding slightly more accepting. Ella, however, stared at him.

Diana leaned across the table, placing her hand over Ella's. "I know this is hard, darling. I really do. Would you like to know what we did in our world?"

"Please," Ella replied, her voice soft, almost childlike, sadness evident in every syllable.

"Well, we did something similar to what we do here. I'm a Healer, not a vet, and your dad is an environmental engineer."

Kal's eyes widened in awe. "Cool, Dad! That sounds awesome."

Rowan's face lit up, about to say something with excitement, but a glance from Diana told him it wasn't the time to go on. He smiled and said nothing.

Ella's curiosity deepened. "Do you use the same type of medicine there as we do here?"

Diana could sense her daughter wanting to believe, yet still hesitating. "In some ways, yes. We use medicines that come from plants—like Aspirin, Morphine, Digitalis—but we use them in their raw, natural form. The world above only uses a fraction of the medicinal plants available, though the Eastern countries do a bit better."

Ella's heart pounded so loudly in her chest that she wondered if her mother could hear it too. She asked, almost nervously, "Can you hear that, Mum?"

Diana's eyes softened with tears that sparkled like crystals. "I can not only hear your heart, but I can feel its rhythm."

Ella's eyebrows shot up. That was it—the final string tying her to disbelief was cut. She was ready to accept that she was Fae.

CHAPTER FIVE

Monday morning came, and Ella wished she could talk to Rhi about everything that was happening, but even if Rhi were still speaking to her, she couldn't. Their parents had made it clear: they weren't to tell anyone about being Fae, especially since they were Fae twins. They were also warned to keep away from others, not wanting the wrong people to discover their secret. That meant no more school for either of them.

Kal, devastated, didn't understand why he couldn't just go in and pick up extra work to do from home. But Diana and Rowan had been firm—school was now off-limits.

Before they could transition to the World Below, Diana insisted they needed to become more familiar with their heightening Fae senses. So, she told them to go for a bike ride and experience nature as newly awakened Fae.

Clipping her turquoise helmet onto her head, Ella stepped outside into the crisp autumn air. The cool breeze felt welcoming, as if the day itself was greeting her. She took a deep breath, and suddenly her senses came alive. As she sat down on her bike, she looked back at Kal stepping out of the front door. He, too, paused for a moment, his head jerking up like a dog that had caught a scent.

"Wow, can you smell this? It's like I'm in Willy Wonka's Chocolate Factory," Kal exclaimed, marvelling at the intensity of the scents surrounding him.

Diana stood at the front door, watching them. "Enjoy your ride, and remember, your Fae senses are just starting to settle in. Let yourselves feel them."

She smiled softly as the twins raced down the path toward the road, their usual playful competition sparking as they reached the gate, immediately bickering over who had won. Diana turned back into the house and sat next to Rowan in the kitchen, resting her head on his shoulder.

"This is it, Diana. This is the start of their *Shift*," Rowan said with quiet intensity.

Diana smiled, though not convincingly. "I know they can do this... I just wish they didn't *have* to."

Out in the fields, the twins spent the day revelling in their heightened senses. They laughed as they smelled the fresh earth, the wildflowers, even the distant scent of rain in the air. They raced through the farmer's fields and dared each other to leap over the small river at the village's edge, their laughter echoing in the crisp air.

As the sky began to tint with evening light, Kal came to an abrupt stop. "El, we should head home. I'm starving— and we totally skipped lunch."

Ella nodded, the ache in her stomach finally catching up with her. The ride back felt almost effortless, even the hill that usually slowed Ella down seemed easy to conquer. It was as if the wind was gently guiding them home, through the waves of different smells and birdsong that felt like it was playing just for them.

As they got off their bikes at home, Ella and Kal exchanged exhilarated glances, both of them beaming with the same rush of energy.

Ella unclipped her helmet, her voice breathless with excitement. "That was so easy! It felt like I was being pushed all the way home."

"I know, right? It was amazing. I could've kept going for miles, no problem." Kal grinned as he opened the front door, immediately hit by a wall of delicious aromas that made his mouth water. He sniffed the air and moved instinctively toward the stove, drawn to the smell like an animal following a scent. Ella wasn't much different, heading straight to where Kal stood, eager to see what delights were cooking for dinner.

Diana heard the twins bustling around the kitchen and walked in to find Ella peeking under the foil of a dish in the oven, while Kal poured them both glasses of juice from the fridge.

Ella looked up from the stove and saw her mum gliding into the kitchen with the calm grace of a wave meeting the shore.

"Mum, what's for dinner? This smells amazing!" she asked, her eyes wide with anticipation.

Diana's eyes sparkled knowingly, fully aware of how incredible everything must smell and taste to them now. She pulled the dish from the oven and peeled back the foil, revealing the hearty meal underneath.

"It's just a vegetable cottage pie," Diana said with a grin, her eyes twinkling with a flicker of delight.

Kal spat out his juice, partly from hearing what was for dinner and partly because the taste of the juice was so strong it made his tongue tingle.

"What? We hate vegetable cottage pie! You must have done something different—this does *not* smell the same!"

Diana chuckled. "Nothing at all. It's one of your Fae senses strengthening. You'll find that smells and flavours are far more intense now. It can be overwhelming, so take it slow."

Kal wiped the spilled juice off the old flagstone floor but then paused. "Does this Fae sense thing also explain why we got home ten minutes faster than usual without breaking a sweat?"

Diana's eyes widened in surprise. "You're progressing much faster than I expected!"

Just then, Rowan entered through the front door, making Diana jump. "Who's progressing fast?"

"Ow, Rowan, you scared the life out of me!" Diana gathered herself, then nodded toward the twins. "Your son and daughter. I think they're going through their strength Shift as well as their senses Shift!"

Rowan's usual calm expression shifted into one of puzzlement and surprise. "We should talk about this over dinner. If the Shift is happening faster than usual, you need to be prepared. Now, go wash up before we eat, you two."

Both Ella and Kal stepped into the bathroom for their usual pre-dinner hand-wash. As Ella rinsed the soap off, Kal gently nudged her with his elbow. "Sure, the vegetable cottage pie smells good, but if it actually tastes good, then I'll know this Fae business is real!"

Ella laughed, drying her hands, then hurried back into the kitchen, where her mum was about to serve up.

Sitting down at the table, Ella and Kal eagerly watched as a large spoon broke through the crisp potato and herb topping, releasing a cloud of fragrant steam. The smells were intoxicating—Ella could pick up the fresh thyme, sweet cherry tomatoes, and the earthy richness of lentils, root vegetables, and mushrooms. She inhaled deeply, savouring the blend of smells.

"Mum, is this how you guys smell food every day?" Ella asked, half-joking, she couldn't imagine living with this heightened sense all the time—she'd probably end up a dribbling mess, not to mention several dress sizes bigger.

Diana smiled. "Not quite as intense as what you're feeling now. When you first start your Fae Shift everything is heightened. You've gone from smelling just a fraction of a scent to experiencing every particle of it. It will calm down a little once you get used to it."

Kal was loading up his plate with enthusiasm, and Ella glanced at him, amusement dancing in her eyes. But beneath the laughter, there was a flicker of anxiety, hinting at the weight of everything they were still trying to process.

"ERRR, Kal, don't you think you should try it first?" Ella teased.

"Nope," Kal replied confidently, loading his plate. "I'm sure it's going to taste amazing, so I'm filling up before you decide you want seconds."

Their dad laughed heartily, anticipation lighting up his face. "Come on then, try it!"

Ella and Kal both picked up a forkful and took a bite at the same time. The expressions of pure euphoria that spread across their faces brought tears to Diana's eyes. They exchanged a glance, remembering just how those first taste as a Fae felt.

Between mouthfuls, Ella began asking questions about their Fae Shifts and what else they could expect.

Diana settled back into her chair, her gaze shifting between her children as she spoke. "You've already experienced your sense of taste. You've also started to gain strength. Soon, you'll find your physical power equals that of about five human adults, maybe even more. Your hearing will sharpen, too. You'll start noticing small things—like the different bird songs in the morning. This 'awareness' will continue to grow until you can hear even the smallest changes, like the direction of a breeze shifting or the first raindrop of a storm as its released from a cloud."

Kal's mouth dropped open in amazement as his mum continued to talk. Ella noticed and kicked him under the table to snap him out of it.

"Ouch! What did you kick me for?" Kal grumbled.

"Sorry, but your food was about to fall out of your mouth. It was kinda gross," Ella replied with a smirk.

Rowan jumped in to keep the conversation moving. "So, basically, everything you could feel, smell, hear, and do as a human is the same, but now it's far more enhanced. While it's incredible in so many ways, it has its downsides too. A smell you wish you didn't have to experience will be more intense, and you'll need to use these heightened senses for defence at times. But that's a topic for another day."

"Yes, let's save that for later," Diana said, relieved not to dive into that conversation just yet. "You both have plenty to process after today. Let's take it one step at a time."

Ella and Kal were beginning to feel the exhaustion of the day, and now there was only one thing on their minds: rest.

Kal stood up and rubbed his stomach. "Mum, dinner was literally life-changing. Do you mind if I just go lie down for a bit?"

Diana chuckled at his words, knowing just how true they were. "Of course, go ahead. This next week will be tough, so rest while you can."

Ella followed her brother into his room. "Can you believe how amazing everything tasted?"

"I know, normally we have to cover that dish in tomato ketchup to make it palatable!" Kal said, letting out a gassy burp. "But right now, I'm too full and tired to think about it. I'm staying right here for the rest of the night." He flopped onto his bed with a groan of relief. "Night, sis."

"Night, Kal." Ella quietly closed his door and headed into her own room. As she sat by the window, watching the first signs of the sun setting, a familiar icy grip tightened in her stomach, twisting until she felt sick. She tried to dismiss it as being too full, but deep down, she knew something wasn't right.

Staring out the window, Ella's eyes followed the vibrant rainbow hues that broke through the evening haze, as she was hypnotised into a comforting daydream. Suddenly, her dream sharpened into focus. It felt real, like she was truly there, she and Rhi were sat on the low branch of their tree. But she couldn't see their faces as she was stood behind them. Compelled, she walked around the tree, eager to see her friend. Yet, something was wrong. Rhi looked different. Her hair and mouth were the same, and her mannerisms were familiar, but her eyes and nose... they were off. It was Rhi, and yet it wasn't.

Muted tones floated past her, and when Ella turned to see who they were talking to, she saw Rhi—running through the field, heading toward them. She hadn't even had time to process it before the dream shattered with the sudden, sharp ring of her phone.

Startled, Ella jumped onto her bed and grabbed her phone. The screen flashed Rhi's name.

Her heart twisted with the same icy grip she'd felt earlier, her stomach lurching with unease. She took a deep breath and answered.

"Rhi, hi, how are—"

She didn't get to finish. Rhi's voice cut through the air, filled with venom Ella had never heard from her before.

"Well, I now know it was the right choice cutting you and your disgraceful family out of my life. And to think I almost didn't listen to my parents when they warned me not to have contact with you."

Ella's throat tightened painfully. The icy grip in her stomach spread upward, choking her words. She was too stunned to speak, too shocked to process the hatred in Rhi's voice.

"I didn't think you'd have anything to say," Rhi sneered.

"There's nothing you *can* say. Your family and their Fae Clan have ruined my family's lives!"

The mention of the Fae Clan sent a jolt of electricity through Ella, unlocking her voice. She blurted out words in a desperate rush, hoping to speak before Rhi hung up.

"Wait! Rhi, why are you talking about Fae Clans?" Ella's voice trembled as she tried to make sense of what was happening.

Rhi's reply was chilling, her voice deepening with anger Ella barely recognised. "Your Clan killed my twin sister. You all think you're better than everyone else, which is a load of crap. You will all pay for what you've done!"

The line went dead, leaving Ella breathless. Slowly, she sank down into the chair by the window, gripping the arms to steady herself. She tried to focus on the sunset that had mesmerised her moments earlier, but all she could see now was black—a bottomless void with no stars or moon to guide her. It felt like a thick blanket had covered the earth, not to keep out the light, but more worryingly to trap the darkness within.

In the living room, Diana, who had been quietly reading, felt an uneasy shift in the air. She walked quickly toward the kitchen, drawn by the sudden change in energy.

"Rowan, do you feel that?" she called. Rowan, already drying his hands from washing up, was on his way toward her.

They met outside the twins' bedrooms, exchanging nervous glances at both doors. Diana kept her voice as calm as possible. "Ella? Kal? Are you guys okay?"

Kal's voice floated through his door, sounding relaxed

and sleepy. "Yup, all good, Mum. Can't move much, but I'll sleep it off."

Ella, however, said nothing.

Taking a deep breath, Diana stepped forward to knock on Ella's door. "I'll check on her," she said softly.

Rowan placed a comforting hand on her shoulder. "It could be nothing. The kids have been through a lot today, and their connections are bound to feel a bit off."

Knowing how sensitive she had been during her own transition as a young Fae, Diana braced herself for whatever she might find behind Ella's door. In the past, Shifting Fae had caused town-wide blackouts, birds to scream in the dead of night, and even triggered small earthquakes. Quietly, she knocked on the door. No response. But behind it, she could feel a vast, aching emptiness.

"Ella, I'm coming in," she said softly, pushing the door open. Cold air immediately rushed past her—Ella was sitting by the window, which was wide open.

"It's freezing in here. Come on, let's warm you up before you turn blue." Diana took the blanket from Ella's bed and wrapped it around her motionless daughter, then closed the window. Kneeling in front of Ella, she was startled to see her daughter's wide, unblinking eyes.

"What happened?" Diana asked gently, knowing all she could do was be there for her. She helped Ella over to the bed, holding her close, hoping her warmth would coax Ella to speak.

After a few moments, the icy grip on Ella began to thaw. She nestled into her mother's arms, her voice small and fragile. "It's Rhi."

Diana's heart sank. She closed her eyes, taking a deep breath to steady herself. This was the conversation she had been dreading for eight long years. She had always known this moment would come.

Ella looked up, her tear-streaked face filled with confusion and desperation. "Nothing makes sense anymore, Mum. Our whole lives have been turned upside down. Rhi called me—she was furious. She said she was glad to be out of our lives, and that our Fae Clan killed her twin sister!"

Diana felt a weight settle in her chest. This was the moment she had tried to prepare for but now that it was here, all her plans vanished, leaving only raw emotion and the sight of her broken daughter before her.

"You're right, Rhi does know about our Fae Clan," Diana said quietly. "And the reason why... is because she's Fae, too."

Ella sat up straight, her eyes searching her mother's face, trying to comprehend.

"Rhi is from a different Clan than ours. Unfortunately, we've been estranged from her Clan for many years."

Ella's mind raced, trying to process everything, but her thoughts were tangled and overwhelming. After the chaos of the last few days, this revelation felt like too much to bear.

Diana continued, her voice as calm and measured as possible. "The reason Rhi hasn't spoken to you since her birthday is because she would have learned the truth—that she's Fae, just like you. And just like we told you not to reveal anything for your own protection, Rhi would have been told the same."

"So... the reason my best friend wasn't talking to me...

was because she was protecting me, not because she hated me?" Ella asked, her voice trembling as she tried to make sense of it all.

Diana nodded. "Since she turned sixteen before you, she had no idea you were Fae, and neither did her parents."

Ella almost felt relieved, knowing her best friend hadn't truly hated her. But then the memory of the phone call came crashing back—the venom in Rhi's voice. That wasn't her best friend trying to protect her; it was someone who now utterly despised her.

"So why was she so angry on the phone? And what was she talking about—her twin being killed?" Ella asked, her voice trembling.

Diana gently cradled Ella's face, meeting her gaze with calm reassurance. "I promise you, Ella, we didn't kill her twin. She's still very much alive."

CHAPTER SIX

The room seemed to darken as Ella stood up, her face twisting in horror.

"WHAT? How could you let them think Rhi's twin was dead? How could you do that?" Ella's voice cracked, her body trembling with rage.

Diana knew she had to set things right before the situation spiralled out of control. The air in the room was already charged with dangerous energy, and she could feel Ella's emotions building to a breaking point.

"I know, and it's been incredibly hard for your dad and me. We... we didn't feel good about it, especially knowing we were having twins ourselves. But it wasn't as simple as you might think. Their family was becoming a threat."

Ella's eyes blazed with fury, emotions surging to the surface. The woman in front of her, the mother she had trusted so deeply, suddenly felt like a stranger.

Pushing past Diana, Ella stormed out of her bedroom and into the hallway, where she bumped straight into her dad. Rowan quickly raised his hands, trying to calm the situation, his face etched with concern, as if he were standing in front of a loaded gun.

"Ella, listen. Let us explain why this had to happen," Rowan said, his tone more firm than apologetic, which only fuelled Ella's rage.

"There's nothing you can say that'll make this okay, Dad!" Ella shouted, her voice rising with every word, her arms flailing in disgust.

Kal opened his door, his face a mix of tiredness and surprise. His family had never spoken to each other like this before.

"Whoa, whoa, Ella, what's going on?" Kal tried to grab his sister's arms to calm her, afraid she might hurt herself or someone else.

Ella spun around, her voice low and filled with fury. "Don't believe a word they say, Kal. This Faerie shit is a mess of lies and hate, and I want nothing to do with it." She stormed through the kitchen and out of the front door, slamming it behind her.

Kal stood frozen, torn between his parents and his sister. Ella's words echoed in his mind, and a creeping doubt began to stir within him. He wasn't sure whom to trust anymore.

Diana stepped toward her son, arms outstretched, as if needing reassurance that he would listen. Kal saw the desperation in her eyes but instinctively stepped back. His trust wavered, then settled on the side of his sister. He said nothing, shook his head, and turned toward the front door. Walking out into the black, moonless night, he hoped to find Ella sitting on the steps. Instead, he saw the empty spot where her bike should have been. Without a second thought, he jumped on his own bike and sped off into the night to search for her.

Inside the house, Diana paced the kitchen, crying and trembling with shock. Rowan gently took her hands and sat her down at the table as she sobbed uncontrollably. She wiped her tears and looked up, heartbroken and ashamed.

"I wish this had never happened, Rowan. We should've never let them become so close."

Rowan tried to comfort his wife but couldn't find the words. He simply held her, letting her cry in his arms.

Out in the thick darkness, Kal peddled as fast as he could, hoping to catch up with Ella. Without lights on his bike, and no streetlights in the country lanes where they lived, he struggled to see. He relied on his familiarity with the roads to avoid crashing into a hedge or ditch. But then, as he continued riding, everything around him began to glow with a faint, ambient blue light.

Kal guessed that his Shifting sense of sight was taking over, much like when his taste had changed. This new ability didn't worry or overwhelm him; instead, he felt a rush of excitement, his mind already racing with how useful such an ability could be. But soon, his thoughts shifted back to the present, and he wondered if Ella was experiencing the same changes.

Further down the road, Ella was indeed experiencing the same Shift, but unlike Kal, she wasn't excited. Instead, her rage intensified, growing with every pedal stroke as she felt her old self slipping further away.

The only place Ella wanted to be was under the

comforting presence of her Tulip tree. She raced through the winding lanes until she spotted the farm gate, barely slowing down as she jumped off her bike and let it crash into the hedge. Without a second thought, she sprinted into the cornfield, the sharp remnants of harvested corn whipping at her bare ankles. When she finally reached the clearing, she looked up and stopped dead in her tracks.

All the anger and hate that had consumed her moments before evaporated, slipping away like water beading off a leaf. The Tulip tree, which had always felt alive to her in some intangible way, now visibly glistened with a vibrant emerald glow. Iridescent light rippled up its trunk and along its branches in flares, making the whole tree shimmer as if breathing. As Ella moved closer, she realised that the flares of light were actually thousands of fireflies, moving in perfect murmuration, following the tree's branches as though they were part of its living structure.

The tree wasn't just alive—it was alive in ways she had never imagined.

When she reached the familiar, massive branch shaped like a giant bear's arm, the one that had always been there to scoop her up, she ran her hand along its surface. She stroked it tenderly, the way one might pet a beloved animal. And then, something extraordinary happened.

The branch, which Ella usually had to leap for, slowly lowered itself. Whether it was a trick of the wind, an imbalance of weight, or something far more magical, the result was undeniable. For the first time, Ella didn't have to jump at all—the branch had lowered itself to meet her.

Ella's voice slipped from her lips in a hushed whisper as

she spoke to the only friend she felt she had left. "You're alive."

The branch seemed to wait for her, as if offering its comfort, and so, tentatively, she sat down upon it. Gently, the tree lifted her. It stopped at the height she had always climbed to, but this time, it was different.

Ella's heart and mind raced, not with fear or nervousness, but with a kind of electric anticipation, as though the air itself was alive with possibilities. Glancing down, she saw for the first time what lay beneath the bark—a network of glowing, sun-yellow veins, pulsing with energy, running up and down the entire tree like lifeblood.

She stared in awe, captivated by the strange, hidden beauty of the tree. At first, delight and wonder filled her, but the steady pulsing soon had a hypnotic effect, drawing her mind back to darker thoughts. It hit her then—the last time she'd been here was also the last time Rhi had been her friend. The weight of everything that had happened over the past week broke free, flooding her with uncontrollable sobs. Tears flowed down her cheeks, unchecked, her cries wracked with a raw urgency she couldn't stop—and didn't want to.

Through tear-blurred eyes, she noticed something—a figure standing in the cornfield, about half a football pitch away, gazing up at her... or the tree. She couldn't be sure which. The figure stepped forward, and as it neared, the outline became clearer. It was Kal, his familiar face tilted toward her, his expression one of pure astonishment. From the way his eyes were locked on the tree, Ella knew he could see it too—something magical, something utterly different about their ancient Tulip tree.

"Kal!" Ella yelled, snapping him out of his trance.

He jumped slightly and blinked at her, looking like a startled deer. "Oh, sorry, sis. Didn't see you there. It's just so... wait, you're seeing this too, right?"

Ella nodded, grinning, though words seemed to escape her. It was hard to find any that could explain what they were witnessing.

"Can you get down? I hate climbing up there. Last time, I nearly broke my leg, remember?"

Ella placed her hands on the massive branch, ready to jump, when the tree reacted. It lowered her gently to the ground, like a personal elevator. She stepped off, barely believing what had just happened.

Kal stumbled backward, tripping over his own feet and landing on his backside. "Did the tree just—? How...?" He stared at her wide-eyed. "Ella, we need to tell Mum and Dad about this."

Her mood darkened in an instant, and as if mirroring her, a sharp flash of red rippled through the tree's glowing veins. Both Ella and Kal whipped their heads toward the tree, then back to each other.

"What the..." Kal muttered, slowly getting back to his feet, eyes fixed on the shifting tree. "Alright, alright, we won't tell Mum and Dad. Happy?"

The red veins softened back to their golden glow.

Kal planted his feet, looking half ready to bolt and half prepared for battle. "Or... maybe we should chop this thing down," he said, not quite serious but testing the waters.

"NO!" Ella whipped around, her voice booming before he could even finish the thought. At the same moment, the veins in the tree's bark flared up, not with soft crimson but a deep, angry red—like the rush of real blood coursing through its limbs.

"Okay, okay! I take it back!" Kal raised his hands in surrender, both to Ella and the tree, as the red slowly faded back into its calm sunny glow. He shot her a nervous grin. "I'm pretty sure this tree can understand us—and it has feelings. So, let's stay chill, yeah? I don't fancy getting smacked by that bear arm." He nodded toward the massive branch, a cheeky grin slipping onto his face despite the tension.

Ella smiled at the Tulip tree. It felt like she was looking in a mirror, though she couldn't understand how that was even possible. She sat down at the base of the tree, leaning her back against the protective trunk, and motioned for Kal to do the same. Slowly, Kal moved toward the tree, keeping his eyes fixed on the massive low-hanging branch.

"Don't be silly, it's not going to punch you," Ella said with a chuckle. "I think you're almost right, with what you said before— but I think the tree is reacting to *my* emotions. I can feel... a connection with it. But I don't know how or why."

Kal hesitated before sitting down, but as he lowered himself, Ella playfully pushed him over. He landed with an awkward "Oomph," and they both laughed, sending hundreds of fireflies scattering into the air.

After their moment of silliness, Kal sat next to Ella. "Do you want to talk about what happened at home? I've never seen you like that before."

"It's Rhi. She called and told me she's a Faerie too, and that our clan killed her twin sister!"

She didn't need to look at her brother's face to know his reaction.

"Wait, WHAT? Rhi is a Faerie? WHAT... Rhi has a twin?!"

"HAD a twin, Kal—HAD. And she said that whatever group, sorry, *clan* we're from killed her when she was a baby! Mum tried to tell me she wasn't really dead, but I don't know if I can believe anything she says anymore."

Kal was speechless, staring down at his feet, unsure of what to feel or how to continue the conversation.

Ella's voice grew quieter, more solemn. "Mum didn't deny it either. Kal, I don't understand what's going on, but I know I don't want to be part of anything—or anyone—that thinks it's okay to do that to a family, to a baby, to twins. What if that had been us, Kal? What if one of us had been killed as a baby or kidnapped, and Mum and Dad thought we were dead?"

A faint red mingled with the golden glow in the tree's veins, and Kal took a moment to decide how to respond. After a pause, he put his arm around his sister and hugged her with all the love he could muster. "I'm with you on this one, sis." He thought for a moment, then, with a gentle squeeze he added, "Hey, how about we camp out here tonight? It actually doesn't seem that cold."

Ella wasn't sure about camping without sleeping bags, but after considering everything, she realised it was the best —and maybe the only—option. "Anything is better than going home right now."

As those words left her mouth, a thick, warm, creamy air surrounded them. It felt safe and comforting, like they were wrapped in their own bed blankets.

Neither of them wanted to talk about what had happened at home anymore, so they chatted about whatever else came to mind: Kal's crazy science projects, who was dating who at school, who hated who at school, and anything else silly and insignificant to distract themselves from the chaos swirling inside their heads.

Kal then spat out a laugh, "Ella if you tell anyone I've been gossiping like a drama queen for the last hour, I'll tell everyone I know about you farting loudly in Maths class and not owning up to it." Both of them fell into silent fits of laughter, unaware of how similar their own mannerism were to the other. As the laughter faded, so too did the last remnants of stress and both Ella and Kal were left in a bubble of contentment.

The day had been draining, especially for Ella, and she was starting to feel sleepy, though she wasn't sure if she'd be able to fall asleep given their unfamiliar sleeping arrangements.

"Kal, I really need to get some sleep, I think," she said, her voice heavy with exhaustion.

"Yeah, me too. I hope you sleep okay, El."

"You too. And Kal—thanks."

Kal nodded, a silent acknowledgment that it was all part of being her big brother—20 minutes older, but a lifetime more protective. Ella lay down on her side, their backs to each other, as if by instinct. They had always slept like that, though they never really questioned why. It was as if some ancient part of their minds knew it was best to keep watch in all directions. She wriggled around, trying to get comfortable, when suddenly a thick, spongy moss began to grow up from the ground beneath them. It wasn't harsh or jarring; it was comforting, like a soft mattress slowly rising to cradle them.

"Kal, you're feeling this, right?" Ella murmured sleepily.

"Mmmhmm," Kal's equally drowsy voice replied.

As they lay, roots began to push up through the ground, weaving together to form a protective nest around them. It wasn't frightening, though. It felt natural, safe even. Neither of them said a word, but the sense of connection between them—and to the tree—was undeniable. They both drifted off into a deep, dreamless sleep.

Ella woke early the next morning to the soft sensation of the Tulip tree's roots gently retreating into the earth. The first rays of the sun were stretching across the horizon like a tidal wave, filling the sky with shimmering colours. She watched in awe as the sky transformed before her eyes, a kaleidoscope of pinks, purples, greens, and gold.

In that moment, she felt completely at peace.

Kal stirred next to her, stretching out with a groan, then wiped a line of drool from the corner of his mouth.

"That was literally the best sleep I've ever had, EVER," he declared with a grin.

Ella laughed and encouraged, "Come on, open your eyes, you're missing the sunrise."

Kal squinted toward the east, his eyes still half-closed in sleepy reluctance.

"I don't think I'll ever get bored of seeing this," he said, his voice filled with wonder. "I guess this is another good thing about being a Faerie." He was trying to stay positive, to keep both their spirits up, but Ella knew he was thinking about the inevitable: they'd have to face their parents today.

Kal spoke quietly and gently, not wanting to pressure her. "We should go home today, you know that, right?"

Ella sighed, her eyes still fixed on the ever-shifting colours in the sky.

"I know," she whispered, not yet ready to face the storm waiting for them back home.

"But we have to at least listen. We can work out the rest from there."

Ella nodded with a faint smile. They both got up and started to walk back to their bikes. Ella suddenly turned and ran back to the tree, giving it a huge hug. "Thank you," she whispered, not caring how silly she might look.

Their ride home was slow, neither of them eager to face what awaited. But as they rounded the corner to their house, a new sense of strength ebbed through them both.

Ella took a deep breath as she stepped through the front door, with Kal close behind. They walked into the kitchen to find their parents seated at the table with a cold pot of tea between them, looking like they hadn't slept. Ella noticed the look of relief in her mother's puffy eyes, and her father had a stern expression, though not one of anger.

Ella and Kal had braced themselves for a lecture—how they'd worried their parents sick, how neither of them had slept... but the scolding never came.

Their dad opened his mouth to speak but hesitated, no words coming out at first. That pause, more than anything, revealed how hard this situation had been for him. Finally, with a deep breath, he said, "Come sit down."

Ella sat across from her mother, and Kal followed, making sure their parents knew he was siding with his sister on this one.

Rowan was clearly going to be the one to lead this conversation. He was always better at getting straight to the point, whereas Diana tended to get tangled in her emotions.

"Firstly," Rowan began, "we are very sorry you found out the way you did. It makes an already difficult situation even harder."

Diana nodded in agreement, her eyes wet as she tried not to cry.

"I'll start from the beginning, and you can stop me if you have any questions."

Both twins nodded, bracing themselves for more revelations.

"As we told you before, Fae folk can only have one child, and twins are very rare. They're dangerous because the magic you create together is more powerful than the strongest Fae warriors combined."

Kal interrupted, "I don't feel particularly powerful. Maybe these strength powers have skipped us?"

"They'll come in time. It's still early days," their dad replied matter-of-factly, enough to make Kal hold off on more questions for the moment.

Diana, who had been watching Ella closely, reached out to touch her daughter's hand, but Ella pulled away. Rowan saw the desperation in his wife's eyes and quickly continued.

"The reason Rhi's sister was taken and presumed dead as a baby was because of the power they would have held together as twins when they went through their Shift."

Ella didn't look convinced, her lips tightening in frustration.

"Dad, you're contradicting yourself. If the magic twins hold is so dangerous, why are we still together?" Ella pointed to herself and Kal. "Why didn't anyone try to split us up or even... kill us?" Her voice carried a sharp edge, aiming to make her parents understand Rhi's family's perspective.

"Because no one knew about you. We kept you a secret from almost everyone. The only people who knew of your existence were the council heads, the Birth Seer, and Warren."

Ella and Kal exchanged looks, having forgotten about their uncle.

Kal squinted, his hand scraping over his face, "So... this makes Uncle Warren a Faerie too."

Diana hadn't yet figured out how she would break this next piece of news to them.

"Yes, he is," Diana confirmed softly, "but there's more. He's not actually your uncle. Warren is one of the highest-ranking Fae Warriors, and he's been your bodyguard since you were born."

Ella put her head in her hands. When she looked up, her expression was a mix of shock, and betrayal.

"This just keeps getting better and better," she muttered sarcastically. "I guess that explains his awkward affection towards us."

Diana nodded. "Yes, Warren is a great man, and he's become part of our family in many ways, but he's not a family man by nature."

Rowan, wanting to keep the conversation on track, almost talked over Diana as he continued, "There's a key difference between your mother and I having twins, and Mr. and Mr Byrne having twins. They were once part of the Fae Clan that we, and most other Faeries, are a part of. But Mr Byrne decided to leave and took many followers with him."

Kal, now sitting forward in his chair, looked as if he were listening to a bedtime story, rather than the truth about their lives. "Why did he decide to leave?" he asked, his curiosity getting the better of him.

"Because he wanted more power," Rowan explained. "He felt that the Fae should be in charge of the *Realm Above*, not the humans. Fae have always been the protectors of the Earth since time began, serving as a balance to keep her alive. But the world has been through many changes—some out of our control—that have wiped out millions of species."

He paused, giving Ella and Kal space to ask questions, but they remained silent, still processing everything. Seeing they were ready to listen, Rowan continued.

"Humans have placed themselves at the top of the food chain, above all apex predators, destroying animals that aren't even natural prey to them. This has created a massive imbalance, and the world as they know it will soon come crashing down. They're dangerously close to extinction."

Kal couldn't stay silent any longer. "I'm sorry, Dad, but I don't agree. We are—the humans are—the most intelligent species on the planet and have done amazing things to further the evolution of the race. You can't seriously expect us to stay living in caves and be hunter gatherers!" His frustration was palpable. He wasn't ready to think of himself other than human, even though he had accepted who he truly was.

Ella, meanwhile, had been sitting quietly, absorbing the conversation. She felt torn between what she had always believed and what she was starting to feel.

Rowan could see he was losing Kal, but before he could say more, Diana spoke up, her voice gentle and soothing. "Hold on, Kal. Take a breath." Her slow, deliberate words immediately diffused some of the tension. "You're right. Humans have done many amazing things for this realm. But unfortunately some of those achievements are in response to problems they created themselves."

Kal's posture began to relax, the frown on his forehead easing, but then Rowan straightened up, a darker expression crossing his face.

"You need to listen very carefully, as this is integral to a Faerie's knowledge of their history and a Warrior's reason for strength and courage," Rowan said, his tone more serious than ever.

Ella shifted uncomfortably, sensing the weight of the information her dad was about to reveal.

"There are five elements hidden within both the Human and Fae Realms. When brought together, they can be used to heal the Earth. But they were all separated a millennia ago... because healing the Earth would also cause mass genocide of humans." Rowan paused, letting the gravity of his words sink in. "The head of each Fae

Clan appointed a trusted warrior. These five warriors each hid an element somewhere it couldn't be found and then took their own lives so they could never reveal its location."

Kal looked horrified. "Are you serious? That's barbaric! How could anyone order their warriors to kill themselves?"

Rowan continued, unflinching, as if Kal's outrage hadn't fazed him. "The five elements correspond with the Earth's natural forces: Earth, Wind, Fire, Water, and Ether."

Ella glanced at her mum, noticing how drained and exhausted she looked. It wasn't just the day's revelations—Diana appeared more worn down than Ella had ever seen her. Concerned, Ella reached over and gently placed her hand on her mother's arm. Diana flinched at first but then softened, her eyes filled with gratitude and love as they met Ella's.

"Ella?" Rowan's voice pulled her attention back to him. "This next part is crucial."

"The Fae Council has learned that the Byrne Clan has started searching for these five elements. They plan to use them to completely and irreversibly eradicate the human race."

Kal shot upright in his chair, disbelief evident on his face. "WHAT? They can't do that! Why would they even want to?"

A tense silence followed Kal's question, broken only by Diana's exhausted voice. "They're not content with maintaining the balance anymore. They've grown tired of watching humans destroy their own realm."

Diana pushed herself up from the table and went to the

stove to put the kettle on. "I'll make us a tea to pick us all up, I sure need something."

Diana reached up to the dusty shelf above the stove and brought down her largest teapot, the familiar sound of it hitting the counter filling the room. She moved methodically, clattering through glass jars of dried herbs and flowers. Ginseng, Liquorice root, and Ginkgo were carefully spooned into the pot before she filled it with boiling water. It was a little ritual, one Kal and Ella had watched countless times, but today it felt like more of a comfort for Diana than for anyone else.

Kal and Ella exchanged glances, both remembering how much they disliked their mother's herbal tea concoctions. They winced as the heavy teapot thudded onto the dining table.

"There, that should do it," Diana announced, her tone a little too bright for the moment.

Kal cleared his throat, trying to soften his words. "Mum, could you pass the honey, please?"

For a brief moment, a flicker of disappointment crossed Diana's face, but she nodded and retrieved the honey from the shelf. Kal wasted no time, scooping four large dollops into his cup, hoping his mother wouldn't notice.

As the herbal tea brewed, Ella's mind churned with thoughts and questions. She looked up, her voice unsure but curious. "Dad, if humans are destroying the planet as much as you say, wouldn't it be better if the Faeries did take over? Couldn't they make the Earth a cleaner place again?"

Rowan leaned back, preparing for a complicated explanation. "It's a good question, Ella. It might seem that way at first, but it's not so simple. When the Earth was created, Faeries were formed as its caretakers. For billions of years, we nurtured the planet, ensuring it flourished. As more species evolved, we became guardians of all life. If we didn't maintain that balance, the natural magic that sustains the Earth would collapse."

Both Kal and Ella sipped their tea, eyes wide as they absorbed what their father was saying.

"So, is Darwin's theory... wrong?" Kal's face lit up with curiosity, his love for science and history evident.

Rowan smiled. "Darwin wasn't entirely wrong. He was right in many ways, but there were things he didn't know. There are species he missed—species you'll get to meet in time."

Diana gave Rowan a pointed look, urging him to stay on track.

"Right..." Ella said with a smirk, half-joking, "Please don't tell me unicorns are real."

Diana's smile held a mix of joy and sadness as she replied, "They were, but they've been extinct for hundreds of years."

Ella's mouth dropped open in shock. "Wait... seriously? What happened to them?"

"Humans," Diana said softly. "Most of what you've heard in fables is true. Unicorns were hunted for their horns and skins because of their powerful magical properties."

Ella struggled to process that unicorns had once been real, let alone that humans had driven them to extinction.

Diana continued, "Unicorn leather was believed to

protect against plague and disease, while their horns could purify water, neutralise poison, and serve as antidotes."

Kal, however, wasn't convinced. His brow furrowed in disbelief as he shook his head. "Mum, I'm sorry, but that's hard to believe. If unicorns were real, why haven't we found any remains? People were hunting Narwhals in the 15th century and passing their horns off as unicorn horns. There's no actual proof unicorns existed."

Rowan calmly poured himself another cup of tea, then reached for the biscuit tin. Sitting back down, he met Kal's eyes, his expression serious yet patient.

"Kal, I understand this is a lot to take in, especially for someone who thinks like you do. But sometimes, you have to accept that the world holds things beyond logic. Just think about where you are now—if I'd told you about Faeries a few weeks ago, would you have believed me? As for the remains of unicorns and other magical creatures, they belong to the World Below, not the human world."

Kal's frown deepened, but he didn't argue further. The weight of the conversation pressed on them all, but the quiet presence of the tea, the herbs, and the history they were learning somehow kept the moment grounded.

Kal rolled his eyes at his mother's last words, but Diana caught the look and knew she had to explain more.

"Unicorns were the first and last magical creatures humans had direct contact with," Diana began, her voice calm and measured. "There was a time when the Fae council hoped to unite the magical and human worlds. Unicorns were chosen as the first attempt to bridge that gap, but when the council saw how they were hunted and slaughtered, they abandoned the idea entirely."

Kal remained skeptical, his scientific mind wrestling with the fantastical claims. "Okay, even if that's true, that was centuries ago. People are different now. We're not as barbaric. If someone saw a unicorn today, they wouldn't kill it for its horn and skin. They'd want to protect it."

Diana sighed softly, appreciating her son's faith in humanity, but knowing he was far from the truth. "I wish that were the case, Kal, but unfortunately, it's not. Take the rhinoceros, for example. Even today, poachers hunt them for their horns, which are used in traditional Chinese medicine to treat fever and high blood pressure. Yes, there are people who care—many do—but too many don't. If unicorns were discovered today, they wouldn't be killed outright, maybe, but they'd likely be captured, studied, and exploited for their magical properties."

Kal fell silent, the weight of his mother's words settling in. Diana's voice was soft but firm, each fact she shared pulling at his trust in science and logic.

"There are many beautiful creatures that have gone extinct on this Earth," Diana continued, her tone tinged with sadness. "Not all of them were lost because of humans, but enough were. We're just not willing to take that risk again. The Fae decided long ago that some things are better left hidden."

Kal didn't respond, but he filed the information away, knowing he'd have to process it later. It was getting harder to hold onto his doubts, and even harder to reconcile the world he thought he knew with the one his parents were revealing.

Chapter Seven

The next morning, Ella and Kal were told they'd be leaving for the Fae Realm that afternoon. The suddenness of the move left Ella feeling uneasy. She knocked on her brother's door and walked in.

"Kal, have you packed yet? I have no idea how to fit my whole life into a small bag. What are you taking?" The twins had been told they'd only need one backpack each, as everything they needed would be provided in the Fae Realm.

Kal was just zipping up his bag as Ella came in. "I'm done. Wasn't that hard, really. I just brought my favourite books."

Ella wasn't surprised by Kal's choice. "But what about clothes, your first teddy, your blanket...?"

"Mum said there would be clothes there, and I'm not too bothered about the rest," Kal shrugged. "I just thought about what I'd be most upset to lose if the house caught fire. Come on, Ella, new life, new start. It's not like we're moving countries, we're just moving worlds!"

Kal's words, even followed with a wink, did nothing to ease Ella's anxiety, and she left his room with an annoyed huff.

Muttering to herself, half in her head and half out loud, she rummaged through her drawers and cupboards, hunting for the things she couldn't bear to leave behind. "How can I choose only a few things? This is ridiculous!"

She tried to adopt Kal's approach, thinking about what she'd take if there were a fire. With this in mind, Ella realised she wasn't as attached to most of her clothes as she thought. She grabbed her favourite jeans from the foot of her bed. Next, she picked up her first doll from her pillow— a little Pixie doll she'd had since she was two. Once she started, it became easier than she expected.

Before long, she had a small pile of items packed into her bag. She scanned her room one last time, checking for anything she might've missed, though there was no more room in her bag anyway.

With her hand on the door latch, she paused as a thought of Rhi came to her. Setting her bag down, she went to her wardrobe and pulled out a box hidden behind the clothes she'd left piled on the floor. It was full of photos and cards Rhi had given her over the years.

Blowing out a shallow breath and blinking away the tears prickling at her eyes, Ella picked her favourite photo of the two of them, taken last year at an outdoor concert. She slipped it into the front pocket of her bag and left the room with a sigh.

Every corner of the house seemed to call out to the

twins, urging them to remember the life they were leaving behind.

Ella felt a wave of nausea wash over her as the reality of the situation started to sink in. She glanced at her mum, searching for reassurance. Diana, sensing her daughter's discomfort, held out her hand and offered a warm, calming smile—the kind that said everything would be okay. Ella grasped it and, for a moment, the nausea subsided, though she knew it was lurking just beneath the surface, ready to return.

Kal, standing beside her, shifted uncomfortably. He broke the silence with his usual attempt to lighten the mood. "So, what now? Do we grow wings and sprinkle pixie dust everywhere?" His grin was wide, but Ella could see the tension beneath his bravado.

Diana chuckled softly, amused by her son's humour. "You might be disappointed to learn that Faeries don't actually have wings."

Kal exaggerated a groan, rolling his eyes dramatically. "Great. Well, there goes all the fun," he said, but the slight dip in his voice betrayed a tiny shred of genuine disappointment.

Diana's eyes sparkled with mischief as she responded, "Oh, trust me, there's still plenty to get excited about."

They all stepped out into the back garden, a place that had always been a source of mystery for the twins. It was always overgrown, a tangle of herbs, tall grasses, and wildflowers—plants they had always assumed were just weeds. But their mother had corrected them often, insisting each one had a purpose, even if they didn't understand it yet.

At the far end of the garden stood an ancient oak tree, its gnarled branches reaching up to the sky like twisted arms. Hanging from one of the branches was a broken, mouldy swing that had terrified Kal and Ella as children. The trunk itself resembled an old, bad-tempered man, hunched over and scowling, as if waiting to scold anyone who came too close.

Rowan was already standing by the tree, a look of pride etched on his face. In one hand, he held a large, worn-looking bag, while his other hand was casually tucked into his jacket pocket.

"As you've just learned, we don't have wings to get around," Rowan began, his tone gentle but firm. "Faeries move in a different way—silently, smoothly. We travel between the World Below and the other Realms using Faerie Circles." He gestured toward the oak tree's roots, where a natural circle of mushrooms had grown in the soft earth. "These circles are made by nature—by life itself—and they connect us to the places we need to go."

Ella stared at the mushroom circle, a shiver running down her spine. She had seen it before but had never paid it much attention. Now, knowing it was some kind of magical portal, it seemed to pulse with a strange energy.

Rowan reached into his pocket, feeling for two smooth stones that were nestled there. They seemed to hum with energy, as if they had been waiting for him to pull them out. He slowly withdrew them, revealing two simple necklaces with small stones threaded onto thin cords.

"These," he said, holding the necklaces up for the twins to see, "are what we call Holed stones. They're simple, yes, but they're powerful. Most Fae wear them around their necks, like this, so they can *Jump*—travel between places—whenever they need to." The stones were beautiful, Ella's was white with grey mottling and a wide hole with dark green twine wrapped around it, Kal's was bright white with dimples all over it, and brown twine. The twins found themselves transfixed, as though they could sense the power embedded in them.

Kal, for once, didn't have anything to say. He turned the stone over in his hand, feeling the dimples on its surface and the weight it carried, small yet significant. Ella slipped the cord over her head and let the stone rest against her chest. She felt an odd warmth spread through her, like the stone was syncing with her heartbeat.

Rowan continued, "You should always keep these on you. Faerie Circles are hidden all over the place, often in the most unexpected spots. But having these stones on you means you don't have to worry about finding a circle out in nature." He looked at both of them, his expression serious now. "The World Below is waiting, and you'll need to be prepared."

Ella's heart raced with a mixture of excitement and fear. She wasn't sure she was ready for any of this, but seeing the determination on her parents' faces gave her strength. Kal, still holding his necklace, glanced over at his sister and managed a small grin.

"Well, at least we don't have to worry about wings," he quipped, trying to mask his nerves with humour.

Ella shot him a sideways smile. "Yeah, who needs wings

when we've got secret magic stones and mushroom portals?"

Diana and Rowan exchanged a look of calm as they watched their children, knowing full well the challenges ahead, but also confident that together, their family was ready to face them.

Ella, standing close to her mum, felt a wave of nerves wash over her. "Is it hard? Jumping, I mean—into another world? It doesn't sound easy."

Diana chuckled softly. "It's easier than you think. It feels like taking a quick, deep breath, like this." She exaggerated a loud, sharp inhale, "HHUUUUUUH!" to demonstrate.

Without hesitation, both Ella and Kal mimicked their mother, inhaling deeply. As they locked eyes, trying to hold in their breath, they burst into laughter, their nervous energy melting away.

Rowan held up his own necklace, showing them how to use it. "All you have to do is place your thumb and fore-finger over the hole on each side of the stone."

Kal, always eager, had his necklace in hand and was about to press the stone when Diana quickly pulled his hand away. "Not yet, Kal! You could end up anywhere!"

Kal froze, realising he hadn't thought about that. He just wanted to get going.

Rowan continued his explanation, and this time, both Ella and Kal were listening intently not wanting to risk making a mistake. "You must hold the stone in your dominant hand—the one you write with. Think clearly about where you want to go, and only then, press your thumb and forefinger over the hole. In a breath, you'll be there."

Ella blinked, surprised at how simple it all sounded, but then a thought crossed her mind. "But how are we supposed to imagine where we're going if we've never been there?"

"Good question!" Rowan responded, sounding like a teacher who was impressed by his student's sharp thinking. "Your mum will Jump first, and then you'll both follow, one at a time. Instead of picturing the place, just focus on who you're going to. Imagine your mum, and you'll be taken to the same place she is."

"I'll go after Mum," Ella said, "if that's alright with you?" She glanced at Kal, noticing the proud smile on his face as he nodded.

Normally, Ella let Kal take the lead on new things, only following once she felt it was safe. But this time, she was determined to be brave.

Diana pulled Ella into a tight hug, squeezing her as if it was their last goodbye, which unsettled Ella a bit. But, pushing aside her nerves, Ella hugged her mum back, unaware that in doing so, they were strengthening their connection, making it easier for Ella to find her later.

Diana then turned to Kal, who responded with a bear-like hug that lifted her off the ground.

Without any further words, Diana gave Ella one last reassuring look, smiled, and pressed her fingers over the Holed stone on her necklace. In an instant, without a sound, she was gone.

Ella and Kal stood in stunned silence. Before they could fully process what had just happened, Rowan gently urged Ella to take her necklace.

"It's OK, Ella. Your mum is waiting for you. It's best to do it quickly while she's still fresh in your mind—the connection is strongest now."

Ella hesitated, feeling her earlier confidence wavering. She looked at Kal, her anxiety growing.

"You can do it," Kal whispered, seeing the fear in her eyes. "I know you can."

"Don't look at Kal, Ella. You need your Mum in your mind. 3... 2... 1... Go!" Rowan's voice was steady as he counted down.

Ella closed her eyes, focusing on the memory of her Mum's emotional hug just before she disappeared. Her thumb and finger met at the centre of the Holed stone without her even thinking. Time seemed to pause, and then a breath rushed into her lungs like a waterfall, filling them until she thought they might burst. Just as panic began to set in, everything stopped.

Ella hesitated, not wanting to open her eyes, but knowing she had to. She slowly peeked through one eye and there, standing in front of her, was her Mum, smiling with tears in her eyes. At first, she wasn't sure if it was real, but the moment she felt her Mum's touch, the breath she had been holding slowly released.

"It's OK, Ella, you did it," Diana whispered.

Ella could only focus on her Mum; everything else around them was a bright, comforting haze.

Back in the world above, Kal was more shocked to see his sister disappear than he had been with his Mum.

"Dad, do you think she made it?" Panic was rising in his

chest, the thought that Ella might have ended up some-where else making him feel sick.

"Yes," Rowan replied calmly. "Your Mum would've been back by now if Ella hadn't arrived within a few seconds."

Kal felt a bit more at ease, but his stomach quickly knotted again as he realised it was now his turn.

"You can do this, Kal. It only takes a moment, and I'll be right behind you," his Dad reassured him.

Kal took a deep breath, exhaled slowly, then closed his eyes. He thought of his Mum and Ella, then pressed his thumb and finger against the Holed stone. In what seemed like a heartbeat, he felt hands on his shoulders and heard his Dad's voice in his ear.

"You did it, Kal."

For a split second, Kal didn't understand and thought he hadn't made the Jump. His stomach dropped in fear, but then he heard his Mum's voice.

"Kal, open your eyes. You're here—you've made it."

He slowly opened his eyes, greeted by a light and warmth he could only compare to sunlight. His Mum and Ella stood in front of him, beaming with relief.

Both Ella and Kal then turned to look around, taking in their new surroundings. Kal frowned in confusion—every-thing looked different, yet strangely familiar at the same time.

Ella, meanwhile, was wide-eyed, staring in awe at the inside of their new home. She had never seen anything like it. Though it seemed smaller than their old house, the light-ness and openness of the space made it feel both comforting and welcoming.

They all stood in what must have been the living room. Both Kal and Ella's attention were immediately drawn upwards to where hundreds of tiny, white leaves blanketed the ceiling. Around these leaves were thousands of flickering lights, moving from branch to branch, never straying too far.

Ella couldn't believe the surreal beauty of what she was seeing. "Kal, are you seeing this too?" she asked, her voice barely above a whisper.

All she got in response was a mesmerised, "Mmmhmm."

Ella's delicate gaze began to drift down the curved walls, which were covered in light wood panels that cocooned the room in a gentle, reassuring embrace. She marvelled at how organic everything felt, as if the house had grown from the ground itself.

Finally, her eyes met her mum's. "Mum, this is unbelievable! But... why is there a tree in the house?"

Diana smiled knowingly at her daughter, understanding that this question was just the tip of an iceberg too vast for words. "This is The Solar Tree. It's the living source of energy within our Realm. We have no direct sunlight from above, so this tree gives us our sunlight below. Its roots reach all the way down to the Earth's core, bringing the light back up to us."

Kal, still entranced, followed the branches of The Solar Tree with his eyes, tracing their path as they seamlessly passed through the walls, continuing outside. Curiosity got the better of him, and he walked over to the curved wall where what appeared to be the front door stood. It reached as tall as the ceiling, adorned with coloured glass arches and intricate mosaic patterns around the top.

Kal stepped through the door onto a wide, sweeping veranda that encircled the entire house. His breath caught as he gazed out over hundreds of homes similar to their own, all connected by an intricate network of The Solar Tree branches, which were pulsing with energy. Each home glowed brightly against the deep, dark surroundings, making the view resemble stars scattered across a night sky.

Turning to his dad, who had joined him on the veranda, Kal asked quite matter-of-factly, "So, how exactly do we get off the house? I don't see any lifts or stairs, and you did say we can't fly."

Rowan chuckled softly. "Your Holed stone will take you anywhere you need to go. Once you're out of the residential area, there are plenty of places to explore on foot, so you won't need the stone for that."

From behind him, Kal heard Ella call out excitedly, "Kal, quick! Look at this!"

Kal jogged back inside, but Ella was no longer in the living room. Her voice called out again, and he followed the sound, realising she was upstairs. As he climbed the strangest but most beautiful staircase he had ever seen, curling like the inside of a Spirula shell, Kal couldn't help but feel like every corner of this new world was designed to captivate his imagination.

Kal ascended the shallow steps, which gracefully led him to the second floor. He heard Ella's voice calling again from inside a dimly lit room. As he reached the doorway, he paused, "I can't see you, Ella. What are you doing in a dark room?"

"Just walk in," she said, her voice laced with excitement. "You'll soon see."

Stepping further into the room, Kal's vision began to shift, much like it had that night when he'd ridden out after Ella to the Tulip tree. Slowly, the room blossomed into a soft, ethereal glow. It felt just as homely as the living room downstairs, with a large arched window occupying the entire back wall. The view outside was breathtaking, with twinkling lights from the homes surrounding them and as far as the eye could see, each glowing with energy from the Solar Tree. The same intricate mosaic pattern that adorned the front door framed the window, and a familiar blanket of white leaves lay sleepily across the ceiling. A raised bed appeared to float in mid-air, with a delicate spiral staircase winding up to it.

Kal's attention was drawn to a section of the tree branch near the door. It had a hole in it that was perfectly round, glowing a vibrant yellow, and emitting a soft hum, beckoning him closer.

Ella turned from the window just in time to see Kal reach out toward the glowing section of the tree and placed his hand inside. "Kal! You can't just go around touching things when you don't know what they are!" Her voice reverted to the tone of her six-year-old self. "MUM!"

Diana entered the room, noticing Kal's slightly guilty expression, as if he were a child caught sneaking an extra cookie. She laughed gently at his worried look. "Don't worry, Kal. It's something we were going to have you both do anyway. What do you feel in the tree?"

Kal hesitated, unsure how to describe it. "It kind of feels like… warm, thick jelly, rippling over my hand."

"Good," Diana said with a smile. "That's exactly what you should be feeling. The Solar Tree is reading your essence. Since it's a source of energy and we're all connected to it, we can control how to use it. Essentially, this is your light switch."

Kal's eyebrows shot up in surprise. "Wait, how do we control it? Do I have to stick my hand in this thing every time I want the lights on?"

Diana walked over to the tree and gently stroked the branch. As she did, the hundreds of tiny white leaves began to open, casting a clear, pure light across the room. Then, as if summoned by magic, millions of tiny fireflies appeared, twinkling like stars in the air.

Kal, still unable to remove his hand from the tree, looked slightly panicked. "The tree will let go once it's finished reading you," Diana reassured him. "Just relax."

A moment later, the rippling sensation stopped, and Kal's hand was released from the tree's grasp. He sighed in relief.

Diana motioned toward another branch. "Now, gently touch the tree and, in your mind, ask for what you want."

Kal hesitated for a moment before reaching out and touching the branch. In his mind, he thought, *I'd like the lights to go down.* Instantly, the room softened, darkening as smoothly as the setting sun. A huge grin spread across Kal's face, his amazement uncontainable.

"That was incredible!" he exclaimed. "Ella, you *have* to try this!"

Diana led Ella into the adjacent room, her future bedroom. Spellbound by the vibrant yellow glow of the tree branch, Ella stood transfixed. It pulsed with life, drawing her closer. Only when her mum gently nudged her did she snap out of her daze, ready to experience the magic for herself.

Ella reached out and placed her hand in the glowing section of the tree, just as she had seen her brother do. Instantly, she felt the warm, jelly-like substance engulf her hand, rippling over her fingers. A few minutes later, the tree released her, and Ella gently stroked its surface. In her mind, she asked for the lights to come on, and with a blink, they did.

Even though she had just watched Kal do the same, the experience of controlling the light herself felt entirely different. This made Ella think of her Tulip tree and the night she and Kal slept underneath it. That tree had certainly responded to her, and she began to wonder whether all trees would now react to her in this way, or if it was only her special Tulip tree and the Solar Tree here.

Diana left Ella and Kal to explore, returning to the living room where Rowan was organising items that hadn't been touched in 16 years.

"The kids have really taken to the Solar Tree. It didn't take long at all for them to link with it. I can't believe we're here, back in our old home," Diana said, wrapping her arms around Rowan's waist, squeezing him tightly with excitement.

Rowan smiled and responded with a squeeze. "We will have to take them to meet the Council soon. We can't have rumours flying around about twin Fae before they've met them."

Diana knew Rowan was right, but she also knew that once they went to see the Council, the real work would begin for the twins. After that, they would have little control over their own lives anymore.

CHAPTER EIGHT

Rowan went to find the twins, who were both sitting by the large windows in Kal's new bedroom, pointing out different houses and laughing at the craziness of seeing people popping in and out of their homes, obviously using their Holed Stones.

"Kal, Ella, there are some people we need you to meet, and we have to do it sooner rather than later." Rowan tried to keep the sense of urgency out of his voice, but he wasn't sure he'd managed it.

Kal looked back at his dad while Ella continued staring out of the window at the strange new world that was now their home. Kal tried to read his dad's tone, but couldn't, which always worried him.

"Do we have to go right now?" he asked.

"Yes, I'm afraid so. It's important for you to meet the Fae Council before word gets out that twin Fae are here. The head of the Council knew about your birth, but he was the only one, and he's waiting for us to arrive."

Ella was now looking directly at her dad with a little-girl, *do we have to go* expression. Her dad picked up on it immediately and smiled.

"I'm sorry, Ella, but yes, this is completely out of my hands. The head of the Council is called Lord Archer, and he was once a great warrior—some say the greatest. He's truly excited that twins have been blessed into our Clan during his lifetime."

"Dad, I really don't think I'll be a very good warrior. Couldn't we change to be something else?" Ella knew she was grasping at straws by the look on her dad's face, but she had to try.

Rowan sat down on the floor with the twins and looked at them both in turn.

"You will both be brave and strong warriors, I know you will. It's inside you, and once you start training, it will come out for you to see. Now come, Lord Archer is waiting."

The twins reluctantly followed Rowan down to the living and kitchen area, where they found their mum busily organising jars of roots and bulbs in the cupboard. The table was already full of dried and crushed plants.

Diana jumped when she noticed her husband and twins standing there.

"Oh! Goodness, I didn't hear you all come down."

"It's time we went to the Dome to meet Lord Archer. He'll be expecting us," said Rowan, excitement bubbling beneath his calm tone.

"Okay, so we'll do the same as last time. Mum will Jump first, then you, Kal. Just remember to focus on Mum and you'll be fine."

Diana quickly connected with her son by looking him straight in the eyes and touching foreheads. Then, faster than a blink, she was gone.

Kal tried not to overthink what he was doing and focused intently on his mum. Before he knew it, he was standing in front of her, in what had to be the most breath-taking building he had ever seen. Moments later, Ella arrived, quickly followed by their dad.

They stood within a giant Dome, its ceiling towering high, easily the height of a 15-story building. The air was charged with energy, and the space within the Dome radi-ated a sense of ancient magic. In the centre of the Dome was a massive amethyst crystal cavern that sank deep into the ground, its surface gleaming with an ethereal glow that filled the space around it like a soft violet light, alive and pulsing.

Around the edges of the cavern stood several Fae, each of them facing inward, eyes closed, almost as if they were in a trance. The glow of the crystal reflected in their serene faces, and they stood so still it seemed like they were in deep meditation, absorbing something far beyond what could be seen with the eyes.

Ella, drawn to the incredible sight before her, felt herself naturally gravitating toward the crystal, her feet moving on their own accord as if being pulled by an invisible force. Her eyes were wide, filled with awe. The beauty of the place, the gentle hum of energy that filled the air, was unlike anything she had ever experienced. The connection she felt with the crystal was instant and deep, as if the very core of her being resonated with its power.

Kal watched as his mum and sister approached the giant crystal, both of them clearly mesmerised by its energy. He stood still, his mind racing but his body calm. "It's incredible," Kal whispered, almost to himself.

Kal watched as his dad jogged to catch up with his mum. He was fascinated by this whole new way of generating energy and receiving light, and he couldn't wait until his dad could explain it all in greater detail. But for now, he was feeling a growing sense of urgency. Kal called out to his mum, who was now walking slowly back, hand in hand with Ella.

"Come on, Mum, we'll be late!" he said, trying to keep the impatience from creeping into his voice. As nervous as he was about meeting Lord Archer, the thought of being late bothered him even more.

Ella's eyes were wide and filled with awe. "Kal, you have to see it. It's incredible," she said, her voice full of emotion.

"I will, another time," Kal replied, a little exasperated. "Let's just get this over with first."

Rowan waved them forward. "This way," he said, setting off at a brisk pace toward the other side of the Dome. Kal and Ella followed, taking in the grandeur of their surroundings as they went. As they moved, Kal began to notice the other Fae within the Dome, each one unique in their own way.

Kal nudged Ella with his elbow, a grin tugging at the corner of his mouth. "I haven't seen anyone dressed like Tinkerbell yet, have you?" he joked, unable to resist. Ella swallowed a laugh as they passed through a set of towering stone arches, intricately carved with swirling patterns that shimmered as they caught the light.

The arches led into a smaller, pod-like dome. The space was darker but carried a warmth within it. The faint glow of the Solar Tree's leaves overhead gave the area an inviting, golden hue. Ahead of them, a guard stood by a plain-looking door—plain compared to everything else they had seen so far.

Diana approached the guard, offering a polite smile. "Lord Archer is expecting us. It's Mrs. and Mr. Bradshaw," she said. The guard's eyes flicked over to Ella and Kal, clearly curious about their identities, but said nothing as he waited for more clarification.

Diana hesitated, unsure how much she should say. They'd been instructed not to reveal the twins' existence until they had officially met with Lord Archer. She was about to stumble through an explanation when the door suddenly flung open.

A giant of a man, broad-shouldered and towering, ducked slightly to get through the door. His voice was a booming, happy rumble. "Diana! Rowan! It's so good to see you again. Come in, come in!" His deep voice was warm and welcoming, filling the smaller Dome with energy.

Ella blinked in surprise. Was *this* Lord Archer? He didn't exactly look like what she had expected. She had pictured someone regal, perhaps with a crown or a robe—something more like the stories she'd heard about Faerie lords. This man looked like he could crush boulders with his bare hands. He appeared to be in his 50s, though he wore his years well. His beard, streaked with silver, hung about five inches past his chin, neatly bound together by a thick silver ring. His wild, light brown shoulder-length hair, however, was much less tidy, a mess of curls and waves that seemed to spring out in every direction.

Over his clothing, he wore an imposing chest plate adorned with a circular arrangement of various crystals, all pulling your eye to a central stone that resembled molten lava. The stone seemed alive, shifting from a deep, fiery red to an almost cold, hardened black with each step he took. The way it flickered between hot and cold, light and dark, was mesmerising.

Kal glanced over at Ella, he had never seen a man like this before—so rough and imposing, yet covered in crystals. He was used to men like his dad, always in suits and ties, the epitome of businesslike order. But standing before them now was the most rugged, manliest man they had ever encountered, and he was practically shimmering with gemstones and wearing what looked like giant shoulder pads that made him seem even more intimidating.

Lord Archer's presence filled the room, and yet there was something about his demeanour that was warm and approachable, even with all the strength and power he radiated. He reached out a massive hand to Kal and Ella. "You must be the twins I've been hearing so much about," he said, his smile broadening. "Come, sit down the man gestured to them all, in a superior but affectionate manner.

"I have been waiting 17 years to meet you both, Ella and Kalan. It is with great honour that I welcome you into our Clan and into the Realm Below."

There was no mistaking now that this imposing figure

was indeed Lord Archer. His deep voice carried a weight of history and authority that made the room seem smaller, yet warmer.

Ella, who would normally be quiet and allow Kal to take the lead, felt an unexpected surge of courage. She opened her mouth before she even realised it. "Thank you, Lord Archer. That's very kind of you," she said, her voice steady but respectful.

Kal, slightly surprised by his sister's sudden boldness, fumbled for words. "Yes, err... thank you, Lord Archer... mmm, yes," he stuttered, feeling his face flush. Ella shot him a look, her wide eyes sternly warning him to pull it together.

Fortunately, Lord Archer didn't seem to notice Kal's awkwardness and continued speaking. "When your mother and father came to me all those years ago and told me they were expecting twins, my first question was, 'Who else knows?' Luckily, your mother is a skilled Healer and had scanned herself, so the only Fae who knew were the three of us and the Birth Seer.

We appointed our best warrior to accompany your parents to the Realm Above and protect you during the first 16 years of your lives. Warren has been commended for his unwavering commitment in keeping you safe and your identities hidden from those who might wish you harm."

Ella's heart skipped a beat at the mention of "harm." She felt like the wind had been knocked out of her, and she swallowed a cough to cover her sudden gasp.

Lord Archer continued, "It was imperative that we kept your existence a secret, especially from the Byrne Clan.

However, this became far more complicated when you, Ella, formed a close friendship with Rhiannon."

Diana lowered her gaze, feeling somewhat responsible for the situation they found themselves in. If only they had stopped Ella and Rhi's friendship sooner, perhaps things wouldn't have spiralled the way they had.

Ella's eyes stung with the prickle of tears she fought to keep back. The mention of Rhi brought the confusion and sadness of their friendship crashing back into her mind.

Sensing his sister's upset, Kal took a deep breath and decided to confront Lord Archer, hoping to clear up the mystery that was still haunting them.

"Excuse me, Lord Archer," Kal began cautiously, trying to keep his tone respectful. "Could you please clarify why Rhi's twin was taken? It's still a bit confusing for us, and as you can see, upsetting for Ella."

The room seemed to close in as Kal's question hung in the air. He suddenly felt like he had overstepped. But as soon as the silence became too much Lord Archer gave a solemn nod.

"You are right to ask," he began, his voice taking on a more serious tone. "The decision to take Rhiannon's twin was made when we received word that twins were to be born into the Byrne Clan. This would usually be a momentous occasion, but we knew far too well that they would be used as a weapon to destroy human kind, and bring unbalance by becoming the rulers of the Màthair Realm."

Ella's heart ached for her friend. The revelation that Rhi had a twin, one she thought was dead, was overwhelming.

"Does she know, that her twins alive?" she whispered, almost afraid of the answer.

Lord Archer shook his head. "Not yet. But soon, the truth will ultimately come out. And when it is, we must be prepared."

"I still don't understand," Kal said, searching for answers on Lord Archer's face. "How are the Byrnes going to know about us being Fae if we were supposed to be a secret?"

Lord Archer's expression grew serious. "When a Fae child turns 16, a surge of energy is released that can be sensed by all Fae above ground. The Byrnes would have felt your energy as you went through your Shift."

Diana had moved to comfort Ella, wrapping her arms around her daughter. Ella clung to her mother, feeling the weight of the revelation.

"I learned about the two of you when it became clear you would be born just weeks apart from the Byrne twins. We knew we had to keep your existence hidden. If they had discovered you, there was a risk you would have been separated or, even worse, killed," Lord Archer explained, his voice heavy with the memories of those difficult decisions.

Ella began to realise the gravity of the choices her parents had made, and she squeezed her mum's hand as an apology for her earlier anger.

"But how did they believe the baby was dead instead of just missing?" Kal asked, still frowning.

"We had a Fae couple who gave birth on the same day in the same hospital," Rowan began, stepping forward to add to the explanation. "Tragically, their child didn't survive. One of our nurses managed to swap the babies within an hour of the Byrne twins being born. Thankfully, they didn't notice the difference, as their newborns were in a separate room while Mrs. Byrne's rested."

Kal's frown deepened, but this time it was a mixture of amazement and disbelief at how seamlessly the plan had been executed despite the risks. "That could have gone wrong in so many ways," he muttered.

Ella, her voice soft and filled with sorrow, asked, "Where is the baby now? I mean, Rhi's sister?"

Lord Archer's face softened. "She was given to the couple who lost their child, and she's lived here in the World Below with them ever since. We couldn't risk the twins encountering each other. Their connection would have been undeniable, even if they were raised separately."

Ella nodded, understanding the gravity of the situation. She knew that if the same had happened to her and Kal, she would have recognised him no matter where they were or how they were raised. The bond between twins was deeper than any magic, or any secret that could be kept from them.

Lord Archer stood up with great purpose, rubbing his hands together as if to signal a shift in the conversation. "But now," he declared, "you must take your first steps within our Clan and meet the person who will become the most important figure in your life—besides each other, of course!"

Ella and Kal exchanged nervous glances. Their parents' faces, though proud, betrayed a hint of sadness.

"Your Fae Master is called Barrett," Lord Archer continued, "and he will train you to become the greatest warriors of our Realm."

The weight of those words hung heavy in the air. Kal and Ella didn't dare look at each other directly, but both felt the rising fear at the thought of what was expected of them.

Rowan, sensing the tension, hesitated before speaking. "Lord Archer, I thought you wanted them to meet with the rest of the Council first? Shouldn't they know more before we rush into this?"

Lord Archer waved Rowan's concern away with a flick of his hand. "I've already informed the Council about the twins. They understand that time is of the essence. We simply cannot afford too many pleasantries. The training must begin at once, for we don't know when the Byrne Clan will start their search for the first element, or if they've already begun."

With that, Lord Archer placed a firm but nurturing arm around both Ella and Kal, guiding them towards the door. "Come, let's go down to the Training Dome and get you started."

Diana's heart pounded in her chest. She had always known this day would come, but not like this—not on their very first day in their new Realm. Panic flared in her chest, and before she even realised it, words flew from her mouth.

"No! Not today!" she burst out, her voice trembling. "Please, let them settle in. This has been an overwhelming week for them, and…"

Before she could finish, Lord Archer interrupted, his voice gentle but firm. "Diana, I understand how difficult this is for you, truly I do. But we must begin their training now. We are at the brink of war, and time isn't something we have to waste."

CHAPTER NINE

K al looked up with sheer panic etched across his face. "Um... First element? War? What does that mean?"

Lord Archer didn't respond, instead leading them back towards the massive Dome with the glowing Amethyst at its centre.

"I'll take them down to Barrett. They'll be home later on, I'm sure," Lord Archer said, dismissing any further questions. Before Rowan or Diana could say anything to the twins, Lord Archer was already guiding them away.

Diana's face crumpled as she collapsed into Rowan's arms, tears streaming down her face. "What have we done? I knew we shouldn't have come back. Rowan, can't we do something?" Her voice was thick with desperation as she looked up at her husband, pleading for answers.

But Rowan's face remained stoic. "This is their calling, Diana. They were born for this. It's why we came back."

Diana's eyes filled with pain. "But they might die!

They're not fighters, Rowan. They're gentle souls. This—this will kill them."

Before Rowan could respond, Diana touched her Holed Stone, vanishing from his arms and Jumping back to their home, leaving Rowan standing alone in the Dome.

Ella and Kal walked behind Lord Archer, both wanting to speak but unsure of what to say. They exchanged glances, desperate to talk yet overwhelmed by everything happening around them.

As they continued down the corridor, Kal's eyes widened in disbelief. Ella noticed her brother's sudden jolt and followed his gaze.

Ahead of them were two enormous, church-like windows made of shimmering, multicoloured glass that seemed to pulse with an ethereal glow. The twins stared up, captivated by the vibrant colours dancing across the glass.

It wasn't until they looked back down that they realised Lord Archer had already passed through the glass and was now standing on the other side, waiting for them. Kal and Ella exchanged a bewildered glance. Kal hesitantly reached out his hand toward the glass, expecting resistance, but his fingers passed through as if it were nothing more than a cloud.

Kal turned to Ella, nodding to assure her it was safe. Together, they stepped forward and melted through the glass, their bodies dissolving into the misty, glowing surface.

They found themselves standing on a wide stone balcony overlooking a deep gorge. Both twins instinctively took a deep breath at the same time, drawing in the rich, earthy tones of the air mixed with sweet fragrances they'd never smelled before.

Ella stepped forward to peer over the balcony. The walls of the gorge were lush and green, covered in soft moss and dotted with small trees growing out of cracks in the rock. At the bottom, a clear stream sparkled in the warm light, winding its way over rocks and patches of grass as it carved through the landscape.

For a moment, Ella could do nothing but stand there, mesmerised. The beauty around her was impossible to comprehend. It was hard to believe they were underground. Her gaze traveled upward, following the immense branches of the Solar Tree. The massive branches were as thick as buses in some places, their cracked bark giving them an ancient, rugged appearance. These giant branches stretched up from the earth like towering columns, weaving together into intricate lattice structures that looked as solid as stone. Around these natural frameworks, buildings were nestled, securely cradled within the safety and strength of the tree.

Kal joined her at the edge of the balcony, his eyes wide with wonder. "This is incredible," he said, his voice filled with awe. "I feel like we're on a different planet. Some of this geology just doesn't make any sense scientifically."

Lord Archer stepped forward, placing his large hands gently on their shoulders. "This Realm is very different from the one you are used to," he said, his deep voice carrying wisdom. "You will both learn as you go. Don't get too caught up in trying to understand everything. There are things even I, after all these years, cannot fully comprehend." His gaze lingered on Kal, sensing the boy's scientific curiosity, much like his father's.

"Look over there," Lord Archer said, pointing across the gorge to a tall building with a domed roof that gleamed in the soft light. "That is where you will train. It's a sacred space, only for warriors. No one else is allowed to enter."

Ella followed his gesture and saw the thin stone bridge that arched over the gorge. The path around to it hugged the moss-covered walls, and fern-like plants draped over their heads as they walked, delicate silk-like fronds brushing their faces. The sound of water dripping from the rocks made Ella thirsty, increasing her anxiety as they approached the bridge.

From the balcony, the bridge had seemed small, but up close, it was even narrower than it first appeared—just a simple stone arch connecting the two sides of the gorge. No rails, no barriers, just a thin path over a vast drop that would surely mean multiple broken bones if they fell.

Lord Archer stood to one side, saying nothing, but clearly waiting for Ella to take the first step. She turned to Kal, a look of apprehension etched on her face, and then faced the bridge again. With a deep breath, she stepped forward. As soon as her foot touched the stone, she felt something strange—a sensation she couldn't quite place, as if a missing piece of herself had just clicked back into place.

Kal watched her from behind, his own anxiety evident in the tightness of his jaw. "Ella, you sure about this?" he asked quietly, though he knew his sister well enough to trust her instincts.

Ella didn't respond. Her attention was solely on the

bridge, and the odd sense of calm that was spreading through her. It was as if the stone was alive, responding to her presence, helping her stay balanced as she moved forward.

Lord Archer remained silent, observing the twins carefully. He had seen this before—the moment when young Fae warriors first connected with their magic of the Realm. It was as though the land itself recognised their importance and provided subtle guidance.

Kal, not wanting to be left behind, took a hesitant step onto the bridge. He felt the same strange energy surge through him, a soft pulse beneath his feet. It wasn't alarming, but it was unlike anything he'd ever felt before. His analytical mind struggled to make sense of it, but he forced himself to trust the process.

When they finally reached the other side, Ella let out a breath she hadn't realised she'd been holding. Her heart was still racing, but the sensation of that missing piece sliding into place lingered, leaving her exhilarated.

Kal, wiping the sweat from his brow, looked at Lord Archer. "What just happened?" His voice was steady, but there was an underlying tremor of uncertainty.

Lord Archer smiled, "You've just made your first connection with the Realm. The magic of this place is woven into the earth, the air, the trees. It will help guide you—if you let it."

Ella and Kal exchanged a glance, neither entirely sure what to say. Whatever lay ahead, they were no longer just ordinary teenagers. Something far greater had begun to unfold, and there was no turning back now.

With a nod from Lord Archer, they continued down the path, the towering building of the Training Dome now looming ahead of them, waiting.

Lord Archer showed the twins into the Training Dome proudly, as if *he* were their father.

Ella went from feeling unusually excited to terrified in a matter of seconds. The high-ceilinged room was full of all manner of weapons displayed on the walls. Branches from the Solar Tree stretched from wall to wall and ceiling to floor, creating a jungle-like atmosphere that Ella could barely see into. She hadn't even considered that there might be others training with them until she noticed eight other teenagers standing there, all watching.

At the back of the room, Ella saw a figure moving toward them through the branches. He wasn't overly tall, dressed in dark brown and black leather armour. His face looked stern, and his shoulder-length black hair was messy, falling free from its fastening at the back. As he got closer, Ella became transfixed by his eyes—they were pale green with a bright blue ring around the outside.

"Barrett, I would like you to meet your two newest warriors, twins Ella and Kalan Bradshaw."

He stood firmly in front of the twins, looking them both in the eyes.

"My name is Barrett, and I am your trainer. I am honoured to teach you in the warrior ways of the Faerie."

The rest of the students seemed unsettled, and some started glaring at Ella and Kal.

"Class," Barrett addressed the group, "these are our two newest students, Ella and Kalan Bradshaw. And yes, before any of you ask, they are brother and sister. In fact, they're more than that—they are twins! As I'm sure you're all aware, twins are born to be great warriors and will outmatch every one of you, so trying to challenge them will be a waste of time, although very courageous."

Kal's eyes widened. He tried to swallow the lump in his throat, but his mouth was too dry. He turned slightly to see Ella looking at him with the same panic in her eyes.

Lord Archer bent down and whispered quietly to Ella and Kal, "Do your very best today. This is the start of something truly magical." And with that, he turned and left the room, carrying himself with such authority that no one dared question his departure.

Barrett then spoke quickly to Ella and Kal, in a tone that made it sound like they should already know what he was talking about. "Go and get into your training suits. We've already wasted enough time with this interruption." He pointed toward a door on the left of the dome which was surrounded with weapons.

Ella and Kal exchanged glances before slowly moving toward the door. Ella opened it and stepped through into an equally impressive round room, with a high, glass-domed roof that allowed the Solar Tree's branches to drape protectively overhead.

"What are we supposed to do now?" Kal asked, unsure if he'd missed some important instructions earlier.

"I think we're supposed to get changed," Ella said sarcastically, looking around, "but into what, I have no idea."

They saw the other students' clothes hanging on hooks, but no sign of anything they were supposed to wear. The confusion mounted as they stood there, unsure of what to do next.

Ella started pacing around the cold, stone room, her eyes searching for anything that resembled a locker or a place where they might find their training suits. The light stone walls were intricately carved with images of battle scenes that stretched all the way up to the glass roof and encircled the room. The carvings were mesmerising, filled with strange figures, creatures, and what looked like ancient warriors mid-battle.

"Kal, come over here and look at this," Ella called.

Kal had been inspecting the central column, still hoping to find their clothes. Hearing his sister, he wandered over, his eyes lighting up when he saw the battle scenes etched into the stone walls.

"What do you think it is?" Ella asked. She knew this kind of thing would excite Kal. He loved history, often reading extra books about ancient civilisations in his spare time. Unlike Kal, Ella had always found history dull, right along with maths.

Kal's face was full of awe. "I don't know," he muttered, completely absorbed. "But this is incredible."

Just then, a voice from behind startled Ella.

"These are depictions of the great battles we've fought over millennia. They're beautiful, aren't they?"

Ella jumped and turned to find herself face-to-face with a girl about her age, with short dark hair that framed her face in a way that made it look strikingly feminine against her smooth olive skin. Her almond-shaped hazel-green eyes sparkled with curiosity.

"Hi, I'm Alana," the girl introduced herself, her voice friendly. "I thought I'd come check to see if you were finding everything you needed."

"Um, no, actually," Ella admitted, feeling a surge of relief. "We don't know where to find the clothes we're supposed to change into."

Alana raised an eyebrow in mild confusion. "You weren't shown around or told how to open your lockers?"

Ella shook her head. "No, we just got here today from the Realm Above, and honestly, everything has been a bit crazy."

Alana smiled sympathetically. "That makes sense. Let me show you."

She led Ella to the side of the room, while Kal remained entranced by the carvings, completely unaware of what was happening.

"See these flat, smooth lines running down the walls where there aren't any engravings?" Alana pointed to an area that seemed less intricate than the rest of the stone wall.

Ella nodded, leaning in to get a better look.

"All you have to do is place your hand flat on the stone and wipe it downwards, like this." Alana demonstrated, her hand moving down the smooth part of the wall.

Ella did exactly as Alana had instructed, and as soon as she took her hand off the wall, a glass panel appeared in front of her. She gasped in disbelief, a broad smile spreading across her face. "This is amazing. How... I can't believe it!" She turned to find Kal, who was still engrossed in the wall carvings, tracing his fingers along their intricate designs. He came across a flat strip of wall and instinctively brushed his hand over it.

In an instant, a glass door appeared in front of him, though it revealed nothing inside. Kal turned to share his excitement with Ella, only to see her standing beside her own glass door, and a girl he hadn't noticed earlier.

"Oh, hi! Sorry, I didn't hear you come in. I was... just looking at the walls," Kal mumbled, his cheeks flushing as he realised how stupid he sounded.

The girl smiled kindly. "Hi Kalan, I'm Alana. I was showing your sister how to open your lockers, but it looks like you figured it out already—impressive." Kal blushed even more at the compliment, feeling his ears heat up.

"That's actually Griffin's locker," Alana added with a grimace, pointing to the locker Kal had opened. "You might want to close it incase he comes in. Just swipe your hand upward."

Kal quickly swiped his hand, and the glass door melted back into the stone wall as if it had never existed. Embarrassed, he hurried over to join Ella, who was still marvelling at her own locker.

"My sword!" Ella exclaimed, excitement bubbling up before she even realised what she was saying. Kal couldn't help but laugh at the absurdity of his sister being thrilled about a sword.

"I know, right?" she chuckled, shaking her head. "I'm not sure I'll ever get used to saying *my* sword."

Alana walked over to the last flat panel of wall and beckoned Kal over. "I'm guessing this one's yours," she said.

Kal swiped his hand down the stone, and sure enough, his locker opened to reveal his bow and arrows, gleaming like old friends waiting for him. His face lit up as he took a deep breath, and pulling his floppy blond hair back in anticipation.

Alana smiled, amused by the twins' reactions to their weapons. "You should both get changed quickly. Barrett doesn't have the best patience. And bring your weapons with you when you're ready." With that, she walked out, leaving Ella and Kal to themselves.

As Alana left, Ella suddenly reached for her brother's messy hair and pulled it back. "Kal, look at your ears! Are they the same as mine?"

Kal, puzzled by her question, humoured her and checked her ears under her hair. His face showed a mixture of surprise and amusement. "You've got pointy ears... have you always had them?"

Ella smirked punching his arm playfully. "You know I haven't. You have them too! Alana's hair is short so I've not noticed them on anyone before now, everyone else has had long hair over their ears."

Kal touched his ears, feeling the subtle points. He wasn't sure how to process this new feature, and for a moment, he felt thankful that wings weren't going to sprout from his back anytime soon.

"Okay, let's focus on getting dressed before Barrett comes in and gives us the drill-sergeant routine," Ella said, her nerves rising at the thought of being late.

They both hurried to change into their training gear. Ella's suit was a sleek, black one-piece with bronze flecks that shimmered in the light. Over it, she wore a sleeveless green jacket that, despite looking thick, felt weightless on her. She marvelled at how it felt like she wasn't wearing anything at all.

Kal, on the other hand, was struggling a bit. His trousers, though seemingly heavy, felt surprisingly light. The large, buckled belt he wore had flag-like pieces of fabric hanging down from both the front and back, making him feel slightly ridiculous.

"I don't think this is right... What do you think?" Kal asked, looking awkward and unsure.

Ella tried to suppress her laughter but couldn't hide her smile. "Honestly, I'd normally say you've got it all wrong, but given where we are, you're probably right. I think I saw someone else wearing something similar before we walked in."

Ella caught her reflection in the mirror inside her locker and barely recognised herself. Pulling her hair back into a messy ponytail, she caught sight of her pointed ears and was struck by how delicate and beautiful they looked.

Both siblings grabbed their weapons and closed their lockers with a swipe. As they stepped out into the training dome, Ella was relieved to see that no one was waiting for them. Across the room, Alana was sparring with one of the boys, and from what little Ella knew about fighting, it looked like she might be winning.

Barrett walked over to Ella and Kal, both of them looked uncomfortable and clearly nervous. Kal instinctively raised his hand, then immediately put it down, realising how ridiculous it must have looked. This wasn't school, and the gesture made him feel out of place. He stammered out his words, making the moment even more awkward.

"Uh, sir... I mean, Barrett. We, uh... we're a little nervous about this training. Neither of us have done anything like this before. Well, unless you count that one time Ruben pushed me down a grass hill at primary school, but..." Kal trailed off, catching Ella's widening eyes and her lips tightening in silent frustration, clearly begging him to stop talking.

Finally, Kal halted his rambling, looking apologetically at Barrett. Ella rolled her eyes and closed them in disbelief.

Barrett remained silent for a few moments. His expression was unreadable, making both twins feel even more out of their depth. When he finally spoke, his voice was slow and steady, though it was hard to tell what emotions were hidden beneath it.

"So, are you telling me your parents never enrolled you in Taekwondo or Jiu-Jitsu? Not even Tai Chi?"

Both twins remained silent, feeling like they had forgotten to turn in their homework. For Kal, this was an especially unsettling feeling, as it was something that never happened to him.

Suddenly, a memory flickered in Ella's mind. Their parents had indeed tried to enrol them in various martial arts and fighting classes, but they had always refused, saying it wasn't their thing. She remembered how Uncle Warren had even tried to convince their school to add Taekwondo to their sports curriculum, but the school had declined for health and safety reasons.

At that moment, Ella wished she had just taken those lessons. Maybe then she wouldn't be so petrified.

Ella straightened up, trying to look more confident. "Yes, they did, but we didn't go because we didn't want to fight for sport. If we'd known why they were pushing us into it, we would have gone."

Barrett's expression didn't change, and his voice remained steady and calm. "Alana!"

The girl they had met earlier in the changing room jumped down effortlessly from one of the Solar Tree branches. Her soft, angelic face was now hard with determination.

"Work with Kalan on his sparring while I focus on Ella," Barrett instructed. "We have a long way to go, and not much time to get them ready."

Ella's stomach twisted with anxiety. "Wait, shouldn't I go with Alana?" she asked, her voice betraying her growing panic. "It doesn't seem fair if I'm partnered with you." She nodded toward Barrett, feeling more anxious as she and Kal were being separated.

Barrett's response was firm. "In the Fae world, there's no difference in strength between male and female warriors. It all comes down to how hard you work, not how big you are."

Ella took a deep breath, feeling a small sense of relief, though her nerves still simmered beneath the surface.

Barrett continued, "Fighting for your Clan is the greatest honour any Fae can receive when they turn 16. Most warriors come from warrior families, but not always. The fact that you both come from a non-warrior background is rare. The fact that you're twins, that makes this situation completely unheard of."

Ella felt the pressure mounting with every word Barrett spoke. She tried to glance discreetly to see if Kal was having a similar conversation with Alana, but she couldn't find him without making it obvious that she was looking.

Barrett's gaze shifted to the sword Ella held awkwardly in her hands. "That is a beautiful sword you've been made. How does she feel in your hand?"

Ella hesitated. The truth was, it felt unnatural to her, but she knew saying that wouldn't help. Instead, she closed her eyes and took a moment to focus, allowing her fingertips to truly feel the sword. Slowly, a warmth spread through her hands, like dipping her fingers into lukewarm water. The sensation ran up her arms, through her chest, and filled her entire body.

Ella's eyes opened wide, and Barrett noticed a brief red flush in them, quickly disappearing.

"That felt... different," Ella said, almost in awe. "It wasn't like I was just holding cold metal. It was warm, alive, like it needed my heart to survive."

Barrett tuned into the energy between Ella and her sword, recognising something extraordinary. What typically took months for young warriors, he sensed in Ella immediately. She was already beginning the *Bonding* process.

"This doesn't usually happen so early in training," Barrett said, intrigued. "Every warrior is deeply connected to their weapon from birth, though they don't realise it. But the Bonding—when that connection becomes tangible—can take up to six months for some Fae."

Ella felt a swell of pride, not in herself, but for some reason in her sword.

"I can see our training will be a bit different from the others," Barrett continued. "Normally, we start with combat and ease into weapon Bonding, but since you have no combat background, we'll begin with the Bonding. Hopefully, that will assist when we move into physical training."

At first, Ella felt relief at not having to fight today. But the idea of Bonding with a weapon sounded equally daunting.

"So this *Bonding*... does it mean my sword is going to become part of me?" Ella asked, a note of worry in her voice.

Barrett smiled, sensing her unease. "You are already connected to it, but you need to learn how to work together properly. It doesn't mean your sword will literally become part of your body, but it does mean you'll feel its energy as it feels yours. You'll hear each other's thoughts."

Just as Ella was about to ask if the Bonding process would hurt, Alana interrupted with a soft cough. She had brought Kal over and whispered something quietly to Barrett.

Kal, now standing next to Ella, had a look of utter bewilderment on his face.

"What is it?" Ella asked, guessing that she probably had the same dazed look on her face as Kal.

"Apparently, my bow and arrow are calling for me to

Bond with them, and I need to go sit with it for like 24 hours or something. How about you?"

Before Ella could respond, one of the other teenagers approached them. He looked both Ella and Kal up and down with his nose crinkled as though there was something unpleasant in the air.

"So, you're the new flavour of the month, huh? Alana won't be happy about that. And don't think any of us are going to go easy on you just because you're twins. If anything, there'll be a target on your back—whoever can bring down a twin Fae first!"

"Griffin, get back to your sparring," Barrett said, not particularly phased by the threat.

Alana stepped forward with a soft, knowing smile. "That's Griffin for you. Not exactly someone you want to annoy. He holds a grudge... for a long time."

"Great!" Kal rolled his eyes. "How am I supposed to stop annoying him if being a twin is the problem?"

Kal wasn't used to people disliking him, and it was clearly making him uneasy.

Barrett spoke calmly, instantly easing the tension. "He's just jealous. He'll have to overcome those emotions, or they'll block his energy, making it harder for him to progress. Griffin is a powerful warrior, and we'll need him in the war to come."

That one word *war* seemed to freeze time. Ella and Kal both stood still, unable to comprehend the gravity of it. They had never imagined that such a small, simple word could be aimed at them. War.

CHAPTER TEN

Ella sat down on a bench at the side of the training dome, watching as Barrett and Alana continued their conversation.

"How long do you think they've been training to get this good?" Ella nodded toward the others sparring. Kal sat down next to her, shaking his head.

"I have no idea, but they're definitely not new like I'd hoped. From what I can gather, we've got a long road ahead of us."

They both sat quietly, watching the seven other teenagers move with an elegance and precision that neither could imagine themselves achieving anytime soon. The mention of *war* still hung in the air between them, but neither wanted to bring it up just yet.

Ella couldn't help but admire the others' grace and power—even Griffin, despite his earlier hostility. Her eyes were drawn to a smaller girl in the back of the dome, flitting in and out of the tree branches. She moved with such fluidity that Ella imagined she didn't make a sound, like the ninjas in the old movies she and Kal used to watch. The girl didn't look like she was 16, but she had to be at least that. Her opponent was a much taller boy, at least 18 by the looks of him, towering over her.

"Kal, look at that smaller girl over there," Ella whispered, pointing just as the girl leaped backward from one branch to another, scaling at least 15 feet without even glancing back.

"Blimey, she's insanely good," Kal muttered, eyes wide. "And look at the guy she's fighting—he's huge! Size definitely doesn't matter. She's kicking his arse."

Kal's mouth hung open in disbelief, and Ella nudged him, a little embarrassed.

"Shut your mouth, don't give them any more reasons to hate us, Kal. Pretty sure being a suck-up is bad news in any world."

Alana started striding over. She moved with such a commanding presence that Ella instinctively leaned back on the bench. There was something about her confidence that made Ella feel smaller by comparison.

"I've got to finish my last spar, and then Barrett and I will talk to you about what's next. You okay to sit here for a bit longer?" Alana asked, glancing between the two.

"Ah, sure...yup...we're good just sitting here," Kal stammered, unable to hide his awkwardness.

Alana tilted her head slightly, her expression somewhere between amusement and curiosity, before spinning gracefully on her heel and charging back toward the waiting Griffin. Ella had to hold back a laugh at her brother's flustered response.

Griffin, however, was ready for Alana. He seamlessly pivoted as she approached, attempting to block her strike, but Alana smoothly slipped past him and dropped into a low spin kick, sending him sprawling to the ground. In an instant, Alana was on top of him.

Ella and Kal's jaws dropped when they saw a snake materialise from Alana's arm, coiling tightly around Griffin's neck.

"Kal, she's going to kill him! Shouldn't we do something?" Ella's hand gripped tightly onto Kal's arm, half-rising from the bench, her voice filled with concern. But as they watched, the snake slowly retracted and eased off Griffin's neck.

Ella sat back down with a heavy sigh of relief. She hadn't been prepared to witness someone being killed, even if they were unpleasant.

"She. Is. Amazing." Kal was leaning forward on the bench, his mouth slightly open, pupils wide in admiration. Ella stared at her brother long enough that he finally noticed.

"What? WHAT? Don't you think that was incredible, what she just did?" Kal exclaimed, his enthusiasm apparent.

Ella couldn't deny that seeing a snake seemingly come alive out of Alana's arm was pretty amazing, so instead of arguing, she kept her thoughts to herself.

Griffin, now getting up angrily off the floor, brushed the dust from his black training gear. "HEY! Since when do we use Bonded animals during sparring? That was out of order, Alana. You're just trying to show off to your new pet."

He pointed bitterly at Kal, as if somehow this had all become his fault.

"ENOUGH!" Barrett's voice boomed across the dome, sharp and commanding.

"I told Alana to use her Bonded animal," Barrett continued, his tone stern, "and yes, it was to show Ella and Kalan. They've already started Bonding with their weapons, and since Alana is the only one of you to have mastered this first stage, it was necessary for them to see what they're about to experience."

Griffin stormed off toward the changing room, slamming the door behind him.

Alana and Barrett made their way over to the twins, while the rest of the students resumed their training. Ella, wanting to get a question in before Kal could start stumbling over his words.

"Is my sword going to turn into a snake?" she quickly blurted out, though in her head she had sounded far less panicked.

Barrett placed a comforting hand on Ella's shoulder. "Who knows, maybe. It could be anything—from a rat to an elephant, or any mythical creature in between. Although I've never heard of an elephant Bonding. The point is, it could be any creature."

Kal, recovering from his awe, took a deep breath and chimed in. "So how do we find out what our Bonded animal is? Does it just appear one day?"

"In a way, yes," Barrett replied, his voice quieter, more

instructive. "But you must allow it to reveal itself. And the way you do that is by spending time alone with your weapon, in silence."

As Barrett spoke, it felt as though the air around them thickened, turning into a bubble. The others sparred on, but now in a distant, soundless haze.

Kal, secretly relieved at the prospect of sitting still instead of fighting, asked, "So we just sit anywhere and wait?" His tone carried a hint of doubt, but he seemed willing to give it a shot.

Barrett frowned slightly, sensing Kal's lack of enthusiasm. "No, not quite. You'll need to find a place that calls to you, somewhere that feels safe, open, and calm. Then, you sit with your weapon and focus on it until the Bonding begins. This could take hours, or even days. During this time, you mustn't speak to anyone or allow yourself to be distracted. Your only focus is the weapon."

Ella, always the thinker, started to feel the weight of Barrett's words, and her mind quickly filled with questions. "But what if we need to go to the bathroom... or if we're hungry?" She was already feeling a little hungry and couldn't imagine going days without food.

Alana, sensing Ella's nerves, offered a reassuring smile that instantly soothed her. "You'll be fine," she said softly, her gaze shifting between Ella and Kal. "If you stay focused, relaxed, and open, you'll find that time will fly by. You might even enjoy the experience."

As Alana spoke, what seemed like an invisible bubble that had enclosed them lifted, and the sounds of the training resumed—the swift jumps and slams of the other students echoed once more.

Barrett gestured toward the door, his arm outstretched. Ella exchanged a surprised look with Kal, neither of them expecting to leave for their Bonding right away.

Barrett's final words as they stepped outside the Training Dome were filled with encouragement. "This is the beginning of your destiny. Whatever happens next, take pride in it and know that I will be here to guide you."

Ella and Kal, unsure of how to respond, simply nodded, offering small smiles in return. As the door to the Training Dome closed behind them, they stood side by side, wide-eyed, feeling the weight of the unknown pressing down on them.

Ella glanced over at Kal, a small grin tugging at her lips. "So... I guess this is where we figure out where to sit in silence. Surely it can't be that hard, right?"

Kal chuckled softly. "Yeah, how tough can it be? Just find a spot and sit around, waiting for... well, something."

But deep down, both of them knew that this was more than just sitting. It was the start of something far bigger than either of them could comprehend.

Kal looked out over the lush gorge with its endless winding trees as far as his eyes could see.

"I have no idea where to go. I guess we just take a walk and see what feels right; that's what Barrett said in his Yoda speech," he muttered, shaking his head.

Ella hadn't been listening; she couldn't stop thinking about where they were and what was expected of them. "I keep telling myself how ridiculous it is that we're supposedly born warriors, but when I touch my sword, it feels as if it's alive, like a part of me. It sounds completely insane, I know…"

Kal interrupted before she could finish. "…No, it doesn't sound crazy. I felt the same thing. Alana asked me to concentrate on the bow in my hands, and it just came alive. It felt like it had a pulse, beating with mine. I can't understand how any of this is even possible."

Ella walked over the bridge and looked down toward the gorge, deep in thought. She decided to take a walk along the stream at the bottom and see where she'd end up, but she had no clue how to get down there.

"Kal, I'm going to try to find a way down to the gorge and see if I can *feel* where my place is to sit."

"Why don't you use your Holed Stone?" Kal suggested.

Ella turned to look at her brother, feeling slightly nervous at the thought. "Do you think I should? What if it goes wrong?"

Kal placed his hands on her shoulders, trying to reassure her in his usual sarcastic tone. "Ella, you can literally see where your Jump will end, so you can't go wrong."

She pressed her hand against her chest, where the Holed Stone lay nestled against her heart, feeling her pulse quicken. Gripping her sword tightly, she breathed out slowly and pulled the necklace out from her top. Taking another look at the gorge, she pinpointed a little alcove where a mossy rock sat. Tall white flowers surrounded its base, reminding her of daisies, and the wall of rock behind glistened with diamond-like beads of water.

With that, Ella touched the stone.

Kal wasn't prepared for how quickly she disappeared. He jumped forward toward the bridge in shock, but before he could even look down, he heard his sister ecstatically screaming, "WOOOHOO! I did it, Kal! I made the Jump!"

Kal stood there, a grin spreading across his face. "Well, looks like she's got this Jumping thing figured out," he muttered to himself. He gazed down at the gorge, where Ella was now a tiny figure, waving up at him with excitement, her joy echoing through the trees.

"Guess it's my turn next," he sighed, still feeling a bit of apprehension but also a surge of confidence after seeing his sister succeed.

"You try too. Come down!" Ella called up to Kal, her arms wide with excitement.

Although Kal had been all encouragement when it came to his sister Jumping on her own, he wasn't as confident about doing it himself. But Ella didn't give up, shouting from the mossy rock where she sat, grinning up at him.

"Grr, why do you make me do these things, El?" Kal grumbled under his breath. He took a deep breath, closed his eyes for a second, and Jumped. A moment later, he landed with a thud—right on top of Ella. She immediately started smacking him on the back.

"Get off! You could have landed on my sword, you idiot!" Ella scolded him, though a laugh escaped her as Kal toppled forward, laughing at the ridiculousness of it all.

Ella stood up, brushing herself off. Looking up and down the gorge, she couldn't decide which way to go. She glanced left, her dominant hand. "I'm going to walk down here for a bit and see where I end up. Where do you think you'll sit?"

She didn't like the idea of them splitting up in an unfamiliar place.

Kal scratched his head, looking back toward where they had come from. "Honestly? I think I might just head back to my room," he said sheepishly, knowing Ella might not like his choice. "I know it sounds boring, but that's where I feel like I'll be most comfortable and open to Bonding."

Ella was a little surprised by Kal's decision to go back when there was so much to explore, but she understood. She didn't like the idea of getting lost either, especially in such a mysterious place.

"Okay, well, good luck, and I'll see you soon. I'll come back to the house when I'm done." Ella pulled Kal into a tight hug, a part of her reluctant to let go. She wanted to feel the safety of staying together, but something about the gorge called to her, urging her to stay.

Kal squeezed her back, trying not to think too hard about her wandering off alone. "Don't go too far, El. And if you get lost, just focus on me and use your stone." He ruffled her hair and, with a nod, disappeared in a flash.

Suddenly, Ella felt the weight of being truly alone. She glanced around the gorge, hoping Kal had made it safely back to his room and not somewhere else. She had to trust him, just like she had to trust herself.

The gorge seemed more daunting now without her brother by her side, but the pull to explore was stronger than her fear. She took a deep breath, adjusted the strap of her sword, and started walking down the left path, each step taking her deeper into the unknown.

Ella decided to just keep walking and see where the path

led her. As she moved carefully along the side of the trick-ling stream, she noticed tiny blue flecks pulsing in the water with every step she took. Curious, she knelt down and ran her hand through the surprisingly tepid water. The blue flecks sparked and shimmered in the wake of her fingers. She quickly pulled her hand back, uncertain if it was safe.

Continuing on, the gorge opened up wider, and the stream expanded into a small, slow-moving river that she could easily walk across if she wanted to. Looking up, she saw enormous tree branches stretching from one side of the gorge to the other. Tiny windows embedded in the trees glowed with soft light, casting an ethereal glow on every-thing around her. The entire scene was a rich tapestry of deep greens, even the river reflecting its vibrant shimmer on the trees overhead.

Ella soon came across a slight alcove in the gorge wall, where three branches swooped down next to each other, forming a natural seat. The spot reminded her of her beloved Tulip tree back home, and she instantly knew this was where she'd begin her Bonding.

She climbed onto the sturdy branches and, to her surprise, felt a softness beneath her hands. Looking down, she saw plush green moss emerging through the bark, creating a cushion-like surface for her to sit on.

"Alright, Ella, how are you going to do this?" she said to herself, feeling unsure where to begin. She felt a bit silly just sitting there but remembered Barrett's instructions to focus on her sword. Gently, she placed her hands over it as it rested in her lap. Gradually, the warmth she had felt earlier in her fingertips began to return, spreading through her hands and up her arms.

Closing her eyes, Ella was soon enveloped by a strange, pulsing sensation. It felt claustrophobic, and she instinctively tried to pull her hands away from the sword, but they wouldn't move. Startled, she opened her eyes and was horrified to see her fingers being absorbed into the sword itself.

Her first instinct was to scream, but she realised, to her shock, that she wasn't in any pain. Forcing herself to breathe deeply, she tried to calm her racing heart. As she exhaled, it felt as though the sword had somehow entered her bloodstream, merging with her. She tasted something earthy and metallic on her tongue, and a brief flash of green flickered in her vision.

The pulsing sensation suddenly stopped, and the warmth in her hands began to fade. When she looked down, her sword was no longer fused with her fingers but instead lay elegantly across her lap, as if it had settled into a peaceful connection with her, its master.

Ella stared at the sword, unsure of what had just happened but knowing, deep down, that something profound had begun.

CHAPTER ELEVEN

Ella didn't know how long she had been asleep on the mossy branches, but the air felt cooler, and the light from the Solar Tree had dimmed, making her think it must be evening—though whether it was the evening of the same day, she couldn't be sure. She swung her legs off the side of the branches, sitting up with her head in her hands, rubbing her face to wake herself up. Her gaze wandered over the clear, sparkling river.

Suddenly, the gentle sound of the rolling water became slightly disturbed. Ella looked out, expecting to see someone approaching, but there was no one. Then, right in front of her, she saw the blue flecks in the water, the same ones she had seen earlier, start to flicker and dance. Curious, she jumped down from the branches and stepped closer to the water's edge.

Something was definitely disturbing the water, but she couldn't see what it was. The blue flecks of light floated closer to her and paused just before the water's edge.

Kneeling down, Ella leaned in for a better look, expecting to find tiny fish beneath the surface. Instead, all she saw was her own reflection, rippling with the movement of the river. Then, faintly, another shape appeared in the water beside her own. It was hard to tell what it was—she could barely recognise her own face in the distortion—but something else was there, standing in the water next to her.

Ella heard a noise—a deep, smooth sound, almost like a dog's bark, but quieter, more controlled. It should have terrified her, but instead, it felt oddly comforting. Slowly, she lifted her head and came face-to-face with the biggest wolf she had ever seen—or perhaps it was something more than a wolf. Its face was broad and shaggy, with a long muzzle and a glistening black nose that was now sniffing her hair. Its eyes, a brilliant orange, sparkled with a mix of intelligence, bravery, and kindness.

The enormous wolf-like creature bowed its head and gently nuzzled against Ella's face. Overcome with affection, she wrapped her arms around its thick neck, holding it close in a warm embrace.

"Hello, you," she murmured, leaning back to take in the creature's full size. "Where did you come from?"

The animal's face was pure white, with dark flecks around its ears and cheeks. As Ella looked closer, she noticed that the dark flecks weren't black, but a rich, deep green, blending seamlessly into the rest of its fur.

"Oh wow, look at you," Ella whispered, a smile of amazement spreading across her face. The sheer size and beauty of the creature left her awestruck. She moved back to the branches, leaning against them for support, and the creature followed her. It laid down beside her, resting its massive head on her lap.

"You really are beautiful," Ella said softly, stroking its fur. "I've never seen anything like you before."

The creature seemed to understand her, nodding its head gently as if in agreement.

Ella inspected the creature's coat as it peacefully and trustingly rested against her. Its fur wasn't just green—it was like a living meadow. Thick, grass-like strands covered its body, dotted with tiny white flowers. As she rubbed its fur, she felt a soft, mossy undercoat beneath it, as if nature itself had woven two layers of protection. The wolf's tail was braided with long, fern-like leaves that fanned out gracefully, completing the picture of this incredible creature.

For the first time since before Rhi's birthday, Ella felt safe and content. She gently stroked the wolf's thick head while gazing out over the sparkling river. Time seemed to slip away as she sat there, captivated by the occasional blue spark that jumped out of the water. Near her, a bright green spider, about the size of a coin, was weaving a web between two branches above her head. The web unfolded in a mesmerising flower-like pattern, and Ella couldn't take her eyes off it.

The dense, sweet air lulled her into a sense of calm, making it difficult to want to move. But soon, thoughts of Kal began to creep into her mind. She hoped he had found his way home and was safe. The pull between staying in this peaceful spot and the need to check on her brother tugged at her heart.

As if sensing her thoughts, the wolf stirred and lifted its

great head. Ella, having almost forgotten the creature's weight on her lap, felt a pang of sadness as it looked at her, as if it knew she had to leave.

"I've got to go now," she whispered, gazing into its gentle, fiery eyes. She stroked its head one last time, feeling a deep connection. "I'm sure I'll see you again soon. It's not like I can miss a giant like you."

The wolf seemed to understand. It nuzzled her face once more, then leaped onto the low-hanging branches behind her. Ella turned to where it should have been, but to her surprise, the creature had vanished. Confused, she looked around—there was nowhere else it could have gone.

Her eyes were drawn to the spot where she had slept. There, resting on the thick branches, was her sword. Its crystals gleamed a vivid emerald green, catching the dappled light from the trees. The sword seemed to wink at her, its beauty hypnotic. It drew her closer, and as she reached out for it, it felt as natural as reaching for Kal's hand. It was part of her, an extension that truly understood who she was.

"Kal," she whispered under her breath. Without thinking, she pulled out her Holed Stone, touching her fingers through the centre.

Before she even exhaled, she found herself back in her new home, enveloped by the comforting aroma of her mum's cooking.

"Mum, Dad, Kal, are you guys here?" she called out, her voice echoing softly through the warm, welcoming space.

Diana came running down the curved stairs.

"Oh, Ella, you're back!" She squeezed her daughter

tightly, then held Ella's face in her hands and kissed her forehead. "ROWAN, Ella's home!"

"Mum, is Kal here? Is he ok?" It was lovely seeing her mum, but all she really wanted was to know her brother was safe.

"Yes, he's here, darling. He's been in his room for two days. I'm hoping he finishes his Bonding soon."

Ella's dad came down the stairs wearing the biggest smile she had seen on him in a long time.

"I'm so proud of you, Ella, my beautiful Faerie. How did the Bonding go?"

"Yeah, I think it went well, but... wait—you said Kal's been in his room for two days? So that means I've been gone for two days?" Ella was completely stunned. "It felt like I was gone for half a day, tops!"

"You must be hungry. I've got some vegetable stew cooking and bread baking. It should be ready soon," Diana said, already heading towards the kitchen.

"Thanks, Mum! Now that you mention food, I'm actually starving." Ella could feel her stomach rumbling and twisting as if it was trying to eat itself. She headed to the kitchen to get a glass of water while she waited.

Rowan sat down next to her at the table, not wanting to rush but clearly eager to hear about her Bonding experience.

"Give her some space, Rowan. She'll tell us in her own time," Diana said, placing a loving hand on his shoulder.

Ella picked up her glass of water and stared at it with hazy eyes. Water was water, right? But this looked different from anything that had come out of the taps in their old house.

Tentatively, she took a sip. As the water touched her lips, Ella's eyes closed in complete bliss. The liquid flowed over her tastebuds, down her throat, and she savoured every moment. It was slightly sweet, perfectly fresh, and she could feel it hydrating every part of her body.

"How does this taste so good? It's completely different from the water we had at home."

Diana smiled, remembering that this was Ella's first experience with Wild Water.

"It's amazing, isn't it? Our Wild Water comes from underground springs, untouched by the pollution of the world above."

As Ella savoured her second sip, there was a sudden slam of a door. Kal came running out of his bedroom, shouting as he stumbled down the stairs.

"Ella! Ella! Are you here? Mum, Dad, is Ella home?"

When he reached the bottom of the stairs and saw his sister sitting at the table, Kal bent over, hands on his knees, looking emotionally drained but clearly relieved.

Ella rushed over to help him stand, hugging him tightly while whispering in his ear, "I'm so glad you're here."

Without a word to their parents, they walked heavily to Kal's bedroom. They sat down on his bed, which smelled musty and sweaty from him lying on it for two days. They just stared at each other, not needing words, sharing a silent understanding.

Ella finally broke the silence, curiosity tugging at her.

"We were both gone for two days, Kal. It felt like half a day to me! How did you get on?"

"Two days? Yeah, wow. I wouldn't have thought I could

last that long without food. It was incredible, El. I don't even know where to begin."

Ella knew exactly how her brother felt; there was so much to say, but starting a conversation about something so foreign was harder than they both thought. Kal blew out a deep breath and began nervously.

"I felt my bow and arrows become part of me. It's literally part of me, El. I know every grain of wood and the minerals that bind it together. I can't explain it, but I have complete faith in it."

Ella felt relieved that Kal sounded just as crazy as she knew she would.

"I know exactly what you mean. I felt my sword become a part of me too. It was like my blood was running through it, and its metal was running through me."

Kal's bow and arrows still lay on his bed. He reached out, touched it, and drew it closer to them.

"I can feel my power through it. I'm starting to believe that the Seer might actually have been right." Kal looked hopefully at Ella, nervous she might think he was mad, but instead, he saw a look of total understanding in her eyes.

"Did you find your Bonded animal? Nothing happened with my sword once I Bonded with it; it didn't change into anything." Ella could tell by her brother's expression that he'd had a different experience.

"I did, yeah," Kal said, feeling almost embarrassed that he'd reached a step further than his sister. But her face lit up with excitement, eager to know more, which pushed him to continue. "After I connected with my weapon, I felt exhausted and lay down to rest. But before I could sleep, I felt something soft tickle my face. When I opened my eyes, I saw a fan of brown and white feathers swoop over my head and land on the edge of my chair." Kal nodded to the desk chair, its backrest riddled with holes the size of pencils.

Ella felt confused. "But how did you know it was your Bonded animal? I mean, it didn't seem like your weapon had changed."

"El, it was a huge eagle, light brown feathers and these amazing pale yellow eyes. They were so clear, like I was looking into the sun."

Ella sat quietly, thinking about the giant green wolf she had encountered. Could that have been her Bonded animal? She certainly felt connected to it in an unusual way, unlike any normal first encounter with an animal.

"But how do you know it wasn't just some random eagle that flew through the window?" she asked, clutching at straws, still trying to process if her Bonded animal could be a giant wolf.

Kal laughed, like the answer was obvious, which only irritated Ella. She stood up and walked over to the window, looking out as if searching for answers. Kal sensed this wasn't the time to push his point and joined her at the window.

"These windows weren't open, El. There was no way it could have gotten in here. And... I just knew. He felt like a part of me."

There was a knock on Kal's bedroom door. It opened slightly, and they heard their mum's voice, though she didn't fully enter, seeming not to want to interrupt.

"There's food ready if you're both hungry."

Kal looked at Ella, wide-eyed and desperate for a meal.

"We're coming down," Ella called back. Then, turning to her brother, she teased, "Come on, rubbish bin, let's get some food before you start eating your pillow."

The twins sat quietly at the table, filling their stomachs with hot vegetable stew and freshly baked crusty bread. Diana and Rowan exchanged glances, unsure of whether to speak or let the twins process everything in silence.

After a while, Rowan broke the silence, his words spilling out awkwardly. "So, how did it go for both of you? Did you have similar experiences? How does it feel being Bonded to a weapon?"

Diana shot him a stern glare, and Rowan immediately sat back, looking slightly embarrassed for pushing the conversation.

"It's fine, Mum. I'm sure you both have questions, just like we do," Ella said, though she was clearly exhausted. Despite her fatigue, she knew they had to talk it through, as there were too many unanswered questions on her mind.

Over the next few hours, they discussed the twins' experiences, marvelling at the similarities but also recognising the differences. Ella and Kal learned that weapon Bonding is usually very personal, with no two experiences being the same.

Diana was especially fascinated by Kal's description of the bird he had Bonded with, and after a few moments of contemplation, she spoke up.

"Kal, I think your bird is the *Lolaire sùil na grèine*—'Eagle with the Sunlit Eye.' They're incredibly powerful and revered as Bonded animals. Very rare, too."

Ella sat quietly, unsure if what she had experienced was even real. But soon, the conversation turned toward her, and she had no choice but to recount her encounter with the large, wolf-like creature with grass for fur and fiery orange eyes.

As she spoke, Diana and Rowan remained still, their mouths slightly open as they listened to her describe the peaceful meeting with the mysterious creature.

"I don't even know if it was my Bonded animal," Ella said, uncertainty creeping into her voice. "It could've just been someone's lost dog. I mean, I'm guessing there are green dogs here, right? It feels like the sort of thing Fae would have."

Diana and Rowan exchanged another glance, this time more serious. Diana remained silent, a look of disbelief slowly turning into concern.

"Rowan... it couldn't be... could it? It's never been heard of before, and it can't be tamed anyway," Diana said, her worry growing more visible.

Ella's stomach knotted with anxiety as the icy grip she thought she had left behind returned, spreading across her chest and clutching at her heart.

Rowan, sensing her fear, leaned forward and took her hands gently. "We need to speak with Barrett as soon as possible. If what we think might have happened is even remotely true... he'll be the only one who knows if it's possible."

Ella felt lightheaded, her chest tight with fear. "Dad, you're scaring me. Can you just tell me? Please, Dad!"

Rowan opened his mouth to speak, but no words came.

He tried again, but still, nothing came out. Diana, always one to find comfort in routine, got up to make some tea, her go-to response when situations became difficult.

"Okay," Rowan began carefully, "but please understand, we don't know for sure until we speak to Barrett."

Ella nodded, her heart racing. She felt Kal's hand on her shoulder, warm and steady. She turned to look at him, his touch radiating strength and reassurance. His silent support helped her feel a little stronger.

Diana returned to the table with a steaming pot of tea, filling the room with its calming, sweet fragrance. Ella's tense chest began to relax, soothed by both the tea and the presence of her family.

Rowan finally spoke again, his tone serious but gentle. "The creature you described sounds like the *Cù Sìth,* a legendary hound. Some say it's a wolf, with a coat of grass and eyes of fire."

Ella's eyes widened, her breath catching. She hadn't even mentioned the grass coat to them yet. She stood abruptly, needing to process what she was hearing. She walked over to the cast iron stove, which looked so much like the one from their old home. Leaning against it, she let the warmth from the glass door and the roaring fire behind it melt the last of the icy fear clutching at her heart.

Diana turned in her chair to face her daughter, her voice soft but full of gravity. "The reason your dad and I are reacting this way is because no warrior has ever had the *Cù Sìth* as their Bonded animal—at least, not in recorded history. It was believed that the line of the *Cù Sìth* was extinct. There hasn't been a sighting for millennia. Only one is said to exist at a time, and no one knows where they're born, how they reproduce, or where they come from. But the *Cù Sìth* is a great power in the Fae world."

Kal, who had been listening quietly, finally spoke up, his voice tinged with frustration that Ella shared. "But Mum, why is this even a problem? Ella doesn't need more panic. We're already stressed about becoming warriors. Why add this?"

Diana sighed, sharing a glance with Rowan. "Kal, it's not about adding more worry. It's just... the *Cù Sìth* is more than just a Bonded animal. If Ella has truly Bonded with it, it could mean something far greater than we ever imagined. That's why we need to talk to Barrett."

Ella, still leaning against the oven, felt the weight of her mother's words. She wasn't just becoming a warrior. She might be connected to a creature of legend, a power that no one in the Fae world had seen in years.

Diana knew they had to talk to Barrett as soon as possible. She stood up and walked over to her daughter, who was looking more lost than ever.

"Let's go see Barrett," Diana said gently. "He'll be able to explain better if it is the *Cù Sìth*."

Ella nodded, staring down at her feet. She didn't want her mum to see the emotion welling up in her eyes. Crying was the last thing she wanted to do right now—not after everything she and Kal had been through.

Diana glanced back at Rowan and Kal, giving them a reassuring smile. "We'll see you there." Then she reached for Ella's necklace, pulling it out and handing it to her daughter. They both Jumped at almost the same time, and within moments, Rowan and Kal joined them outside the Training Dome.

"We're not allowed in unless Barrett invites us," Diana explained, gesturing for Ella to open the door. "You go in and tell him we need to speak to him urgently."

Ella and Kal walked into the quiet dome, their footsteps echoing in the vast space. Within seconds, Barrett emerged from a side room.

"Ella, Kalan," he greeted them warmly, it's good to see you back so soon, and together too."

Before Barrett could say more, Kal, unable to hold in his anxiety, blurted out, "Can you invite Mum and Dad in? They're outside, and it's really important they talk to you. It's about Ella's Bonded animal."

Barrett frowned slightly, tilting his head in curiosity, before walking to the doors and opening them. He saw Diana and Rowan standing with worried expressions.

"Come in, you are welcome in the dome," Barrett said, inviting them inside. These words, spoken only by the Warrior Trainer, were essential; entering without invitation had caused serious injury in the past, as the dome's natural energy field only allowed those with pure warrior hearts inside.

Barrett normally didn't let anyone in who couldn't walk through the energy field themselves, but he could hear the gravity of the situation in Kal's tone.

"Diana, Rowan, it's good to see you again. What seems to be the matter? Kalan mentioned something about a problem with Ella's Bonded animal?"

Rowan stepped forward, and Ella and Kal watched with

interest as their father and Barrett clasped each other's arms and pressed foreheads together in greeting. They had never seen their parents do this with anyone outside their family.

Barrett guided all four of them into the side room, a place neither Ella nor Kal had been before. It wasn't what they expected. Three of the walls were lined with bookshelves from floor to ceiling, and an old-fashioned wooden ladder on tracks leaned against them, ready to wheel around the room to access the countless volumes.

His desk was mostly neat, except for the open books sprawled across each other. As Ella got closer, she noticed one of the drawings on a page. The paper was old and brown, and the drawing appeared to be hand-sketched. It showed an elegant face with a long, slim neck. At first glance, she thought it was female, but something about it suggested it could be male. The figure had long, pointed ears—far longer than hers or any Fae she had encountered so far. Markings adorned the side of its head, extending up into its hairline. As she leaned in for a better look, Barrett firmly but gently closed the book, as well as the others scattered across his desk.

He sat down and gestured for the others to do the same. Kal couldn't stop glancing around at all the books, managing to read a few titles off the larger spines—*The History of Fae and Our Place in the Realm, The Art of Shape Shifting,* and *The Worldwide Faerie Ring Guide* were just a few that he longed to explore. Remembering why they were there, he pulled his focus back to the moment.

"So, what's happened that's caused you this obvious concern?" Barrett asked.

Rowan looked at Ella, trying to read her emotions, but her expression was closed off.

"Both the kids completed their Bonding at almost the same time," Rowan explained. "We were talking about what they experienced. Kal told us about the bird he Bonded with, which Diana believes could be a *Lolaire sùil na grèine*."

Barrett glanced approvingly at Kal. "And Ella?" he asked, turning to her, but she didn't respond.

Rowan continued quickly, not wanting to take away from Kal's moment but needing to get to the point. "Ella wasn't sure at first if she'd Bonded with an animal, but she eventually told us about a huge green wolf that sat with her, and its coat was like grass. It couldn't be, could it?"

A heavy silence filled the room, and Ella realised she already knew the answer. She waited for the familiar icy grip of fear, but this time, she sat taller, ready to face whatever came next.

"You were right to seek advice," Barrett said finally. "I'll need to speak with Ella alone. I'll send her home after we're done."

Rowan and Diana looked disappointed not to get an immediate answer, but they knew Ella was in good hands. They stood up to leave.

"Thank you, Barrett," Diana said, her voice tinged with emotion. She kissed Ella on the top of her head before walking to the door.

Once Ella was alone with Barrett, she felt a wave of relief. The panic her parents had stirred began to fade, and she felt more at ease with Barrett. He wasn't creating fear like they had.

"Did your parents tell you what they thought you Bonded with?" Barrett asked, a subtle spark of excitement in his voice that he didn't quite manage to hide.

"Yes, they said it might be the *Cù Sìth?*"

Barrett nodded thoughtfully. "It does sound like that could be the case. Can you tell me what happened and how you felt at the time?"

Ella closed her eyes and took herself back to the moment by the water's edge, watching the blue sparkles approach in the river.

"She was beautiful—a giant of a dog or wolf, whatever she is. Her fur was soft, like grass, with moss underneath and tiny white forest flowers scattered through her coat. Her tail was braided with ferns that fanned out when she rested her head on my lap. And her eyes... they were orange, like fire."

At the mention of the eyes, Barrett's gaze sharpened slightly.

"She lay on your lap willingly and seemed completely at ease?"

Ella frowned at the question, her head pulling back slightly. "Of course, it was her own will. Who could make a creature like that do anything against her will? We sat together, and I stroked her. That's when I got a good look at her fur properly. Then I started thinking about Kal and how worried I was. I said that I had to leave, and she jumped behind me, to where I'd been sitting during my weapon Bonding. My sword was still there, but she was gone. There was nowhere else for her to go, it was really strange."

Barrett leaned back in his chair, exhaling as if in disbelief.

"Ella, your parents are right. You've Bonded with the *Cù Sìth*. This has never happened before in the entire history of Fae warriors."

Ella's heart skipped a beat. "Is that bad? Everyone's been reacting like this is a problem," she said, her voice a little shaky as she tried to restrain her emotions, and Barrett's long pauses weren't helping.

"It's hard to say," Barrett admitted. "She's never Bonded with anyone before. The *Cù Sìth* is known as the 'Omen of Death' for humans. They used to hunt and kill humans for their Faerie masters, who were mostly from small, older Clans that believed humans were destroying the Realm. But over time, those traditions faded, and the *Cù Sìth* seemed to disappear. Many thought she was extinct. Some, however, believed her return would bring great power."

Ella sat down, more confused than ever. "Why would a creature like that Bond with me? I don't want to kill humans. I still think of myself as human most of the time!"

Barrett fell silent, he loathed not having a definitive response, as he prided himself on his knowledge of the Fae Realm.

Ella sat quietly, her thoughts spiralling back to the gentle creature she had met by the river. She found it impossible to connect that serene, comforting presence with the monstrous human killing beast Barrett had told her about.

"Barrett," she said softly, "I don't know what happened in the past, but the wolf—dog—whatever she is, isn't evil. I *felt* something... She would protect me, and—" Ella paused, hesitant, then continued, "I know it sounds strange, but I think she loves me too. It's hard to explain, and I know it sounds silly having said it out loud, but it's true."

Barrett looked at her, studying the sincerity in her eyes. Her conviction was palpable, and despite the centuries of legends that loomed between them, he found himself believing her. He gave a short nod, acknowledging her words.

With deliberate movements, he walked over to where his old wooden library ladder stood, sliding it along its clunky rails to reach a high shelf on the far side of the room. He climbed almost to the top and pulled out a thick, dark red, leather-bound book. It had something embossed on the front in black, but Ella couldn't make out what it was.

Carefully, Barrett carried the hefty tome back to the desk and set it down as if it were made of glass. As he opened it, the ancient book groaned and creaked, its pages cracking like old bones, stretching after centuries of sleep.

"This book is millennia old," he said softly, reverently. "It was never given a name so that no one could speak of it. It's filled with creatures of our Realm. Some of the information is factual, and some—well, even Faeries have their own fairy tales. The *Cù Sìth* should be in here, and I'm hoping it has something that can shed light on your Bond."

He turned each fragile page slowly, his fingers careful not to tear the delicate parchment. Each turn of the page gave Ella time to glance at the illustrations and names—some familiar, some utterly alien. She spotted a sketch of a half-man, half-horse creature labeled "Centaur" and leaned in to look closer.

"Are Mermaids real?" she asked suddenly, her voice tinged with disbelief as she saw what looked like a half-woman, half-fish sketched on one of the pages.

Barrett chuckled softly. "In a way, yes. But not quite as you know them. Most creatures you know from stories are, in fact, very real."

Ella's mind raced, struggling to reconcile yet another childhood fable turned reality. Just as she was absorbing this, Barrett suddenly slammed his hand down on a page, making Ella jump.

"Got it!" he exclaimed.

Ella's eyes widened at his sudden change in demeanour. He had been treating the book like a fragile treasure moments ago, and now he seemed almost reckless. She stepped closer and looked down at the page he had found.

"This," Barrett announced, "is how the *Cù Sìth* has been depicted since the beginning of recorded history."

Ella leaned over to see a grotesque drawing of a hulking green beast. Its fangs were bared, dripping with dark saliva, and its eyes glowed a menacing red-orange. The image exuded aggression and fury. It looked ready to leap off the page and attack. Without even realising it, Ella took a small step back, her heart hammering. This horrifying creature was nothing like the gentle giant she had Bonded with. Sadness welled up inside her at the thought that such a beautiful being had been so misunderstood.

Barrett began reading aloud from the scrawled script beneath the drawing, while Ella slowly backed into the chair again, her face pale.

"The Cù Sìth is a rare hound that resembles a wolf in its physicality, although it is easily twice their size. Apart from its massive build, it is distinguished by its green fur and fiery red-orange eyes. The Cù Sìth can kill a human through sheer terror and drags their bodies to the World Below for punishment."

He glanced up, noting Ella's distressed expression, and softened his tone. "This was a long time ago, Ella. A small, radical faction of Fae used the *Cù Sìth* for those purposes. Not all of us... liked killing humans."

Ella bit her lip, fighting the overwhelming urge to look away, to deny what she was hearing.

Barrett flipped the page gently and continued reading, this time from a section labeled *Factual Information*.

"It has been documented but never proven that these giant beasts have a more gentle side. A young Niskai once claimed she was helped back to her stream by a Cù Sìth after becoming trapped out in the sun for too long."

He looked back up at Ella, his gaze thoughtful. "If it's true that you've Bonded with the *Cù Sìth*, it means something in her has changed—or you've awoken a part of her that's been dormant for centuries."

"But... why me?" Ella whispered, her voice strained. "What does that mean for me, for my future?"

Barrett sighed heavily, closing the book with a gentleness that belied its content. "That's what we have to figure out. It could be that your presence—your heart—has drawn out her true nature. You might be the first Fae in history to forge a new path for this creature, one of protection and companionship rather than fear."

Ella nodded slowly, taking in his words, but uncertainty still gripped her. She had gone from being an ordinary girl to a Faerie warrior—and now, she was apparently Bonded to a legendary creature thought extinct for centuries.

"How do I even begin to process this?" she murmured, more to herself than to Barrett.

"You start by accepting it," he replied softly. "The *Cù Sìth* chose you for a reason. The key to understanding her—and yourself—is to trust in that Bond. It's not a curse, Ella. It's a gift. One that may change everything."

For the first time since arriving in the World Below, Ella felt a flicker of hope. Maybe, just maybe, there was more to her than she had ever imagined. And perhaps this creature —this *Cù Sìth*—wasn't here to be her weapon, but her guardian.

Barrett stood with purpose and extended his hand to Ella, gesturing for her to follow him back into the Training Dome.

"Our next step is to draw her out and see if she can be tamed, not just for you, but toward others as well."

Ella's mind raced as she followed Barrett, unsure how they would summon the *Cù Sìth* again, or if she was ready for what was to come. Gripping her sword tightly, she felt a surge of protectiveness over it but also a nagging uncertainty about her own readiness.

Barrett's voice took on a low, calming tone as they stepped inside the Dome, the kind that made her feel slightly more at ease. "I need you to focus on the connection you share with your sword," he said softly. "Let the energy flow between you. Move slowly around the room, swinging it gently in a figure-eight motion. Keep your eyes closed and just feel."

Ella's heart quickened. She had never swung her sword before—let alone *any* sword—and the thought made her hands tremble slightly. She took a deep breath, closing her eyes, trying to calm the nerves swirling inside her. With a soft exhale, she allowed herself to concentrate on her sword, letting her other thoughts melt away.

As the seconds ticked by, something strange happened. Ella felt the presence of warmth near her hand, soft and comforting. It moved slowly, guiding her hand with a gentle pressure, moulding her grip perfectly around the hilt of the sword. Curious, she opened her eyes just a sliver. To her astonishment, a soft green mist swirled around her hand, enveloping her in a protective embrace.

The mist felt familiar, almost like the energy she'd sensed when the *Cù Sìth* first appeared. It moved with her, ensuring that each movement she made was fluid and natural. Ella's earlier tension began to fade, replaced by a strange but comforting sensation of being guided and cared for, in a way she'd never experienced before—not even from her parents.

CHAPTER TWELVE

Kal sat at the kitchen table with his mum and dad, the tension in the air thick as they waited for any news about Ella. Diana grew more anxious with each passing minute. "Maybe I should go check if she's alright?"

"You can't go down to the Training Dome again, Diana. We were fortunate Barrett let us in last time. I'm sure we'll hear something soon," Rowan replied, though his calm voice masked his own anxiety. He needed to be the strong one, knowing his wife was on edge.

Kal suddenly straightened, tilting his head as if he could hear something the others couldn't. "I can feel Ella. Something's happening." He stood up abruptly, his senses heightened, almost sniffing out the vibrations in the air.

Diana, already wound tight, shot up from her seat. "That's it! I'm going, and no one is stopping me." Her voice was almost frantic.

Before she could grab her Holed Stone, Kal gently took hold of her arm. "No, Mum, she's fine. I don't know exactly what's going on, but it's incredible. I'll go check on her, but I promise, everything is okay."

Diana and Rowan exchanged confused glances as Kal disappeared, Jumping straight to the Training Dome.

As soon as Kal arrived in the Dome, he froze. His sister was there, her eyes closed, sword in hand, green mist swirling around her fingers as she moved the blade in a rhythmic figure-eight pattern. It was mesmerising, but also unsettling.

Before Kal could call out to her, Barrett approached, placing a reassuring hand on Kal's arm and pulling him aside, urging him to stay silent.

"I knew you would come, Kalan," Barrett whispered, his voice calm and steady. "Do not be alarmed by what you see. Your sister is safe for now."

Kal's gaze snapped to Barrett, worry clear on his face. He wasn't sure what Barrett meant by 'for now,' but it didn't sit right with him. His hand unconsciously tightened around his bow.

"What do you mean, 'for now'?" Kal's voice was taut with concern, his protective instincts in overdrive.

Barrett, undeterred by Kal's intensity, continued in a low, steady tone. "Ella's Bonded animal indeed seems to be the *Cù Sìth*, but we need to bring the creature out and tame her."

Kal's grip tightened even more around his bow. "So you're just going to coax a giant green wolf out of her sword, that may or may not want to kill her?" His voice was filled with disbelief, but he was desperately trying to keep a calm tone as not to distracts Ella.

Barrett remained calm, slowly moving closer to Ella while signalling Kal to stay back. "Do not worry, Kal. I won't let any harm come to her. But you do need to trust me."

Kal watched in tense silence as Barrett slowly circled around Ella, his focus entirely on the swirling green mist that sparked around her hands. Kal's heart raced, but he trusted Barrett, though every instinct told him to step in.

Ella was lost in the rhythmic movement of her sword, her eyes still shut, completely absorbed by the connection she was feeling. Unbeknownst to her, the mist around her hands began to spark more intensely. With one final upward sweep of the blade, she paused, and as she brought the sword down, a massive, ghostly trail of green mist flowed from the sword, shaping into a familiar form.

Within seconds, the mist solidified into the huge green wolf Ella had seen by the stream. Its powerful, graceful form descended onto the floor with a thud that reverberated through the Dome. As soon as the beasts feet touched the ground, Ella opened her eyes.

Standing in front of her was the great beast she had Bonded with earlier. But now, it was growling deeply, so low that her gut quivered uncomfortably. It was a terrifying sound, rumbling through the air like an approaching storm. Its eyes were locked on Barrett, hackles raised, fur rippling with barely contained fury.

To Kal's surprise, Barrett didn't retreat. Instead, he bowed deeply, head low, left hand turned slightly outward in a gesture of submission.

The wolf's growl didn't cease. It seemed ready to attack, its energy radiating rage.

Ella, her heart pounding, stepped forward and spoke softly, her voice gentle. "Hey you, it's nice to see you again."

As soon as the *Cù Sìth* heard Ella's voice, it whipped around fast. Kal instinctively raised his bow and arrow, hoping he wouldn't have to use it, especially since he had never actually fired one before.

"Kal," Ella calmly gestured for him to lower his weapon. Under normal circumstances, this would have seemed completely foolish, but there was something about how Ella and the *Cù Sìth* looked at each other—almost poetic.

Ella knelt down, allowing the beast to come to her. Slowly and steadily, with the reassurance of her voice, "It's okay, come on, it's okay," the creature came face to face with her once again. There was no fear in either of their eyes, only love. They were Bonded, and Ella knew it now, even Kal and Barrett could see it.

The connection between them was like that of a mother and her newborn, a beautiful wonderment that transcended any other love. Tears welled in Ella's eyes as the large, shaggy head buried itself into her neck. She could smell the sweet scent of spring flowers drifting from its lush green coat.

Kal broke the moment, stepping toward them like a proud uncle wanting to connect. The *Cù Sìth* flicked her head toward Kal, assessing him. Seeing no threat, she allowed him to move closer. She sniffed his hand, then looked into his eyes with her head tilted, as though she was reading him.

"She knows we're family, Kal. She can feel our connection," Ella said softly. Kal looked at his sister in awe.

Ella stood up and glanced over at Barrett, who wore a look of immense pride and amazement.

"I never thought this was possible," Barrett murmured, "for the *Cù Sìth* to be Bonded and tamed."

Barrett didn't move closer, cautious of how the creature might react toward him. He wasn't sure how this would affect her training, but the possibilities raised countless questions in his mind.

"What do we do now?" Ella asked, her voice filled with uncertainty. "I mean, I don't even know how she got here, or if I could do it again."

Kneeling slowly to the floor, Barrett bowed his head and extended his hand slightly, trying to show the *Cù Sìth* that he meant no harm. After a moment, he felt the warm, spongy moss of her coat brush against his hand, followed by deep, bear-like sniffs. Then, she walked away, her regal braided tail swaying behind her.

Ella smiled and stroked her new friends head when she returned. "She knows you won't hurt me. She trusts you because I trust you."

Barrett nodded and bowed. "You both should go home and rest. You have a big day tomorrow. Your intensive training begins, and there's much to learn in very little time."

Ella looked at the beautiful beast, unsure if her parents would be thrilled about her bringing the *Cù Sìth* home.

"To return your Bonded animal to your weapon, hold your sword out toward her, blade facing down. The same goes for you, Kalan. They will return as smoothly as they arrived."

Ella raised her sword, pointing it toward the giant wolf, who was now sniffing around the dome. As she did, the creature swirled into a mist and was absorbed back into the sword. Ella's eyebrows shot up in shock, while Kal laughed with sheer excitement.

"Go home, rest, and I'll see you both at solar rise tomorrow," Barrett said as he turned and calmly walked back to his office, the door closing gently behind him.

"That's the same as sunrise, right?" Kal asked, his confused face making Ella laugh. She nodded, shrugging with the same tired assumption as her brother.

Without another word, they both touched their Holed Stones and were back home before they could blink. Their dad was in the living room, reading a book on the sofa. He jumped slightly at their sudden appearance, still adjusting to people Jumping in and out of rooms again. He looked tired, the weight of worry clear on his face, but there was peace in his eyes as he saw Ella and Kal return safely.

"How did it go? Was Barrett able to help at all?" Rowan asked, his eyes full of concern.

Ella smiled wearily at her dad and nodded.

"Where's Mum?" Kal chimed in, his voice edged with worry.

"She's fine," Rowan replied. "She went back to work earlier. The Healing Medics are short-staffed, so she decided to help out. Not sure how late she'll be."

Kal started gently pushing Ella toward the stairs. "Come on, lazy bones, Barrett said you need to rest. I'm starving and can't be babysitting you all night."

Ella barely protested, stumbling upstairs. Kal called to his dad as they went up, "Be back down in a minute, Dad."

He opened Ella's door, and she practically collapsed onto her bed, falling asleep within seconds. Her sword lay protectively beside her. Kal, a bit concerned, carefully rolled her blankets over the weapon, hoping it wouldn't harm her while she slept.

Rowan listened to Kal coming back down the stairs, feeling a sense of relief that he'd finally get some answers about what had happened.

"Is she okay? Honestly?" Rowan asked nervously.

"Yeah, she's fine, just drained from the day," Kal assured him. "Dad, I actually saw her Bonded animal come right out of her sword. It was incredible."

Rowan looked completely bewildered. "She was able to call on her animal and release it? That usually takes months of training. And did Barrett think it was the Cù Sìth?"

"He said it was, yeah," Kal replied, still in awe. "Ella was amazing dad, you'd have thought it was our family dog by how it responded to her—though calling it a dog doesn't seem right. It's more like the size of a cow! We have to be back at the Training Dome at solar rise, so I better get some rest. Something tells me tomorrow won't be easy."

Rowan smiled at his son's use of the phrase "solar rise." "Rest up. I'm proud of you, Kal."

Kal nodded, his mind racing as he climbed the stairs. The thought of being hungry slipped away as exhaustion took over. All he could focus on now was switching off his brain and recharging before the gruelling day ahead. As he lay down on his bed, Kal silently willed his dreams to take him far away, not knowing where they'd actually lead him.

CHAPTER THIRTEEN

Kal opened his eyes to find himself plummeting through a sweltering darkness. Far below, veins of red pulsed across a barren, black landscape, resembling rivers of blood. His body tumbled weightlessly through the void, heart pounding in his chest.

A sharp, protective birdcall pierced the silence, and he instinctively turned his head. Racing toward him was a massive bird, wings pressed flat to its sides as it hurtled downward like a diving missile. Fear clenched at Kal's heart as the creature closed the distance with terrifying speed. But as it drew nearer, relief surged through him—he recognised the broad wingspan and distinctive white tail feathers. With a powerful sweep of its wings, the eagle swooped beneath him, lifting him from his free-fall and saving him from the terrifying drop.

Now safely perched on his eagle's back, Kal adjusted his bow and arrows under his arm, allowing him to take in his surroundings. What he had first thought looked like bloody veins below now revealed themselves as vast rivers of fire, winding through tar-like, bubbling black pits. The searing heat radiating from the landscape was overwhelming, forcing the eagle to ascend higher, seeking a refuge from the scorching temperatures.

The eagle carried him to a rocky ledge high above the fiery wasteland. With a grateful sigh, Kal slid off its back, though his dismount was far from graceful. Relieved that no one was around to witness it, he gave the bird a reassuring pat on its soft brown feathers before facing it.

"What are you doing here, boy? And where on earth are we? This place looks like... well, actual hell," Kal muttered, his voice shaky but filled with awe. The eagle, as if sensing his thoughts, nuzzled its feathery head against his neck, reminding him of how Ella's Bonded beast had once done. The bird's yellow eyes, bright and piercing as the sun, seemed to glow with an unspoken understanding.

Kal met the eagle's gaze and felt an overwhelming sense of connection, as though he were looking at a part of himself he hadn't known existed. "I guess you need a name, huh? I can't keep calling you 'boy.' Let me think... How about Sonny? That seems to fit, doesn't it?"

The eagle gave a sharp, approving cry, sealing its acceptance of the name. Kal smiled, a strange sense of comfort washing over him as he settled onto the ledge. Below, the rivers of molten fire cast an eerie glow over the rocky cliffs, illuminating hundreds of embedded stones—amber, gold, and deep red—sparkling like fireworks against the pitch-black depths.

Kal frowned, a feeling of unease creeping over him. "This

doesn't feel like a dream," he muttered. "Sonny, why are we here? How did I even get here?"

In response, Sonny flicked his head toward his back, gesturing for Kal to climb on once more. Though confusion weighed heavily on his mind, Kal found himself trusting the eagle. He swung himself onto Sonny's broad back, gripping the bird's feathers tightly as they launched into the air again. The wind roared in his ears as they ascended into the black void. He was forced to close his eyes against its intensity of the heat, burying his face into Sonny's neck for shelter as they soared higher into the unknown.

With each wingbeat, Kal's questions deepened, but he sensed that answers lay somewhere within this dark, scorching realm—if only he and Sonny could endue the heat and find them.

Suddenly, everything went silent. The air cooled, and the wind had stopped. Kal realised he had been holding his breath and gasped for air, his lungs expanding painfully as he filled them with sweet, cool oxygen. As the rush of air stabilised, he opened his eyes, unsure of what he would see next.

Kal sat up in bed, disoriented, his eyes adjusting to the serene flicker of the Solar lights above. The peaceful ambiance did little to calm his racing mind as he tried to make sense of the vivid dream he'd just had. He jumped out of bed and quickly checked on Ella, who was still fast asleep. He thought about waking her but knew she needed the rest.

Returning to his own room, Kal noticed his sheets were damp from sweat. Feeling restless and unsure if he'd sleep again, he reached for his bow and arrow on the chair. To his surprise, the bow was almost too hot to touch. Confused but exhausted, he lay back down and soon drifted into a deep, dreamless sleep.

The next morning, Kal woke to the most amazing smell, one that filled his senses and pulled him out of bed faster than anything else could have. As he stepped out of his room, he noticed the Solar Tree lights rippling down the corridor toward the kitchen, like neon signs leading the way. Barely touching the floor, Kal hurried down, following the delicious aroma.

Entering the kitchen, he saw everyone already up and eating.

"I was just about to come and get you," Ella said, her voice tinged with nervousness. "Remember, we have to be at the Training Dome at Solar rise." She looked as if she feared they were already running late.

"Ella, you'll be fine. We set the alarm early so you'd have plenty of time to eat," Diana reassured her, placing a steaming mug of tea in front of Kal before setting down a plate of green pancakes.

Kal eyed the strange-looking pancakes with suspicion, but after a nod of encouragement from Ella, he took a bite and was immediately lost in the incredible flavours.

"Mum, what's in these? They taste amazing, even if they look weird," Kal asked, his mouth full of pancake. Diana smiled, remembering her early experience with Fae food and the explosion of flavours it had brought to her senses.

"You don't have time for a culinary lesson right now," Diana said, shooing them both upstairs once they'd finished their food. "You need to get washed and changed out of those clothes."

"You each have a shower room through the inner doors in your bedrooms. It'll start working when you walk in— and see if you can figure out the soap." She smiled playfully.

Kal chuckled as they reached the top of the stairs. "Thanks for making that perfectly clear, Mum," he called out, rolling his eyes at Ella as they both opened their bedroom doors.

Kal stepped into his bedroom and searched for the shower room his mother had mentioned, noticing it was tucked beside the large window at the back. He walked into what looked like a cocoon-shaped room, with plants growing across the ceiling and down one of the walls. There was no visible shower head, but within seconds, a fine mist began to cover his face and clothes. Kal laughed in amazement as he quickly undressed, letting the warm mist wash away the stale sweat from the night before. He noticed some plants had small brown berries hanging from them. He plucked one, feeling its slippery texture and inhaling the incredible scent. The berry acted as soap, and soon Kal was enjoying a warm, soapy shower that he didn't want to leave.

After pulling himself away from the shower, Kal dressed and cautiously picked up his bow and arrows. This time, they were cool to the touch.

When he returned to the kitchen, Ella was already there, sword in hand, looking as though she was halfway to becoming a warrior. Their parents gave them gentle kisses, no words needed, as Ella nodded to Kal with her Holed

Stone in hand before Jumping. Kal lingered a moment, gave his parents one last look, and Jumped as well.

Barrett stood waiting for them in the middle of the Training Dome, hands behind his back. When Ella arrived first, she was relieved to see the other students weren't there yet. She didn't have long to wait, though—Kal Jumped in just moments after her.

"You're both late," Barrett said, his tone laced with disappointment. "The rest are already getting changed. I suggest you change quickly."

Ella and Kal exchanged glances. If they were late, it could only have been by a minute or two, but they knew better than to argue. Barrett wasn't interested in apologies or excuses; he simply wanted them on time.

Ella pushed the changing room door open, and the tension hit her immediately. Griffin stood in front of them, arms crossed, already dressed in his training gear. His smug expression made Ella want to wipe the grin off his face.

"So, first day of training and the favourites have already fallen behind. How disappointing," Griffin sneered.

Ella and Kal ignored him, quickly swiping their lockers open and changing into their gear as fast as they could. But as they emerged from the changing room, Ella's stomach sank. Everyone was standing there in silence, waiting for them.

"Now that everyone is present, I want to let the rest of you know that Ella and Kalan have Bonded with their animals and will start learning how to call upon them during battle," Barrett announced.

Kal couldn't help but notice the flash of irritation cross

Griffin's face, his smugness vanishing. It was hard for Kal not to smile.

"Griffin, you'll partner with Ella. Alana, you'll work with Kalan," Barrett instructed, his voice calm but firm. "I want to see you all use what's naturally within you, and we'll build from there."

Reluctantly, Ella moved toward Griffin, while Kal tried to hide his eagerness as Alana approached him.

"Hey, Kal, congratulations on Bonding. What did you get?" Alana asked, her gaze steady and warm.

Kal felt a sense of familiarity with Alana, as if he'd known her for a long time. It made him open up easily. "It's a White-tailed Eagle. I've named him Sonny. He's pretty amazing, actually. I even had this weird dream last night where he was huge, and I was flying on his back. The landscape looked like hell, with fiery rivers and black tar everywhere, I woke up sweating."

At the mention of his dream, Alana's expression shifted to one of concern. She glanced over at Barrett, who was watching the others sparring.

"Have you told Barrett about this dream?" she asked, trying to mask her worry.

Kal shook his head, a bit unsettled by her reaction. "No, why?"

"Let's spar for a bit," Alana said, seemingly brushing off the topic. "We'll see if we can get you to call out Sonny." Kal noticed the sudden change in her demeanour, unsure if she was genuinely moving on or just distracting herself.

As they began, Kal realised Alana carried a bow and arrow as well, though he hadn't noticed it before. She stood in a graceful stance, one foot in front of the other, moving with the precision of a dancer. Kal, a little lost, tried to mirror her, but Alana's fluid movements made him feel clumsy.

"Come on, Kal, do as I do. Don't worry about your bow yet. You need to move with the flow of energy, feel the earth beneath you. Let her know you're here for her, and she'll protect you," Alana instructed, her voice calm but commanding.

Kal unintentionally wrinkled his nose at the spiritual tone of her words, and Alana noticed, stopping her movements. "I know this is hard for you. Life here is different, but the sooner you accept that we're all connected through the Màthair earth's living energy, the sooner you'll be able to fight as a warrior."

This was the first time Kal had noticed any annoyance in Alana's voice. He didn't want to be difficult—that had never been his way. He'd always tried his hardest at school, and in that moment, he realised that this was his new school. He needed to start treating it like one.

Kal positioned himself to mirror Alana's stance and waited for further instruction. She gave a small nod of approval, and they resumed their practice.

Ella, glancing over at her brother, couldn't help but wish she had been paired with Alana. Griffin, on the other hand, seemed determined to assert his dominance, spending the first ten minutes bragging about how he was the strongest in the class.

"Okay, Griffin, can we actually start now?" Ella said, her patience wearing thin. She was on the verge of walking over to Barrett to complain when a soft murmur rippled through the group. Curious, Ella turned to see what had captured everyone's attention.

Her eyes landed on Kal, who was moving with Alana in what looked like a primal dance. They were circling each other in perfect unison, every footstep and breath in sync. Ella watched as Kal brought his bow and arrow into position, and Alana mirrored him. It was then that Ella understood why Barrett had paired them—so Kal could learn from someone who also wielded a bow.

Ella glanced down at Griffin's hand, noticing the long dark sword with red crystals embedded in the pommel. For a brief moment, she found herself wishing she didn't have a sword. But just as the thought crossed her mind, the hilt of her weapon vibrated gently in her grip. Ella squeezed it, feeling a wave of guilt wash over her for even thinking such a thing.

When she looked back up at her brother, she was transfixed. A shimmering white light began to seep from Kal's bow and float above him, and the same ethereal glow emerged from Alana's. The shimmering lights mixed and then separated, drawing Ella in as if they held some magnetic pull.

Suddenly, a loud screech echoed through the dome, followed by a warm gust of wind. Before everyone stood two magnificent white-tailed eagles. Kal said nothing; he could only stare at Alana, who smiled back at him, her face glowing with excitement.

"Okay, everyone, back to your own sparring. Kalan needs

to concentrate," Barrett called out as he walked over to Kal, who was still staring at Alana in awe.

"I'm proud of you, Kalan. You managed to tune into Alana's energy and replicate it as your own. This will give you great strength in battle. Now, you must learn to control your eagle and master your bow and arrow." He gave Kal a firm pat on the shoulder before turning to walk away, catching Ella's eye. "Your turn next, Ella."

As the surprise of what had happened wore off, the others returned to their sparring. Kal, still processing what had just occurred, turned to Alana, his voice low. "I thought your animal was a snake?"

Alana didn't break her concentration, keeping her gaze focused on him. "I'm on my second-level Bonding, which means I have two animals I'm Bonded with."

Kal's eyes widened in surprise. "Two animals? How many levels are there?"

Alana smiled, sensing his amazement. "There are five levels a warrior can obtain. So, you could potentially Bond with up to five animals. Not everyone gets another animal after their first; some receive another weapon. But don't worry about that now. Let's focus on training you and Sonny first."

Kal nodded, still trying to absorb the idea. "Okay. But... he's not going to attack you, is he?" The thought of ending up in an all-out eagle fight on his first day didn't exactly thrill him.

Alana shook her head with a smile. "No, he won't. He can sense we're friends from our body language and conversation. But if he does see me as a threat, that's where Flare comes in. She won't let anything happen to me."

Kal glanced up at the second eagle perched gracefully on the branch beside Sonny, her sharp eyes keeping a steady watch.

"Alright, let's start with some basic target practice. Sonny and Flare can stay up on the branch and observe."

"Great," Kal muttered with a hint of humour. "Just what I needed, an audience to watch me make a fool of myself."

Alana chuckled softly, then guided Kal by the shoulders to face a small target on the far wall, about 60 feet away. Kal's confidence wavered as he saw the distance, his jaw dropping slightly.

Behind him, Alana moved closer, her breath light against his ear, sending a shiver down his spine. Her voice came out in a soft, almost hypnotic whisper that Kal barely registered. At that moment, it didn't matter. His focus was entirely on the bow in his hands and the calm presence guiding him.

Alana gently helped Kal raise his arms, positioning the bow. With only the lightest touch, she steadied him, then whispered one final word that he did not understand. Kal instinctively placed the arrow on the string, drew it back, took a slow breath in and with the release of his breath came the released of the arrow.

He eyes grew wide as the arrow flew smoothly through the air, hitting the target dead-on. Kal stood frozen in shock, his mind racing.

"I hit it! Alana, I hit it!" he exclaimed, disbelief flooding his voice. "How is that even possible? I've never shot an arrow in my life!"

Alana's face radiated with pride. "It's possible, because you're a warrior. This bow and arrow were forged with your life's essence from the moment of your conception." Her voice was firm, encouraging him to stand tall and embrace his calling.

Just as Kal started to process her words, Alana's expression shifted, a mischievous grin spreading across her face. "Now, this is where the fun begins."

Kal followed her gaze, turning to see that five smaller targets had appeared around the original one. His stomach dropped. Worse yet, the new targets were moving!

"Uh, Alana, don't you think this is a bit of a leap in my archery skills?" Kal's voice cracked slightly. "I thought we'd stick with one target for a few days, then maybe work up to something harder, but this—"

"Kal," Alana interrupted firmly, "I believe in you, and so does Barrett." Her tone brooked no argument. She knew there was no time to waste. A war was looming, and Kal and Ella had to be ready.

CHAPTER FOURTEEN

Ella had been watching Kal and couldn't help but feel a twinge of jealousy at how nurturing Alana was being towards him. All she had gotten from Griffin was aggressive annoyance. Barrett noticed Ella's lack of enthusiasm toward Griffin and called her over, sensing she needed some guidance.

"Ella, I can see you're having trouble connecting with Griffin. He is the most competitive and also difficult in the class, but apart from Alana, he's also the best. I paired you with him because he wields a sword like you do, and I have every faith that soon you will be more accomplished than he is. He also needs a lesson in humility, and you are the one to teach it to him." Barrett's gaze suggested that he was counting on her to knock Griffin down a peg.

Ella nodded and tried to stand taller, feeling her resolve harden. The thought of putting Griffin in his place was enticing, and it helped her pull her shoulders back as she strode toward him, determined to make Barrett proud.

"Did you get told off by the teacher? Well, don't cry about it. Just listen to my instructions!" Griffin sneered, his tone laced with cruelty. But Ella stayed calm, focusing on one thing: beating him, no matter the cost.

"Come on, then," she said coolly, as if he was the one delaying them.

Griffin's face twisted in irritation, but Ella knew that staying composed gave her the upper hand. For the next hour, she mirrored his every move, honing her technique. Soon, she could predict his steps, his strokes. He was stronger than her and clearly wanted to prove it, pressing his advantage with brute force. But Ella was faster, her movements becoming smoother and more precise.

Barrett had been watching closely. He saw that Ella had begun to move beyond Griffin's instruction, developing her own rhythm. As she swung her sword downward, the crystals embedded in the hilt began to glow, and a green mist swirled around her. Ella panicked momentarily, unsure how to control what was happening. But before she could process it, the giant Cù Sìth bounded out of the mist.

Griffin fell backward, scrambling toward the wall in terror. The rest of the warriors in the dome froze, retreating in shock at the sight of the massive creature.

But Ella felt strangely calm. She approached her friend, her hand stroking its raised hackles as she knelt beside the creature's snarling face. "Ssshhh…" she whispered softly, her touch reassuring the beast that there was no danger. Slowly, the Cù Sìth relaxed, its fiery eyes dimming.

"What is that?" Griffin had regained his feet, trying to pretend he hadn't been terrified just moments before.

Barrett stepped forward, walking slowly to where Ella stood. He moved carefully around the beast, his head low and his hand outstretched, allowing the creature to sniff him. Once she recognised him, Barrett gently stroked her.

"This, Griffin, is the Cù Sìth," Barrett said gravely. "She is the only one of her kind, long thought extinct, until she Bonded with Ella. These creatures have never Bonded with a warrior before, so how she reacts to being tamed is still an unknown. Treat her with the utmost respect. She is a queen among all creatures."

Griffin was visibly holding back his words, his face turning red with the effort. The Cù Sìth noticed his tension, and slowly turned her massive head toward him, her hackles rising and teeth bared once more.

Ella stood by, intrigued by how the creature seemed to sense Griffin's dislike for her. She didn't intervene, curious to see what would happen next.

Griffin, now backing away slowly, gripped his sword tightly, ready to defend himself.

"I wouldn't do that if I were you, Griffin," Barrett warned, his voice steady. "It will only end badly for you."

Normally, Barrett would welcome a spontaneous spar, but not this time. Griffin wouldn't stand a chance against the giant, and everyone in the room knew it.

Griffin wasn't one to normally back down, but this time, he knew the sensible thing to do was listen to Barrett. His grip on his sword relaxed, but the beast continued to stalk him slowly, close enough to bite.

Ella approached, stroking her Bonded animal's back and whispering softly. The giant wolf finally backed down, allowing Ella to lead her protector back to Barrett. She gave Griffin a look that said, *Don't expect an apology.*

Barrett, looking proud of how calmly Ella had handled the situation, addressed the whole dome with a warning:

"Ella, I want you and Kalan to take your Bonds around the dome and introduce them to everyone. They need to know who is on their side so that when the time comes for battle, we don't have any... mistakes. Everyone stay calm and still, it will be your own fault if you choose to ignore these words."

The mention of battle startled Ella, but she walked over to Kal and Alana. Kal was grinning as she approached.

"Haha, you showed that idiot, didn't you?" Kal said, laughing as the massive wolf jumped up, placing her two paws on his shoulders. She towered over him, more than half a body taller, and Kal's grin widened as the rest of the dome stared in awe.

"El, you've got to name her! We can't keep calling her 'The Cù Sìth.' Oh, and by the way, meet Sonny." Kal's graceful eagle flapped his wings and perched elegantly on Kal's arm.

"Nice name," Ella said, smiling. "I haven't felt like I've found the right name for her yet," she added, stroking her wolf's velvety head. "But I will."

For the next twenty minutes, Kal and Ella walked around the dome, introducing both themselves and their animals, as they hadn't met most of the other trainees properly either. It was slightly awkward, but necessary.

As they finished their rounds, Kal noticed Alana speaking with Barrett in the corner. He couldn't make out the conversation, but whatever it was didn't look good, judging by the expression on Barrett's face. When Alana turned to face Kal, guilt was written all over her.

"Kalan, Ella, over here, now!" Barrett's voice was sharp, with an urgency that made Kal's stomach churn. Ella was just as shocked, but she and Kal hurried over to where Barrett and Alana stood, their faces serious.

Barrett gave orders to the rest of the trainees. "Everyone, keep sparring, but this time, two-on-one. I don't want to see anyone lagging behind. Keep your energy up and draw strength from the Màthair."

There was a subtle panic in his tone that only Kal and Ella seemed to pick up on.

Barrett's attention then shifted fully to Kal. "Kalan, Alana told me about the dream you had last night. You should have come to me immediately."

Kal frowned, realising he had underestimated the importance of what he'd seen. "I'm sorry, Barrett. I did think about it when I woke up in the middle of the night, but I figured it wasn't urgent. Plus, I didn't think you'd appreciate being woken up."

Ella looked utterly confused, her brow furrowed deeply as she tried to follow the conversation.

"When it comes to dreams, I need to know everything," Barrett said, his tone hardening. "Dreams in this Realm are never just dreams—they're windows into possible futures."

Kal's heart skipped a beat. "So you're saying I can see the future?" He started to feel a sense of wonder, but that excitement faded quickly as he saw the grave expressions on Barrett and Alana's faces.

Barrett's voice was steady but grim. "Think about what you saw, Kalan. It wasn't just a dream. It's a vision of war—a war that could destroy our Realm."

Kal's stomach twisted as the reality of his dream settled in. The blackened wasteland, the fiery rivers—it wasn't just some nightmare. It could be their future.

He slumped down into a chair, overwhelmed by the images flashing through his mind. "But how? It looked like the end of the world…"

Ella, growing more worried by the second, stepped forward. "What is this about? Kal, why didn't you tell me about this dream?"

Barrett motioned toward his office. "Both of you go with Alana. I'll be in shortly. I need to finish up with the group. And return your animals to your weapons."

With a flick of their wrists, Ella and Kal's Bonded animals dissolved into mist and were absorbed back into their weapons.

"Come with me," Alana said quietly, as Barrett resumed instructing the others. She led the twins into Barrett's office, where they had been once before with their parents. They were both equally impressed the second time, though the tension made it hard to focus on anything other than what was coming next.

Kal took the opportunity to scan the shelves for book titles while Ella wandered over to Barrett's desk, curious if the old books from before were still open.

"I would sit down if I were you," Alana said, her voice uneasy. "Barrett doesn't like it when people touch his things without permission."

The tension in the room thickened as they waited for Barrett to join them. Something was coming, something bigger than either of them had expected.

Even though Kal was sat down, it still didn't stop him from looking around the room, captivated by the endless shelves of books. "Have you read any of these?" he asked Alana, his curiosity getting the better of him.

She smiled and nodded. "I've read most of them."

Kal did a double take, unsure if he had heard correctly. Alana's face was sincere, which caused Kal to stare a little longer than was usually polite. He fumbled to get his words out, managing only, "But how, when... but you're only..."

Before he could finish, the door opened and in walked Barrett. Kal really tried to focus on Barrett, but Alana kept drawing his attention away. He had never met anyone like her, and yet, she felt so familiar, as if he had known her for years.

"Kalan, please, you must concentrate. These are very serious times, and unfortunately, it's only the beginning," Barrett said firmly.

Ella could feel that all-too-familiar icy grip tightening around her throat, but then she felt a gentle, firm hand on her shoulder. She turned and saw Alana standing behind her.

"Don't give into it, Ella. Accept that it's there, but move on. You're more powerful than you think," Alana said softly.

Ella didn't know what to say, but to her surprise, she realised the panic had faded. She took a deep breath, feeling calm wash over her. Turning back around, she sat straighter, ready to listen.

"I'm sure you're both feeling confused," Barrett said, leaning back in his chair. "And there is no easy way to explain what's happening, but I will try."

He paused, gathering his thoughts before continuing. "The Realm that we and every other creature on this planet belong to is close to death. This is due to the Byrne Clan and their greed for power. They separated from all Fae Clans many centuries ago because they didn't believe that humans should have the honour of running the world."

"I can almost understand why, though," Ella blurted out before quickly backtracking. "Well, I mean, we only have to look at how humans have messed things up..."

Barrett raised an eyebrow but did not seem upset. "Ella, from the outside, your perception is understandable. But once you realise the lengths to which the Byrnes have gone to manipulate humanity's self-destruction, you will see the darker truth."

Kal's face was filled with questions, his mind buzzing. "But why were humans put in charge of the world in the first place, and not the Fae?"

Barrett seemed pleased by the question. "Put it this way: Is it right for a mother to do everything for her children? To live their life for them without letting them experience the world for themselves? A mother should guide and nurture, yes, but also allow her children to make their own mistakes."

Barrett fell silent. No one spoke for what seemed like an eternity. Ella's confusion deepened. Then Kal broke the silence.

"So, you're saying the Fae are like the mother, and

humans are our children?" Kal's face scrunched up in confusion.

Ella half-laughed, glancing at Alana, but her straight-faced demeanour killed any sense of humour Ella had been feeling. "Hang on a minute. How are we the 'mother' of humans? That makes no sense."

Alana stepped in, her calming presence soothing Ella once more. "The Earth is the true Mother - Màthair - but we are part of her essence. The Fae were forged with the Earth over 5 billion years ago. Other life forms didn't come until much later. We've been here to welcome and guide every new life that has appeared since. We are the Earth, and the Earth is us."

Kal found himself staring at Alana again and had to force himself to look elsewhere. He blew out a slow breath, his lips wobbling slightly. "Wow, this is... a lot. But I believe you," he said, turning back to Barrett. "So, how do we stop the Byrnes?"

Barrett stood and moved toward the shelves, his fingers brushing along the spines of ancient books. After a moment of searching, he pulled out a slim, leather-bound book and placed it gently on his desk. Beckoning Ella and Kal to come closer, he opened the book slowly, revealing its fragile, time-worn pages.

The pages were stained, the ink barely legible in places, but the bright, intricate paintings that adorned large parts of the text captivated Ella. She couldn't take her eyes off them.

"What are these?" she asked, pointing at the paintings, which had lasted better than the faded text.

"This is *The Book of Elements*," Barrett explained, "It

contains all the known information about the five elements and predictions for the future." He turned to a specific page and stepped back. Kal immediately leaned in, his eyes wide with recognition.

"This is it—this is my dream! But how is it in here?" Kal asked, turning to Alana for answers, who looked toward Barrett.

"Kalan, your dream felt real, didn't it?" Barrett asked, though it sounded more like a statement than a question.

"Yeah," Kal replied. "I could feel the heat from the fire and how soft Sonny's feathers were when I was on him. Even my bow was hot when I woke up from the dream."

"You felt all of this because your essence traveled there with Sonny," Barrett explained. "There's a reason you were there: it was a warning. One of the five elements has been stolen, and your dream showed us it was the Fire element."

Kal was still trying to process everything. "What exactly do you mean by 'element'? I mean, I know about the periodic table, but I'm guessing this is something different?" He needed to understand because being dragged into a fiery apocalyptic world in his dreams was unsettling, to say the least.

Barrett looked visibly upset, and Alana stepped in to explain. "There are five elements in this Realm—Earth, Air, Fire, Water, and Ether. They're the forces that connect life. If any of them fall into the wrong hands, the balance shifts, and darkness is brought out in all of them. Light cannot exist without darkness."

Kal glanced at Ella and saw she was just as perplexed as he was.

"Alana, I get that this is serious," Ella said cautiously. "But how are we supposed to help? We've only known about the Fae for less than a week."

Barrett fixed them with a determined gaze, realising they still didn't grasp how crucial they were. "You are both our chosen warriors. Twins are only ever born when there's a major shift in the Realm. You were both born to protect the Earth. Whether you realise it or not, you've been warrior Fae since the day you were born."

Barrett's words left them both momentarily speechless. But when Ella snapped out of it, her eyes burned with fierce determination. "So, what are we going to do about it?"

Kal, jolted by his sister's resolve, sat up straighter, the same look of readiness flashing across his face.

Barrett placed both hands on his desk and looked down at the painted image of the fiery rivers. Then he looked up at the three of them, his eyes filled with purpose.

"We need to find out who has stolen the Element and retrieve it before it can be delivered to the Byrne Clan. Alana, you and Kalan gather the other warriors in the dome. We need everyone prepared for battle."

Ella felt a surge of concern at how quickly things were escalating and the fact that her brother had been separated from her.

"What about me?" she asked, hating how vulnerable the question sounded. Trying to compose herself, she stood taller and gripped her sword with newfound determination.

Barrett looked at her, sensing her unease. "Ella, you and I need to visit the Seer immediately. I need to know that your Cù Sìth is fully connected to you and won't become a danger to our clan during battle. The Seer will be able to sense if the Bond is strong enough. Focus on me and follow my Jump." His eyes locked onto hers before he disappeared.

For a brief moment, Ella hesitated before she focused hard and Jumped after him. When she reappeared, she found herself in a dimly lit, leafy tunnel, just high enough for Barrett to stand. The thick, spongy leaves around her shimmered with a pearlescent glow, catching her eye and making her feel for the first time that she was truly underground. A ripple of claustrophobia washed over her, and she instinctively tightened her grip on her sword. As she did, a wave of warmth spread through her hands, calming her. Her subconscious walls seemed to melt away, and she was able to hold her head high, breathing deeply. Without thinking, she whispered, "Thank you."

CHAPTER FIFTEEN

Barrett led Ella to the entrance of what appeared to be a small mud hut.

"You'll need to go in alone. She's been waiting for you. Remember to always speak the truth, and you'll be fine. I'll be right here," Barrett assured her.

Ella hesitated for a moment, her foot resting on the bottom step. She didn't turn around, but a wave of apprehension froze her in place. She wasn't sure if she could handle any more bad news. With slow, deliberate steps, she approached the wooden door, noticing the metal symbol etched on it: five overlapping circles forming a flower-like shape. It was familiar—her mother had books with that same symbol, and she even wore a necklace bearing it.

Bracing herself, Ella expected the door to be heavy and creaky, but it opened with surprising ease, gliding silently on its hinges. Inside, she was met not with the dark, cold space she anticipated but one of breathtaking beauty. The entire room was bathed in shimmering gold, so smooth and liquid-like it seemed to flow down the walls. In the centre of the room, a perfectly circular pool mirrored the golden glow, casting shimmering reflections on the ceiling. Ella approached the pool, marvelling at how clear the water was, almost as if it weren't there at all.

She could have stayed lost in that moment forever, but a soft, deep hum of a voice greeted her, pulling her back to reality. "Hello," it said.

Ella turned, and her gaze landed on a woman seated on the floor gracefully at the far end of the room. She was sure the woman hadn't been there when she first entered, but now, she sat with regal poise. The Seer's large, bright, white eyes, without any colour or pupils, captured Ella's full attention.

The woman before her was like a queen. Her dark, radiant skin seemed to shimmer against the golden surroundings. Her long, elegant neck supported a serene face framed by thick, black, wavy hair cascading over her shoulders. Ella felt awestruck by her beauty and the immense calmness radiating from her presence.

A voice, so smooth and hypnotic, drifted across the water towards Ella.

"I have been expecting you, Ella. It was an honour to feel your Essence at birth. Now, you come to me with your Cù Sìth, as a war approaches."

For a few moments, Ella stood silent, still absorbing the Seer's words and the captivating beauty of her voice.

"Uh, yes," Ella stammered. "Barrett thought I should come to make sure my Cù Sìth has Bonded enough with me —so she doesn't, you know, kill anyone on our side." As those last words left her mouth, the reality of what lay ahead hit her like a wave, nearly knocking her off her feet.

The Seer's smooth, silky voice reached her again, steadying her.

"You have nothing to fear. Your Bonded animal is entirely loyal to you. However, she will destroy anything that stands in your way. You must remain strong and in control."

"Thank you, Seer," Ella replied, unsure of herself. "I'll make sure I stay in control."

Feeling slightly awkward, Ella began to step back toward the wooden door, thinking perhaps the conversation had ended.

"Ella." The Seer's voice was filled with care. "You and Kalan are essential to the survival of the Fae. You will face hard decisions, but trust that the answers are within you both. Just remember to breathe—always remember to *breathe*."

Ella felt this was the end of her time with the Seer. She gave a slight bow, uncertain if it was the proper thing to do, and backed away some more until she reached the door. The Seer remained seated in serene silence, her tranquility unbroken.

As Ella clumsily stumbled down the steps, not wanting to turn her back on the Seer, the door quietly closed behind her. When she finally turned around, she met Barrett's eyes, feeling a new sense of strength and purpose. Her Essence had been awakened, and she understood what she needed to do.

Barrett, sensing the change in her, nodded knowingly.

"I take it everything went well?"

"It did, yeah," Ella responded. "I can't really explain how I feel, but I just know that I'm ready."

"Good. Let's get back to the dome and get your armour rea..." Barrett Jumped out of the leafy tunnel before he could finish the sentence.

Ella took one last glance at the wooden door, recalling the golden light that had surrounded her inside. Thick, heavy vines began to weave across the door until it was completely sealed. "No popping in unannounced, I guess," she muttered to herself. Taking out her Holed Stone, she closed her eyes and Jumped back to the Training Dome, where Barrett was already leading her towards the changing rooms.

"Alana will meet you inside. You'll need to get your kit on and meet the rest of the warriors out here."

The Dome was packed with warriors—men and women, all looking strong, battle-hardened, and full of an intensity that Ella could feel from across the room. The sheer power in the air was like a punch to the stomach. Weapons of all kinds filled the space: swords, bows and arrows, axes, slingshots, and weapons Ella had no clue what they were. As they reached the door, a rippling silence fell over the crowd. Ella thought it was because of Barrett's presence, but the truth was, all eyes were on her —the fabled twin.

Once inside the changing room, the atmosphere shifted entirely. The room, filled with warriors preparing for what lay ahead, hummed with a mixture of fear and uncertainty.

From behind a changing wall, Kal's head popped out, relief washing over his face when he saw his sister.

"What took you so long? It's been a bit crazy here!" Kal stepped out fully, grinning. "Hey, check out my kit."

Ella stopped in her tracks, speechless. There was a part of her that wanted to laugh at how un-Kal he looked, but another part that felt like he had finally stepped into who he truly was.

Kal was dressed in metal armour over his shoulders, chest, and forearms, with intricate etchings she had never seen before. The breastplate bore the same symbol she had seen on the Seer's door—five circles overlapping like a flower. His dark trousers were tucked into calf-high boots, and leather straps crossed over his shoulders to hold his bow and arrows, with loops for other weapons around his waist.

"Well, you certainly look the part," Ella giggled, knowing he'd do the same when he saw her dressed up.

Alana, who had been helping prepare Ella's kit, glanced over at Kal and smiled warmly. Then, regaining focus, she grabbed Ella's arm. "Come on, you need to get changed. Lord Archer will be addressing everyone soon, and you can't miss it."

Ella followed Alana behind one of the changing walls, where her armour was hanging. Her breath caught when she saw it.

"This is mine?" Ella stepped closer, her fingers brushing over the beautifully etched breastplate. In the centre was the same symbol as on Kal's armour and the Seer's door, but encrusted with a deep red crystal that reminded her of the stone in Lord Archer's breastplate.

Alana smiled. "Yep, that's yours. You'll need to get used

to putting it on by yourself. I'll be out here if you need help."

Left alone, Ella slowly undressed and began to figure out how to piece her kit together. First, she pulled on the dark trousers that tucked into her calf-high boots, then buckled the armoured skirt that had a front slit. The leather top, which felt like cotton once she put it on, was surprisingly comfortable, and over that went the breastplate and shoulder armour.

Realising she couldn't do the back buckles by herself, she peered around the corner and found Alana pacing in the now-empty changing room. A slight wave of irritation hit her—Kal hadn't even waited for her.

"Alana, could you help me with the buckles at the back?"

Alana was by her side in an instant, fastening the straps with ease and showing her how to secure her belts for her sword and any other tools she might carry. Once everything was in place, she turned Ella toward the mirror.

At first, Ella was hesitant, but as she looked closer, the reflection began to feel natural. It wasn't just the armour she wore—it was as though she was finally seeing herself as the warrior she was meant to be.

Alana, meanwhile, was quickly tying Ella's hair back into a messy side braid.

"Sorry, I'm not great at doing hair," she admitted, looking slightly embarrassed. "I don't really need to bother with it much myself."

Ella smiled. "It actually looks pretty good, and don't worry—I'm not much better. Anything more than a ponytail is fancy for me."

They both chuckled lightly, a brief moment of levity before stepping back into the intensity awaiting them in the Dome.

Ella remembered the Seer's words: *Always remember to breathe*. She drew in a slow, deep breath, letting it filter through her lungs, steadying her body, until all the fear drained away, leaving only focus. Alana gave her a reassuring nod toward the door, and together they stepped back into the dome where everyone seemed to be waiting for her.

Kal stood nearby, giving her a look that said, *'Sorry, I had no idea and didn't have time to warn you.'* Before she could respond, a booming voice cut through the charged atmosphere, and all eyes turned toward Lord Archer.

"Welcome, Ella and Kalan. We are all proud to witness this moment, though it has come sooner than we would have liked," Lord Archer said, his voice commanding the room. "Barrett informs me that you are both ready for what lies ahead."

Ella's eyes darted through the crowd, searching for Barrett. She had no idea how to react. Suddenly, she felt Kal's hand grip hers tightly, offering a silent reassurance.

"Come up here, and let's have a look at you both in your kits," Lord Archer waved them over. Both twins stood frozen, looking like they wanted to run. Barrett and Alana appeared beside them, whispering encouragement they could barely hear over the sound of their own nerves.

Before they knew it, they were standing next to Lord Archer, though neither of them remembered walking through the sea of warriors. The room fell silent, expectant, and for a brief moment, Ella feared they were supposed to speak. To her relief, Barrett stepped forward.

"Here before us stand Ella and Kalan, our first Fae twins in over a thousand years," Barrett began, his voice filled with pride and solemnity. "They join us at a time of great uncertainty and fragility within the Clans. Kalan has had a vision revealing that the Fire Element has been stolen. We don't know if the Byrne Clan has it yet, but if not, it's only a matter of time."

A murmur rippled through the crowd, bouncing off the walls and reaching Ella and Kal, who tried their best not to look completely overwhelmed.

Barrett continued, bringing the twins closer to the crowd. "We all remember what it's like to discover we are warriors after 16 years of believing we are human—or most of us anyway," he said, nodding to Alana, who smiled gracefully. This caused Ella to frown, unsure of what it meant. " Some of us have had to fight before we felt ready, but the truth is, your training is never truly complete. You are warriors now, and soon, you will be stronger than anyone here. Believe in yourselves, in your purpose. It will all come together in time."

Ella felt a surge of strength rise within her, and she could sense Kal beside her, breathing deeply and steadily, his own confidence building.

"Kalan," Barrett said, motioning him forward, "call on your eagle. Let Sonny feel the energy of the warriors around you. We need all warriors and their Bonded animals to work together as one."

With pride, Kal took his bow and called upon Sonny, who

swooped out like a dragon descending on its prey, fierce and majestic. Kal whispered softly to his eagle, words only Sonny could hear. The eagle circled the room, as if reading the essence of every warrior present. Heads nodded in respect, and a sense of unity filled the space, strengthening Kal's resolve. Sonny returned to his shoulder, letting out a loud screech of approval.

Ella knew it was her turn now, but her heart raced at the thought of keeping her Cù Sìth calm amidst the crowd. She glanced over at Barrett, who raised his eyebrows and nodded, signalling it was time.

Standing tall, Ella swiftly drew her sword. With a flick of her wrist and a whispered command, the green mist began to swirl and coalesce into the terrifying form of the Cù Sìth. Gasps of disbelief echoed through the dome as the older warriors stepped back, unsure of what they were seeing. The massive beast stood before them, its moss-covered fur rippling with latent power, its fiery eyes blazing. Even Lord Archer, who had been briefed about the Cù Sìth, seemed taken aback by the magnificent creature.

Ella placed a hand on the Cù Sìth's head, her touch calming the giant creature almost instantly. Barrett stepped forward confidently, careful not to let the beast sense any uncertainty in him. He addressed the warriors again.

"This, warriors, is the Cù Sìth. A beast thought to be extinct, now Bonded with Ella. She has never been tamed before, but Ella has shown us that it is possible. Treat her with the utmost respect. She is a Queen among creatures."

Ella could feel the weight of every eye on her, but instead of fear, she felt calm. She had control.

As Ella walked around, she was relieved to see her friend's demeanour shift from snarling with raised hackles to calmly sniffing and getting acquainted with everyone. Standing back next to Kal, they exchanged a look of mutual relief. Ella leaned over and whispered to her brother as Lord Archer continued speaking.

"I've thought of a name for her—Artemis, Art for short. You know, like the Greek goddess of wild animals."

Kal smiled, nodding in approval. "It suits her."

He scratched Artemis's head, and her big, fiery orange eyes stared at him with something that resembled respect.

"Hey, Art. It's really nice to meet you," Kal said softly. Artemis leaned her solid head affectionately against him, almost knocking him back from the sheer weight of her.

Ella refocused on Lord Archer, who was assigning different "team clans" to search for information on the missing Fire Element. Some were sent to the Niskai waters, others to the Dryads in the Oak Woods. Ella and Kal exchanged confused glances; they had no idea where these places were or what kind of Fae they were meant to find. Judging by the confident warriors around them who were already disappearing to their destinations, it was clear they were the only ones out of the loop.

Barrett stepped forward, placing a hand on each of their shoulders. "This is where I leave you for a while. You'll learn a lot from Lord Archer and Alana. Keep your spirits high, and always remember—this is what you were born to do."

Before either of them could ask where he was going or

why he was leaving, Barrett Jumped out of the Training Dome.

Ella couldn't help but feel a little abandoned. "Where is he going? Isn't this the time he needs to be here?"

Lord Archer's face tightened slightly as he responded, almost nervously. "Barrett has gone to seek council with Cerridwen, goddess of the Underworld. She holds great wisdom, and Barrett has a unique affinity with her."

Kal's face showed his growing concern. "How long will he be? Is he going to meet us later?"

Speaking gently, as though comforting a disappointed child, Lord Archer replied, "It's difficult to say how long he'll be. There are greater issues at hand, beyond just the Fire Element."

He placed a firm, reassuring hand on Kal's shoulder. The weight of it was solid and strong, the hand of a warrior, and it brought a lump to Kal's throat. He swallowed hard, pushing away nerves, knowing there wasn't time for them.

"We'll go meet with the Dwarves," Lord Archer continued. "Their mines run deeper than any other part of the Realm. They might have heard rumours of disturbances within the fiery pits."

Alana buckled on her bow and adjusted her arrow pack, looking every bit the battle-ready warrior. Kal, watching her, fumbled to copy what she was doing, his nervous hands struggling with the buckles. Alana smiled and walked over, helping him secure the tricky straps across his back. She patted his shoulders and said with a grin, "Ready to go hunting?" She winked and walked back to Lord Archer, leaving Kal unsure if she was serious.

Lord Archer straightened his back and pushed out his chest, the blood-red crystal on his breastplate glinting in the light. Ella's eyes were drawn to it, and she felt an immediate connection. Her own breastplate seemed to mirror his, straightening her posture and pushing her shoulders back. At first, Ella thought her kit was moving on its own, possessed, but then she felt it was the crystal reacting to Lord Archer's.

He looked at her gently, speaking with a nurturing tone. "You are both warriors—always have been. Trust your instincts and believe in what you see, hear, and feel."

This gave Ella a boost of confidence as she followed the others out of the dome. Standing on the bridge, she watched as Lord Archer and Alana suddenly Jumped out of sight. Then, hearing his booming voice from below, she saw that they were down in the gorge where she had Bonded with Artemis. Ella and Kal followed, Jumping down to meet them.

"This is where things get a bit darker," Lord Archer said. "The Solar Tree connects to most places within our Realm, but the deeper tunnels that lead to the Dwarf kingdom are not among them. Stay close, and a light will guide us when needed."

Alana pulled back a thick curtain of vines and flowers that draped over a sparkling, dewy door made of gnarled, ancient wood that looked so thick Ella wasn't sure it could be moved. All over the front were strange tree like symbols, definitely not Runes but Ella felt they must be similar. The rusted metal hinges looked like they'd not been opened in a long time. There was no handle, no lock, nothing to indicate the door could be opened from the outside. In the centre, a hole was carved deep into the wood. Ella peered into it, startled by just how far it went.

Lord Archer rolled up his sleeve, revealing a wide metal cuff on his arm, etched with markings similar to those on his breastplate, centred with the same glowing blood-red stone. He inserted his arm into the hole, and the stone pulsed, radiating warmth. Ella looked down to see her own stone flicker faintly, sending a soft glow from her breastplate.

Before she could say anything, Lord Archer twisted his arm inside the hole, and a heavy clunking sound began. He muttered something under his breath, and to Ella's surprise, she found herself quietly repeating the same words.

Lord Archer pulled his arm out as the giant door creaked open. Kal nudged Ella, a little harder than he intended, and she shot him a look.

"Sorry! But seriously, that was the classic horror movie door creak, don't you think? All we need now is for someone to say, 'I'll be right back.'"

Ella giggled and almost said those exact words but stopped when she saw the look on Kal's face—one that said, *Don't you dare.*

Alana led the way through the door, with Kal close behind. Ella took a deep breath, bracing herself as though diving underwater, her hand resting comfortably on her sword, ready for whatever came next.

Instead of the dark, dirty tunnel she'd expected, she found herself in a high-ceilinged passage adorned with ornate arches every twenty feet, each glowing red and illuminating the otherwise dim but beautiful space. The strange symbols that covered the door were also etched along the archways and lit up like fire.

Ella's breastplate crystal glowed brighter, casting a soothing light ahead. She became mesmerised by its shimmering glow and stopped walking, causing Lord Archer to bump into her. She turned, about to apologise, but froze when she saw his expression.

"You have the Painite crystal," Lord Archer said, stunned. "But how is that possible?"

Ella had no answers, but she could tell this wasn't expected. "I... I don't know, Lord Archer. Maybe I was given the wrong kit? This could belong to someone else?"

"No," he said firmly. "A warrior's kit is made for them from the moment of birth, just like their weapon. This stone was meant for you... but why?" He seemed to be talking more to himself now, pacing slightly as if searching for an answer.

"You can't have any Dwarf blood in you as Kalan doesn't have the crystal, you must be connected to them somehow though, this has never happened before."

Ella, feeling confused, asked, "Could it be some kind of mistake? I mean, how would I be connected to the Dwarfs?"

Ella, growing more curious, ventured to ask, "How do *you* have one of these crystals, Lord Archer? How are you connected to the Dwarfs?" She couldn't understand how someone as tall and strong as him could be linked to a race known for their smaller stature.

"Let's walk," he said, gesturing for them to keep moving. "We don't want to lose the others down here."

They continued down the glowing tunnel, the light shifting and dancing across the walls like a gentle breeze. "Believe it or not, I am half-Dwarf," Lord Archer revealed. "My father was a Dwarf Chief, and he fell in love with my mother, a Faerie. Cross-Fae relationships are rare and dangerous. Most offspring don't survive. But I was raised by the Dwarfs until my father died in battle when I was seven. My mother brought me back to her people, I've been fortunate to be accepted by both Faerie and Dwarfs."

Ella found herself fascinated by his story, imagining what life might have been like growing up in the World Below. Part of her wished she had been raised there too—she might have felt more prepared for everything they were now facing.

As they caught up to Alana and Kal, they arrived at the edge of a vast pit that seemed to have no bottom. A winding staircase clung to the walls, lined with arches glittering with gemstones that burst into a kaleidoscope of colours as Ella and Lord Archer's crystals illuminated them.

Ella stared down into the depths, feeling both awe and apprehension. '*I guess there's no turning back now,*' she thought, gripping her sword a little tighter as they prepared to descend into the unknown.

Kal hadn't noticed at first, too busy looking down into the endless pit. But when he lifted his head, his eyes widened in awe. His gaze traced the source of the light back to Ella's breastplate, and he did a double take.

"Uh, Ella, you're glowing! What's going on?"

"Apparently, these Painite crystals come from the Dwarfs, but you only get one if you're a Dwarf or connected to them somehow. We can rule out us being Dwarfs, but I guess I must be connected to them in some way."

Kal looked over his own kit, searching for any sign of a crystal, but there was nothing. Lord Archer noticed the disappointment on his face.

"Just because Ella has this crystal doesn't mean you will too, Kalan. Every Fae has their own path. Although yours is closely intertwined, there will always be elements that differ."

Alana suddenly raised a finger, signalling them to be quiet. Her expression had shifted from gentle and sweet to fierce and alert.

She glanced over at Lord Archer and tapped under her nose. He lifted his head and took a long, slow sniff of the air, nodding in understanding. Then he tapped his ear, and Alana mimicked him, sniffing the air as well. She nodded in agreement with whatever Lord Archer had sensed.

Without speaking, Alana turned to Ella and Kal, motioning for them to copy her. She took a slow, deep breath in through her mouth, then exhaled just as slowly, putting a finger to her lips to signal the need for absolute silence.

Lord Archer placed a hand on Ella's shoulder, startling her. She turned to see him covering his Painite crystal. He gave her a knowing nod, and she understood—she needed to do the same.

Taking a deep breath, Ella covered the glowing crystal with her hand. Instantly, the stairs went dark, all the vibrant light and colour vanishing, plunging them into pitch-black silence. They stood in the suffocating darkness, unsure of what might be lurking nearby.

CHAPTER SIXTEEN

The four of them stood still in the darkness, Ella's heart pounding in her chest as she strained to listen. Who or what were they hiding from? Would they need to fight? And were they even ready for that? She tried to focus on her breathing, slowing it down to keep herself calm. A faint smell drifted into her nose. Ella sniffed gently, trying to place the scent without making too much noise. It reminded her of something... and then it clicked. It smelled like a tea her mum used to make sometimes.

At the thought of her mum, a wave of homesickness hit Ella hard. Everything had been so chaotic since they'd arrived in the World Below that she'd hardly had time to think about her parents. She wished she could be back home, sitting in the kitchen while her mum brewed one of her magical pots of tea. No matter the occasion, her mum always knew the perfect combination of herbs, flowers, and roots to energise, heal, or comfort.

Ella opened her eyes, exhaling slowly, and then her

breath caught in her throat. She gasped quietly, quickly clapping her free hand over her mouth, making sure she didn't move the hand that was covering her crystal. The others turned toward her, their lips pressed tightly in silent warning. In the dim light, they looked like shadows, their outlines glowing slightly. It was like the night she and Kal rode out to the Tulip tree, able to see in the dark. It still startled her when this ability kicked in.

Lord Archer signalled for them all to stay where they were, which Ella and Kal were more than happy to do. He moved silently forward, his hand still covering his crystal, inching down the steps around the ever-curving tunnel.

Suddenly, a loud cry echoed down the tunnel, and in an instant, the kaleidoscope of colour exploded back onto the walls and ceiling. The light could only mean one thing— Lord Archer had uncovered his crystal, or someone had uncovered it for him!

Without thinking, Ella yanked her hand from her crystal, her sword drawn as she sprinted down the stairs, ready to face whatever danger lay around the corner. She slammed into Lord Archer's broad back, barely making him budge. He turned, concern flickering in his eyes as he raised his arm to block her sword.

"Ella, stop! This is no enemy—it's my cousin, Orek."

Ella stood there, sword still raised, staring in shock at the dwarf before her. It took her a few moments to process, probably longer than was polite. Despite the obvious size difference between them, there was a definite resemblance between Lord Archer and Orek—both had unruly brown hair and beards streaked with white. Orek's beard, however, was so long it looked like he could tuck it into his belt. Their faces shared the same kindness, though their eyes were different.

"I could smell that Mugwort you're smoking from miles away, Orek," Lord Archer said with a chuckle, though concern lingered in his eyes. "What are you doing this high up, and why are you traveling alone?"

Orek let out a throaty laugh, followed by a rough cough, before taking another puff from his enormous pipe, which looked more like a musical instrument than anything used for smoking. His voice was deep and raspy, but warm.

"Well, I needed something to take my mind off the long journey up to your parts."

By this time, Alana and Kal had caught up to them. Alana practically jumped on Orek, wrapping her arms around him and ruffling his long beard. "Uncle Orek! How are you? It's been ages! What brings you here, and why are you alone?"

Orek's initial joy at seeing Alana quickly faded as he took another deep puff of his pipe, his face clouding over. "I came to see you, cousin, and to warn you. There's been a shift below—many of our Clan are leaving. The Fire Element was taken yesterday. I volunteered to journey up here and inform the Clan Council."

Lord Archer and Alana exchanged worried glances. "Do we know who took it?" Lord Archer asked, his voice tight.

Orek's face contorted with frustration. "It was those blasted Night Elves. Ateful creatures. They left a single arrow behind, just to make sure we knew it was em. And we all know where they'll be taking it."

Ella found herself feeling slightly overwhelmed standing in front of Orek, though she wasn't quite sure why. After all, she was a Faerie now. Realising she still had her crystal covered and that there was no longer a need to do so, she removed her cupped fingers from around the stone. Instantly, the stairwell lit up even more, as though stars had been embedded into every surface, sparkling brightly.

The sudden brightness lifted Orek's face. He glanced behind him, as if expecting to see another of his clan approaching from below.

"Orek," Lord Archer said, noticing his cousin's confusion. "This is Ella, and her twin brother, Kalan." His tone left no room for doubt.

"But how does the girl have the Painite crystal? Is she half Dwarf as well?" Orek asked in surprise, seemingly brushing past the fact she was a twins.

Lord Archer gave a slight shrug. "I don't know, cousin. And right now, we don't have the time to figure it out." Turning to Alana and Kal, he instructed, "You two need to return to the Council and inform them of what we've learned. Warn the other warriors about the Night Elves. We'll meet you at the edge of the Black Woods before Solar-down."

Alana nodded and turned, running back up the stairs. Kal followed close behind her, trusting Lord Archer's orders.

"Ella, you and I are staying with Orek," Lord Archer continued. "We need to make our way down to where the Fire Element was taken. We must gather as much information as we can before we encounter the Night Elves."

Ella's mind raced. In the stories she'd read, Elves were

always graceful and peaceful folk. But it seemed that wasn't the case here. "So, these Night Elves... they're not on our side then?" She already knew the answer but asked anyway, hoping for some glimmer of hope.

Lord Archer gave her a knowing look. "There are grains of truth in human tales, but most of it has been twisted to make the Fae world more palatable to human ears. Something I think is unnecessary."

Orek, unable to contain himself, interjected with gruff bitterness. "Elves are the lowest of the low, especially em Night Elves. They care only for emselves and couldn't care less about the rest of us tryin to live in peace."

Ella blinked, startled by Orek's open hatred. "So Night Elves are worse than other Elves?" She was aware her questions might seem basic, but she needed to understand, so she pressed on. "What's the difference between a regular Elf and a Night Elf?"

Orek practically leapt at her question, his voice booming with frustration. Ella's pulse quickened, her heart pounding in her chest as his energy unsettled her.

"Orek, calm down," Lord Archer said firmly, casting his cousin a sharp look. "This isn't helping anyone—least of all Ella, who's only been in our Realm for a week. What she needs are facts, not emotions."

Orek, apologetically nodded and dialled down his intensity. "Lead the way, Orek," Lord Archer continued," and I'll explain what Ella needs to know about the Elves."

As they descended the spiralling tunnel filled with rainbow hues, Ella felt a strange sense of gratitude for her

Painite crystal. Without it, she wasn't sure she'd be able to navigate this deep, even with her Faerie night vision.

Lord Archer began recounting the long history of the Elves, which gave Ella something to focus on other than the seemingly endless descent. "Elves have been around almost as long as the Faeries," he explained. "In fact, they evolved from us. They were once Faeries who despised the sun and believed that helping to maintain the balance of the Realm was a tiresome and thankless task. So, they made their homes underground, and much of the architecture you see today stems from those early settlers."

Ella tried to concentrate, but the air was growing thick and hot. Lord Archer and Orek seemed unbothered, likely due to their Dwarf heritage. She absentmindedly touched the crystal on her chest plate and found that, as soon as she cupped it, the oppressive heat became much more bearable. It was as though the crystal was shielding her from the discomfort.

Realising she had drifted off in thought and missed part of Lord Archer's lesson, Ella snapped her attention back to the present, refocusing on the words as they continued their descent.

"The Night Elves evolved from the Elves," Lord Archer began, his voice echoing softly in the tunnel, "They still resemble their ancestors, but with charcoal-black skin, allowing them to disappear in the tunnels and forests. It's nearly impossible for any other Fae to see one in the shadows, even Faeries, with our enhanced night sight. The warriors have grey or black hair, while the elders of the Clan have quartz-white hair. Their only light comes from their eyes, which are almost pure white. However, in recent years, rumours have spread about some Night Elves with completely black eyes. I've yet to encounter one myself."

Ella had no trouble conjuring a mental image of the Night Elves, and what she imagined sent chills down her spine. "But why are they so angry? Surely they weren't always like this?" she asked, hoping there was some redeeming explanation.

Lord Archer sighed, the weight of history heavy on his shoulders. "They're angry because we moved into their Realm. When humans came into existence, the Fae knew we would eventually have to leave the World Above. As the human population grew beyond what the world could sustain, we were forced to move sooner than we were ready for. It was time for humans to rule the World Above. So, all Fae went below. The Elves were furious—they felt we were taking over what they had built over billions of years. So, they exiled themselves again, choosing to live in the places the rest of us wouldn't."

Ella walked in silence, unsure how to process everything she was learning, and could understand why the Elves would be so upset. The stories she'd grown up with were slowly unraveling, revealing truths that shook her understanding of the world. After what felt like hours, they finally reached the bottom of the spiralling stairs. The sight that greeted her stole her breath away.

Orek, seeing her reaction, beamed with pride. "I knew she'd love it, Archie. Maybe she's a Dwarf after all."

Hearing Lord Archer referred to as "Archie" made him seem more approachable, a reminder that even the most powerful figures were still people with histories and families. Ella knew she had more questions about the Elves, but she decided to save them for later.

The cathedral-like structure before them was covered in runes, each arch decorated with mystical creatures from her childhood stories and others she didn't recognise. One giant carving, in particular, caught her eye—a tree shaped like a man. His face, gentle and wise, seemed to watch over her like a protective guardian.

"Who is this carving of? He's quite remarkable," Ella asked, unable to tear her eyes away from the figure.

Lord Archer halted, looking at her with curiosity. "You can see the man carved into that tree?"

Ella chuckled softly, thinking he must be joking. "Of course, it's right there. It's hard to miss."

Lord Archer's expression turned serious. "I can see it too, but the fact that *you* can see it is... interesting." He studied her as if she were a puzzle he couldn't quite solve.

"What do you mean?" Ella asked, her concern growing.

"The Green Man is visible only to Dwarfs and mythical creatures, Ella. No other Fae has ever been able to see him."

"But I'm not part Dwarf, am I?" Ella's voice wavered. "Kal doesn't have this crystal, so what does this mean?" Anxiety bubbled inside her as she thought about Kal and Alana, wondering where they were.

As they moved closer to the Green Man, Ella's fingers began to tingle. She looked down and realised her sword was vibrating in her hand, a faint green mist swirling around her knuckles and creeping up her arm.

"Lord Archer!" she called out, panic rising in her chest as

she felt the sword slipping from her control. She struggled to restrain it, nearly striking two Dwarfs who quickly leaped out of the way, shouting in alarm.

Seeing the terror in her eyes, Lord Archer rushed to her side. "Ella, relax. If you fight her, she'll fight back harder."

But his words didn't comfort her. She tightened her grip, trying to force the sword to stop. "Can you just help me?" she begged through gritted teeth, her panic growing as the sword began to whirl around her head like a wild beast.

"I can't, Ella," Lord Archer said firmly, his tone calm but urgent. "No one can touch your weapon but you. I'd only make it worse. You need to relax and breathe!"

Ella didn't want to hear it—how could breathing help when her sword was spinning out of control? But she remembered the Seer's advice: *Always remember to breathe.*

With great effort, Ella closed her eyes, took a deep breath, and slowly let it out. The green mist began to settle, and the sword's wild movements eased. Bit by bit, the sword returned to her control, resting quietly in her hand.

When she opened her eyes, Lord Archer was watching her closely, his expression showing his pride. "Good. You did it."

Ella nodded, still shaken but grateful for his guidance. She realised then that controlling her weapon—and herself —was going to be a bigger challenge than she'd thought.

As Ella relaxed her grip on the sword, a soft whisper seemed to drift past her ear, carried on a gentle breeze. She looked down and knew that Artemis, wanted to come out. With a flick of Ella's wrist, she bounded out, panting heavily and drooling with thirst, as though exhausted from being contained.

Artemis glanced at Ella, nodding as if to say *Thank you*, before stepping cautiously toward the statue of the Green Man. By now, Artemis had attracted quite a bit of attention, and a ripple of panic began to spread through the crowd gathered around them.

Lord Archer quickly moved to calm everyone down, sensing the rising anxiety. Surprisingly, Artemis seemed unbothered by the Dwarfs staring at her—her focus remained entirely on the statue.

Ella approached her friend and knelt beside her, resting her arm over her thick neck. "What is it, Art? What do you see?" she whispered, her voice meant only for her beasts ears.

Following Art's gaze, Ella realised that the wolf was staring directly at the Green Man. To her surprise, Art knelt on one knee and bowed her head, an act of reverence. Glancing up at the statue, Ella thought she saw a fleeting moment of recognition pass over the Green Man's carved face, as if he knew Artemis.

Confused, Ella turned to Lord Archer and Orek. "What's going on?" she asked, feeling a bit self-conscious as everyone's eyes were now fixed on her and Artemis.

Orek stepped forward, a glint of excitement in his eyes. "Oh, I expect these two are old friends. The Green Man is the King of the woods, entrusted with keeping the life cycle going. Every autumn, he dies, and much of the forest with him, but his essence comes here for peace and restoration in the winter. Then, every spring, he is reborn. All creatures of the woods know him, and I'm sure a Cù Sìth has spent plenty of time in his woods."

Ella looked down at Art, who was still gazing up at the statue. She felt even more connected to her, seeing this ancient, unspoken Bond between Art and the Green Man. Unable to resist, Ella hugged Art's neck, feeling the strength of their connection.

Orek straightened up, a mischievous grin on his face as he nudged his cousin. "So, Archie, when were ya gonna tell me she's got a Cù Sìth as a Bond? Guess you're not at the top of the triangle anymore, eh?" Orek chuckled, winking at his cousin.

Ella couldn't help but smile at the dynamic between the two. They seemed more like brothers than cousins, and it amused her to see a Dwarf teasing the towering half-Dwarf, half-Faerie warrior Lord.

Lord Archer, unimpressed but clearly amused, shook his head. "Very funny, Orek. Now, perhaps we should move on and take a look at where the Fire Element was kept."

Ella scratched Art's head gently, guiding her as they continued walking. After about ten minutes, they arrived at a pair of massive metal doors. Unlike the rest of the stunning kingdom, these doors were plain and rusted. Gazing up at their towering height, Ella couldn't understand why they were so enormous. *What could they be trying to keep in—or worse, keep out?* she wondered, deciding she might not want to know the answer.

Orek approached the doors, pulling his axe from his belt and placing the Painite crystal embedded in its handle against the metal. Instantly, the doors lit up as fiery red veins pulsed through the black rusted metal, as if blood were being pumped through a colossal, dark heart. The doors swung open without a sound, despite their immense thickness, and Ella stared in awe. "That's one big door," she muttered to herself, not realising she had spoken out loud.

"It needs to be," Orek said, only noticing Lord Archer's sharp look after he spoke.

Lord Archer clearly didn't want to alarm Ella, considering how new she was to their world. He had hoped to keep certain details from her for a little longer. "Well, she'd find out sooner or later," Orek muttered, shrugging off his cousin's disapproval.

With a sigh Lord Archer turned to Ella, who was looking up at him with wide, curious eyes. "These doors are here to keep out dragons," he explained quickly, before Ella could spiral into panic. "But don't worry, there hasn't been a dragon up here in a very long time. They tend to stay close to the earth's core. This is just a precaution."

Ella's eyes widened, and tiny tears began to prickle in her bottom lids. She blinked them away, forcing herself to stay calm. "Dragons, but wouldn't they just melt through that metal?" she whispered, her voice shaky.

Orek chuckled, "No, this beauty is made from the finest Wolfram and Steel mix, there's nout getting through that."

Ella felt slightly better by Orek absolute tone, but she still took a few steps back, suddenly feeling the urge to run, but her feet seemed glued to the floor.

Lord Archer placed a reassuring hand on Ella's shoulder. "I know the stories humans are told about dragons, and while some parts are true, many have been wildly exaggerated."

Ella wasn't ready to accept vague reassurances. "What parts exactly have been exaggerated?" she demanded, her tone firm. If they wanted her to step foot in that fiery pit, she needed more information.

Orek shot a glare at his cousin, clearly thinking there was no time for explanations, but Lord Archer knew Ella wouldn't move forward without some clarity.

"Alright," he began. "Dragons are born in the centre of the Earth. Once hatched, they move out of the molten outer core and live in the rocky mantle for most of their lives, peacefully. But, like any species, there are always a few who like to cause trouble. The Dwarfs try to track them because, occasionally, dragons pass through the Dwarf tunnels to escape through the tops of volcanos. Humans believe volcanic eruptions are caused by magma buildup, but in reality, it's a dragon trying to break free."

Ella furrowed her brow, skeptical. "So why haven't humans ever seen a dragon? I'm pretty sure that would make the news."

Lord Archer smiled slightly, understanding her disbelief. "There are many magical creatures in the World Above, but they are not seen by humans.

Ella stood still, processing his words. Despite her hesitation, she straightened her shoulders and stepped through the giant, dragon-proof doors.

Not far beyond the doors, they came upon another spiralling pit, similar to the one they'd descended earlier.

Ella sighed in frustration. "Not another one. How far do we have to walk this time?"

Orek's eyes twinkled with mischief. Instead of answering, he pulled a lever, and a large metal cart swung out of the shadows, scooping them up like a ski lift. Ella instinctively grabbed whatever was nearby, her eyes squeezed shut. When she dared to open them, she let out a small laugh—it felt like they were on a roller coaster, the cart rattling along the tracks. But then the cart sped up, whipping around in circles, descending faster and faster until Ella felt sick.

Just when she thought she couldn't take anymore, the cart screeched to a halt. She stumbled out, her head spinning, her legs shaky. Orek nudged her playfully as he passed. "Better than walking, eh?"

All she could manage was a weak "Mmm-hmm" as she tried to regain her balance.

They stepped into an immense cavern, filled with stone bridges crisscrossing the space at various heights. Some were so high above them, Ella could barely see the top, while others had crumbled into jagged ends, leaving a terrifying drop into the abyss below.

Orek led them across one of the sturdier bridges, much to Ella's relief. As they reached the other side, Orek's voice dropped to a near-whisper. "It was kept through there," he said, pointing to a small, smoking archway barely large enough for a Dwarf.

"It's been safe here for millennia, undetected by any Fae. But somehow the Night Elves found it."

Ella crouched to squeeze through the archway. The heat hit her instantly, thick and oppressive. As she straightened up on the other side, she was greeted by a hellish scene. Rivers of bubbling fire snaked through the darkness, casting an eerie glow on the craggy walls. It reminded her of the Dragon door they had passed through—like arteries pulsing with fiery blood around a blackened heart.

The heat was unbearable. Ella had to close her eyes, afraid they might burn. "Can we go back out? It's too hot!" she cried, pushing her way past the others in desperation.

Once outside, she gasped for cooler air and turned to Lord Archer, her face full of questions.

"I know you found the Night Elves' arrow, but how do you know the Fire Element is really gone? It's so hot in there, I'm surprised anyone could see long enough to check."

Orek wiped sweat from his brow, "A Fire Salamander was given to the Fae who hide the element, it was to guard it like an egg and lay on it and never move. I saw this Fire Salamander crawling outside the hole in the rock, I followed it until I reached the Night Elf's arrow."

Ella's breath caught in her throat. "So the Element really is missing..."

Lord Archer nodded solemnly. "Yes. And without the Fire Element, the balance of our Realm is in danger."

For a moment, there was nothing but silence as they considered their next step. Lord Archer's face was etched with concern. "We need undeniable proof that it was the Night Elves. If we venture into the Dark Woods without reason, we may never find our way out."

Just then, a small creature crawled around the corner of the archway. It was so bizarre looking that Ella instinctively stepped back. Its shiny black body was covered in bright orange spots and stripes, and in its mouth, it carried what appeared to be a stick. Lord Archer, seeing the creature, broke into a wide grin.

"Haha, you clever girl! Is that what I think it is?"

Orek started laughing, almost dancing on the spot with excitement.

"What is that? And what's in its mouth?" Ella couldn't help but sound a little disgusted by the slimy, lizard-like creature.

"This, Ella, is the Fire Salamander," Lord Archer explained, beaming. "And she's brought us a gift, an arrow. With it, we should be able to determine which clan it's from."

Orek bent down, gently took the arrow from the Salamander's mouth, and then handed it to his cousin. The creature scurried back into the fiery cave. As Lord Archer examined the arrow, the silence that followed made Ella uneasy.

"This belongs to the Night Prince," Lord Archer said quietly. "They've sent their very best warrior to retrieve the Fire Element. We must warn Kalan and Alana immediately. They must not enter the Dark Woods without us."

Ella's heart clenched at the mention of her brother. "Kal wouldn't go in there alone; he's too sensible for that." She knew her brother well—he wasn't one to take reckless risks.

"Kalan might be cautious," Lord Archer replied, "but Alana... she can be impulsive. It wouldn't surprise me if she's already gone in without waiting for us."

His words hit Ella like a punch to the gut. Her stomach

twisted in knots, anxiety swelling until bile rose in her throat. Unable to hold it back, she bent over and retched, the burn harsh and acidic. She wiped her mouth, trying to steady herself, but the shock and worry gnawed at her.

Orek exchanged a grave glance with his cousin. Without wasting a moment, Lord Archer turned to Ella, his gaze intense. "Come, hold on to me. We'll Jump together. Just keep your thoughts focused on me."

Before she could respond, Lord Archer wrapped a strong arm around her, and Orek grabbed onto his shoulder, in the blink of an eye, they'd Jumped. The sweltering heat of the fiery caves vanished, replaced by the oppressive chill of a vast, dark forest. The sudden, icy cold sent a shiver up Ella's spine, settling as a prickling discomfort at the back of her neck. At first, the cold was a relief from the suffocating heat, but it quickly grew into a sharp, electric unease she couldn't shake.

Ella scanned the dense shadows, her eyes darting through the mist and darkened branches. She was determined to find Kal and prove he wouldn't be foolish enough to enter the forest without them. "I can't see him," she said, her voice tight with worry. "They must not be here yet."

She tried to push aside the nagging doubt twisting in her gut, forcing herself to stay strong and believe in her brother's good sense. But Lord Archer's clenched jaw and gritted teeth told a different story.

"They were here," he said darkly, his voice laced with frustration. "But it seems Alana thinks she can handle this on her own."

Ella's heart pounded. The forest seemed to press closer

around them, its shadows stretching like claws, and an eerie silence hung in the air, broken only by the occasional rustle of leaves. She couldn't bear the thought of Kal wandering these dark woods without support, especially if Alana had already pulled him in with her impulsive actions.

Lord Archer rested a steadying hand on her shoulder, his face a mixture of resolve and apprehension. "Ella, we'll find them. But you have to trust me—stay close, and whatever happens, don't lose focus. These woods are unlike anything you've faced. If you let your guard down, it will take advantage."

She nodded, swallowing her fear. Her senses were heightened, every nerve attuned to the oppressive energy of the forest. The shadows seemed to pulse with a life of their own, whispering secrets she couldn't understand, pulling her deeper into unease. She had to find Kal. She had to believe he was safe.

CHAPTER SEVENTEEN

Ella sat on a rock at the edge of the woods, her voice rising with frustration, "So you're telling me that my brother has gone in there with Alana? Why would she go in without waiting for the others? All they had to do was hold on a little longer!"

Lord Archer quickly placed his hand over Ella mouth and raised a finger to his own lips as he whispered, "We need to stay quiet. We don't have the advantage here, and we must assume they already know we're here."

Just as the three of them were about to step into the Dark Woods, over fifty Faerie's Jumped in from every direction, surrounding them. Ella couldn't hide her relief at seeing the other warriors standing side by side.

Lord Archer gave quick, quiet instructions, his voice barely audible as it was passed through the crowd in a low hum. Ella's mind, however, was fixated on finding Kal. She had nearly forgotten about the Fire Element and the Night Elves until Lord Archer reminded her.

"We now know the Fire Element has been taken by the Night Prince. There is no other choice but to enter their Clan lands and retrieve what is rightfully ours. These woods are all but unknown to us. The Night Elves hold the advantage, which might make them overconfident. Tread carefully, tread light."

Ella watched as many of the Fae turned to touch foreheads with their comrades, a ritual that brought a momentary sense of calm. But soon, that calm was replaced by the overwhelming feeling of being utterly unprepared for what lay ahead. Despite every instinct telling her not to, she found herself stepping into the darkness.

As they ventured deeper, the warriors around her seemed to dissolve into the blackness, as if being swallowed by a thick, syrupy fog. The oppressive silence weighed heavily on Ella, like cotton stuffed into her ears, and the damp air clung to her skin. Soon, the only signs of life were the faint blue outlines of Lord Archer and Orek ahead of her.

They moved cautiously for nearly an hour without a word. Suddenly, Orek raised his hand, signalling them to stop. Lord Archer swiftly extended his arm in front of Ella, halting her in her tracks. All she could hear was the creaking of the trees, and then—without warning—Lord Archer pushed her head down hard until she hit the ground. A shrill whistling sound sliced through the air, followed by a deep thud. Dazed, Ella reached out and felt a long arrow embedded in the tree beside her.

Disoriented, it took a moment for her to locate the

others. Lord Archer had his sword drawn, moving stealthily through the trees. Three more arrows shot through the air, their pale blue streaks cutting through the darkness toward Lord Archer, who deflected them with ease, as though they were nothing but twigs.

"Ella, get over here—quickly," he commanded, his voice sharp but quiet. Ella didn't hesitate. She scrambled over tree roots and crawled around hollow logs too high to climb, her heart pounding as she moved. It felt like only seconds before she reached Lord Archer's side, though her frantic movements made time blur.

"Where's Orek?" Ella whispered, scanning the shadows for a trace of blue light.

"He can take care of himself. Let's focus on keeping you safe for now."

Ella bristled at being treated like a child. Her frustration fuelled a surge of defiance. "I don't need looking after," she muttered, but her tone sounded more childish than she intended, irritating her further.

"I'm not talking about babysitting, Ella. I'm talking about keeping you alive," Lord Archer shot back, sensing her annoyance but brushing it aside. There was no time for teenage moods, not with the danger closing in and the Fire Element still unaccounted for.

They moved cautiously through the towering trees, the canopy so thick that no light filtered through. Every now and then, the creak of a nearby tree would freeze them in place, waiting for an ambush that never came.

"I guess it's a good sign we haven't heard any fighting or

screams, it must mean that everyone is still safe?" Ella was trying to stay positive, but the only response she received was a dubious *hum* from Lord Archer.

Then she heard the faintest sound. Turning slowly to catch it better, she instinctively placed her hand on her sword and drew it out slowly. Her hand trembled, but not with fear. It was Art, her Bonded companion, sensing danger and wanting to be released to protect her.

Before she could fully process what was happening, a pitch-black figure leaped from the branches. All she could see were the glowing green eyes and the strange white markings on its face, resembling war paint.

Ella's trembling hand steadied, and her eyes widened as the male figure approached her cautiously. His bow was still drawn, his hands shaking slightly, but there was something in his expression—an unwillingness to strike. As he drew closer, Ella could make out more detail. His face was charcoal grey around his eyes, forehead, and cheeks, contrasting sharply with the pale white that almost made the rest of him look translucent.

Lord Archer turned and saw the Night Elf in front of Ella. He immediately drew his sword and shouted, "Ella, get down!" But she didn't move. Instead, she glanced calmly at her protector.

"It's okay. I don't think he wants to hurt me," she said quietly, turning back to the Night Elf who had shown her unexpected kindness. But when she looked again, he was gone, swallowed by the darkness as if he had never been there.

Lord Archer grabbed Ella's arm firmly, his displeasure evident. "What were you thinking? That was a Night Elf! You're lucky he didn't put an arrow through your head!"

"But I don't think he was going to hurt me. I saw it in his eyes—he just couldn't," Ella replied softly, almost as if speaking to herself. Lord Archer tugged her arm to keep her moving. His frustration was palpable—Ella wasn't grasping the seriousness of the situation. He knew he had to guide her, take on a fatherly role. The twins came from a non-warrior family, and they didn't have their parents to lean on for this kind of experience.

After calming himself, Lord Archer spoke more gently, his tone filled with concern and wisdom. "He was a Half Night, an Elf that chose to become a Night Elf. Not all are born into it. Those who join have to prove their worth, and only when their skin turns completely grey are they considered pure. By sparing you, he risks being punished by his own kind."

"But how could they know? There's no one here but us," Ella said, feeling a flicker of unease in her chest.

"They will know," Lord Archer said darkly, his voice low. He continued walking in silence, signalling that he was done talking.

Everything was still. The oppressive quiet settled over them until, suddenly, Orek appeared out of nowhere in front of them.

"Oh, Orek! Where have you been? I was begin…" Ella's words were cut off by Orek's rough hand covering her mouth.

A tense exchange of hand signals passed between the cousins, none of which Ella understood. But it was clear from their expressions that the news wasn't good. Lord Archer took a deep breath and continued without a word.

Ella had had enough of being kept in the dark. She yanked back slightly, whispering urgently, "What is going on? You can't expect me to just wander around these creepy black woods, waiting for Night Elves to ambush us. I'm worried about my brother, and I have no idea how we're going to find him in this place."

Orek glanced at Lord Archer, then nodded.

"Orek has found out where Kalan and Alana are. It seems they've been taken to the Night King's palace. The molten flames flowing beneath the earth are heading toward the Black Palace."

"But how does he know this? I thought no Fae knew these woods," Ella said, confused and slightly annoyed by the half-truths she had been told.

"I did say that, yes. And Orek is Fae, but Dwarfs know tunnels better than anyone else in this Realm. There are tunnels everywhere, you just need to know where to look."

Orek straightened up proudly and leaned in close to Ella, his gravelly voice whispering in her ear. "The molten flames follow the Fire Element wherever it goes. I don't fink the Night Elves know that. I was just in a tunnel right under the palace. I 'eard two sets of feet being dragged along the floor, and a boy and girl's voices in distress. Elves an' Faeries ain't the only ones wiv good hearin."

"But that could have been anyone. We can't assume it was Kal and Alana and just go charging in there." Ella's head throbbed as the weight of her concern deepened the frown on her brow.

Lord Archer looked at her, his voice hard, "You got a better idea?" He waited for a response, but Ella remained silent. "Didn't think so."

With nothing more to say, Ella felt cornered, like she was up against an impossible situation with no way out. They walked in silence for the next half-hour, occasionally stopping when the creaking of trees made them pause. Ella soon noticed the trees were thinning, and up ahead, an opening appeared.

Instead of the daylight she had hoped for, the sky beyond was an empty void of black. A waterfall cascaded from nowhere it seemed, the sound soothing, but there was no life in the water. Everything felt drained of light and energy. Without realising it, Ella grabbed Lord Archer's arm, pulling him back.

He covered her hand with his own, his voice calm but firm. "This is where our paths have led us. We must retrieve the Fire Element. If it falls into the Byrnes' hands, our Realm will be one step closer to destruction."

Ella steadied herself. "Okay, so what's the plan?"

Lord Archer looked at her, dead serious. "We walk straight in."

Ella blinked, not surprised but a little unnerved. "I guess I should have seen that one coming."

Desperate to find her brother, Ella summoned her courage and stepped out from the dark tree line alongside Lord Archer and Orek, heading toward the waterfall. Within moments, hundreds of arrows were aimed at them from all directions. The three of them continued walking, hearts pounding as they neared the huge gates.

Ella's adrenaline surged; she could feel her heart beating in her ears. For a moment, she closed her eyes, trying to centre herself. When she did, she was back with the Seer, reminded of her inner strength and her connection to Kal.

Opening her eyes, she felt focused and stronger than before. She scanned her surroundings with newfound clarity. The ground was dark green and slimy, though it didn't feel slippery. She noticed flashes of grey faces among the trees, watching their every move, arrows aimed and ready.

As they approached the waterfall, it parted slowly, like theatre curtains revealing a show. They walked through and found a pearlescent path leading to a huge shimmering black door. The presence of the Night Elves became more apparent—they no longer hid in the shadows but stood boldly, their black soulless eyes following every step.

By the time they reached the door, Ella was completely captivated. Her hand reached out and touched the rough surface - which looked like millions of crystal clusters stuck together - Instantly, a cold sensation crawled up her arm, freezing her to the core. Her skin prickled with goosebumps, and her lips turned blue.

Orek pulled her hand away just in time. "Don't touch nuffin', it'll suck the life outta ya."

The massive dark crystal door opened slowly, even thicker than the Dragon door in the Dwarf tunnels.

"This seems too easy," Ella muttered, her nerves on edge.

"It won't be," Lord Archer responded grimly, fully aware

the Night Elves liked to play games. They were undoubtedly walking into a trap.

Behind the door, the room was smaller than Ella had anticipated. In the centre stood a large round table, and sitting on the most regal chair was an elegant yet menacing Night Elf. Ella could tell from the way others fawned over him that this was the Night Prince.

Ella couldn't help but stare. His matte dark grey skin looked almost dead, his black eyes were like slits, and his ears were long and sharply pointed. A strange crown sat upon his head—two silver arcs that rose from his scalp, crossing each other before curving down and joining beneath his chin, creating a knife-like appearance that suited his angular features. A silvery streak ran down his nose, enhancing his sinister look.

Without even turning to face them, the Night Prince spoke in a slow, deep voice. "Come closer, Fae twin, let me look at you." He beckoned her with a long, slender finger, and a large silver ring nearly covering his black, claw-like nail.

Ella didn't wait for approval from Lord Archer or Orek. She simply stepped forward, drawn by the Prince's command.

The Night Prince stood as Ella reached the opposite side of the table. A surge of bravery swept through her, and she gritted her teeth, her voice unwavering. "Where is my brother and Alana? We know you have them."

Ella could sense Lord Archer and Orek standing firmly behind her, their presence giving her even more strength. The Night Prince smiled, his face twisting into a mocking grin as he began to tut, a sound that unnerved her, but she refused to let him see her falter.

"You young Fae think you can come into my land and make demands of me?" he asked, his voice low and dripping with superiority. "That is not polite. And besides, why would I let either of you leave when I have the famous twins everyone has been talking about?"

His gaze locked onto Ella's, and she instantly felt his eyes penetrate her, filling her skin with an uncomfortable, prickling sensation that seemed to cut right through her. She closed her eyes, desperately trying to shake off the dark feeling crawling inside her. In that moment, a vision of the Seer flashed before her, the same safe, womb-like comfort she had felt in the Seer's presence. Her essence surged forward, pushing back against the Prince's darkness, and she remembered to *breathe*, slowly regaining her strength.

Opening her eyes, Ella clenched her jaw and spoke again, her voice as steady as before. "Where is my brother?"

The Night Prince's smile never faltered. "My guards will happily take you to him, but you will leave your weapons here." There was a glint in his eyes, one that told Ella he was not to be trusted.

Orek reached to touch Ella's shoulder, his intent to calm her evident, but Lord Archer stopped him with a look. Only a few Fae knew that Dwarfs were telepaths, and Lord Archer didn't need to say anything aloud for Orek to understand: *Don't. Something is happening with her—we need to see where this goes.*

Ella's hand found the grip of her sword, her fingers steady as she drew it in one fluid motion. The Night Prince responded, his shoulders squaring as he unfurled his height, making Ella swallow hard. But nothing would stop her from finding Kal.

With a swift movement, the Night Prince grabbed onto his crown and flicked it outward. The metal crown quickly shifted and snapped into the shape of a bow, and with his other hand, he pulled out a quiver of arrows tipped with gleaming black stone. It all happened in less than three seconds, and suddenly Ella was standing in her first real fight.

Behind her, Lord Archer and Orek turned to face the dozens of Night Elves that were surrounding them from behind.

The Night Prince stepped elegantly onto the table, moving toward her. His long, claw-like fingers pulled back the bowstring, the arrow aimed at her. His voice was dripping with condescension as he taunted her. "If you think you frighten me, child, you're mistaken. One small arrow in your sword arm, and it's over."

Just as Ella prepared for the worst, she heard a voice, strong and encouraging in her head—it was Kal. *Ella, believe in yourself. I'm here with you. He doesn't have the heart you have. Use it. It's your strength.*

Ella didn't have time to question how Kal's voice was in her head as the Night Prince let the first arrow fly. Ella watched it wobble toward her, and everything around her seemed to freeze for a split second. She seized the moment, slicing through the arrow with her sword. But more arrows followed, each deflected in turn by her steady hand.

Suddenly, the other elves began shooting their arrows,

and Lord Archer and Orek deflected them with their own weapons. Amidst the chaos, Ella noticed a red mist swirling through the elves—it was coming from Lord Archer's sword.

Just as Ella registered the mist, she heard the whistle of an arrow aimed at her back. Instinctively, she ducked, and the Night Prince's arrow flew straight through the head of an elf standing in front of her. It was the first time Ella had seen someone die, and though it felt unreal, she didn't have time to think. She stayed crouched, her mind in overdrive.

Suddenly, a massive rusty-red lion leapt over her, knocking the Night Prince to the ground. The lion's harness was decorated with red gems, and it fought with incredible strength.

Before she could catch her breath, Ella felt a hard thud from behind that knocked her off her feet. Winded, she realised a powerful arm had wrapped around her waist, lifting her into the air. Lord Archer was holding onto her with one hand while gripping the lion's saddle horn with the other. He swung them both onto the saddle, where Orek was already seated.

The giant lion bounded forward, arrows falling harmlessly behind him.

"Ella, focus on Kalan! His energy could guide us to where they're being kept!" Lord Archer's voice was urgent.

Closing her eyes, Ella tried to concentrate on Kal, though it was difficult while gripping the lion for dear life. *Kal, where are you? We're coming, but you need to tell me where you are.*

Kal's voice came through her mind, and a blurred image was visible on the inside of her eyelids. *Ella, you need to hurry.*

We can hear more guards arriving outside. I don't know where we are, but we went down some steps, and it looks like a prison from the 1700s.

She tried to look back at Lord Archer but almost lost her balance, so she stayed facing forward. "He said they're in a prison, and they went down some steps. That's all he knows, it looks really dark and I can't make out much."

Lord Archer, sitting behind her, was shocked. Telepathy was rare, and he was half-Dwarf, but no Dwarf had ever sent mental images before. He hadn't expected this when he asked her to focus—he hadn't expected it to work.

The lion raced through the pearlescent halls, each turn identical to the last. Suddenly, they entered a large hall with ten different tunnel entrances branching off. Without warning, Ella yanked the harness, pulling the beast sharply to the left.

"He's down here. I can feel it," she said, surprising herself with the certainty in her voice.

The passage grew darker as they sped through, the atmosphere heavy with foreboding. Thick metal rings hung from the walls, with chains dangling ominously beneath them. Dark stains marked the floor. They rounded a corner, and a staircase came into view.

As the lion leapt down the stairs, they skidded to a stop at the bottom, confronted by an army of guards. Standing in the centre, as calm as ever, was the Night Prince. His voice slithered through the air, cold and menacing.

"I think it's time to get everything out in the open, don't you? Lord Archer, I must say I'm impressed by your Manticore. What a magnificent beast. But I'm afraid he'll have to go. If you don't return him to your weapon, I'll be forced to take matters into my own hands."

One of the archers pulled back his bowstring and aimed an arrow directly at the Manticore's neck. The giant beast bared its fangs, growling with pure intent towards every Night Elf in sight.

Lord Archer spoke with a slight laugh in his voice. "You should know that a Manticore can't be felled by a single arrow."

The Night Prince's face twisted into a painful-looking smile, though his eyes betrayed the enjoyment he was taking from the situation.

"I'm well aware of that, Lord Archer, which is why this is no ordinary arrow." The Night Prince seemed to revel in the uncertainty creeping across his foe's face.

Looking closer, Ella noticed a drop of white, foamy liquid at the tip of the arrow. Lord Archer saw it too, and his eyes shifted in panic as he spotted a small golden frog sitting peacefully on the Night Prince's shoulder.

Ella leaned toward Orek and whispered, "What is that? It looks like a frog." She wasn't sure what to make of this supposed secret weapon.

Orek's face went pale. "It is. That's a *golden poison frog*," he said, his tone close to defeat as he saw Lord Archer's shoulders drop.

Ella knew poison in the name couldn't mean anything good, but she found it hard to believe that such a tiny frog could harm the enormous lion which she now knew was a Manticore.

Lord Archer hadn't spoken, just stared at the Night

Prince, while Orek grabbed his cousin's arm. "That arrow will kill 'im instantly. You can't let that 'appen."

"What choice do I have, Orek?" Lord Archer gritted his teeth, clearly aware of the severity of the situation and not needing the reminder.

Ella, feeling helpless, whispered to Orek, "What's happening? Why isn't he stopping the Night Elf with the arrow?"

Orek's answer shocked her. "He has two choices—he either hands you over and sends his Manticore back to the sword, or the frog poison kills the beast instantly."

Ella couldn't understand why Lord Archer was hesitating. To her, the choice seemed obvious.

Before either Orek or Lord Archer could stop her, Ella stepped forward, walking past them and straight toward the Night Prince. Lord Archer's stomach dropped when he realised what she was doing.

"Ella! This isn't your decision to make—get back!" His normally steady and commanding voice cracked and emotional.

"This *is* my decision," Ella responded, her tone firm. "I choose to go. Now, you need to send your Manticore back." She gave them both a look as if she had a plan, though neither of them were reassured by her confidence. Ella had no experience with elves, let alone Night Elves.

Two guards seized her by the arms and led her past their Prince. Lord Archer flicked his sword ever so slightly, and the giant Manticore peacefully dissipated into smoke, reabsorbing into his sword.

A swarm of Night Elves surrounded Ella, sweeping her

away down the darkened corridor. The Night Prince remained alone, seemingly vulnerable. Lord Archer, his eyes narrowing in focus, raised his sword, locking onto the Prince's neck.

"You cannot threaten me," the Night Prince called out. "For you will never see your twin Faeries again. But don't worry—you'll get them back, once they've unlocked the Fire Element for me."

Lord Archer's confusion was clear. "Unlock the Fire Element? What are you talking about?"

The Night Prince's mocking grin widened. "Oh, how interesting. Your loyal cousin neglected to tell you that part, didn't he?"

Turning to Orek, whose face was lined with shame, Lord Archer searched for answers. "You knew the Night King needed the twins to unlock the Fire Element? Is that why you brought us here? Is that why you were on your way to our Realm when we met in the tunnels? Orek, what have you done? This makes no sense!"

Orek met his cousin's eyes with sincerity he'd never shown before. "Archie, I couldn't see no other way. Our Seer foretold that twins would come to unlock the powers of all the Elements. We've all 'eard the rumblings of war. I thought if we took the Fire Element and made it look like it was stolen, we could unlock it and use its power against the Byrne Clan."

Lord Archer struggled to keep his emotions in check in front of the Night Prince, who was clearly enjoying the unfolding drama.

"But why did the plan need to involve the Night Elves?"

Lord Archer's voice grew louder with anger. "As the keepers of the Fire Element, you could have taken it without involving them! We wouldn't be in this situation!"

Orek saw his cousin's chest heaving with fury. "We needed the Byrne Clan to believe it was really stolen, and the only Fae capable of pulling that off are the Night Elves."

Lord Archer's gaze shifted to the Night Prince, and after a moment, he sheathed his sword and walked toward the tall, grey figure. The prince was perhaps the least trustworthy Fae in all the Realms, even more so than his father.

"And why should we trust you? What's in this for you?" Lord Archer demanded.

The Night Prince gave a slow, cold smile. "Right now, you don't have anyone else to trust. So you're not in a position to ask."

With that, the grey figure turned and disappeared into the shadows of the dark hall, leaving Lord Archer and Orek standing alone, a heavy silence settling between them.

Orek broke the aching quiet, hoping to convince his cousin that what he'd done was for the right reasons.

"I'm sorry I didn't tell you, Archie, but there were eyes and ears everywhere. I couldn't trust the Dwarf Clans anymore; our trust had been broken, and deceit was the only way out. It pained me greatly to do so, but I saw no other choice."

Lord Archer could feel the truth in his cousin's words. With a deep breath, he placed his hand on Orek's broad shoulder, accepting his story.

Orek felt relieved by his cousin's forgiveness, but he knew he needed to prove that the trust was well placed.

Both of them turned their attention to the dark hallway ahead, which stretched out before them like a black pool waiting to drown them. The Night Elves darkness was unlike any they had ever faced—it was alive with malevolence, and they knew they were at a disadvantage.

CHAPTER EIGHTEEN

P ushing forward into the darkened hall, they walked in tense silence, every step echoing through the narrow passageway. The oppressive darkness seemed to stretch endlessly, swallowing time as they pressed on. Suddenly, Lord Archer halted, holding up a hand.

"We're missing something," he muttered, his eyes narrowing in thought. "Let's check the walls. There might be hidden side tunnels."

They placed their hands on the cold, smooth stone walls, fingers carefully tracing the surface for any concealed doors or hidden passages. The silence was thick as they moved along the walls, feeling for even the faintest irregularity. Finally, after what felt like ages, both stopped simultaneously—they had reached a cross tunnel. They scanned the area, hoping for some sign that would indicate which direction to take, but there was nothing. Both tunnels looked pristine and smooth, as if freshly carved, giving no hint of which way to go.

Frustration began to bubble up inside Lord Archer. Leaning back against the wall with a heavy sigh, he transferred his full weight onto his heels—and suddenly slipped, hitting the ground hard with an unceremonious thud.

"What are you doing down there? This aint the time for tantrums, Archie," Orek teased, extending a hand to help his cousin up.

"I slipped on something," Lord Archer grumbled, brushing himself off as he inspected the sole of his boot. Frowning, he picked off a small, spongy piece of something dark. Bringing it to his nose, he gave it a quick sniff, and a low chuckle escaped him. "She really is a warrior."

Orek's brow furrowed in confusion. "What in the world are you talking about?"

"She left us a breadcrumb—or rather, a piece of moss," Lord Archer explained with a hint of admiration. "It's from Art's coat. Ella must've dropped it to leave us a trail."

Orek's skeptical expression softened, quickly replaced by a broad grin. "Leave it to Ella, huh?" he said with a laugh. But his amusement was cut short by a sharp look from Lord Archer, signalling the seriousness of their task.

They followed the trail, each small piece of moss leading them deeper into the labyrinthine tunnels. The passage twisted and turned, forming a complex maze, and the darkness pressed closer around them with every step. Yet, after what felt like an eternity, the shadows ahead grew lighter, hinting at an opening. They stopped abruptly, straining their ears; faint, muffled voices drifted toward them, accompanied by the clatter of chains.

Lord Archer spoke to Orek through their telepathic link, *This must be where they're holding them. Be light on your feet.*

Orek gave a curt nod, and the two moved forward, each step as silent as a shadow. The voices grew clearer as they advanced, and Lord Archer recognised them: Kal and Alana. But there was no sign of Ella.

Peeking around the corner, Lord Archer saw them, suspended in metal cages, hanging at head height. Alana was facing away, but he could see her struggling against the bars to try and undo the lock, the source of the clanging noise they'd heard.

Lord Archer motioned to Orek, and they slipped quietly into the room. Kal spotted them first, his eyes lighting up with relief, and he almost shouted in excitement. But Lord Archer pressed a finger firmly to his lips, signalling him to stay silent.

Alana, sensing their presence despite facing the opposite direction, turned around with a smile of relief. She signed to Lord Archer with quick hand gestures, *Took your time—I thought I'd have to handle this alone!*

Lord Archer's response was swift and stern, his gaze unwavering as he replied, *We'll discuss your misjudgment later.* He wasn't about to let her impulsive actions slide, especially after they had nearly derailed their mission.

How many guards have been here? Have you heard anything about the Fire Element? His questions were rapid, needing immediate answers.

Alana replied, *We were brought here after we were captured. At first, it was just us, but then they brought in one of their own. He's down at the other end of the room. I tried to talk to him, but he won't respond. We heard something about 'the other twin'—that's how we knew they were after Ella. The room was full of guards at the time, but they've been gone for a while now. Where is Ella?*

The slight shift in Orek's expression betrayed more than Lord Archer would've liked. *The Night Prince has her. He believes the twins can unlock the Fire Element, and he's using them to harness its power against the Byrne Clan. But trusting a Night Elf is a dangerous game. We need to get you both out of here—now.*

Lord Archer scanned the area for any way to release the cages without making a noise, but nothing presented itself. He glanced back at Alana, who only shrugged in helpless frustration.

They were running out of time.

"I've already been trying to come up with a plan, but I can't see any way out," Alana whispered, frustration evident in her voice.

Kal, feeling left out and increasingly anxious, whispered urgently, "Where is Ella?"

There was no immediate response. A moment later, Alana turned to him, her eyes steady as she whispered back, "Kal, we will find her. She's somewhere in the palace, but first, we need to get ourselves free."

Her calm voice lulled Kal into a brief moment of false security, but the tension remained.

Lord Archer, sensing time was running short, walked toward the other cage further down the room. He approached carefully, not wanting to startle whoever was inside or alert any nearby Night Elves. As he neared, he saw a figure with thick streaks of white hair and both hands gripping the bars—one hand black with long pointed fingers, and the other a gleaming pale hand, almost childlike in its purity. Lord Archer immediately recognised them as the hands of a Halfling, a mix between a Light Elf and a Night Elf.

Halfling's were typically Light Elves who wished to become Night Elves. But to fully transform, they had to prove their loyalty by abandoning their former ways. Over time, the Night swallowed them, until the last bit of Light in their eyes was extinguished during a ceremony before the Night King.

Lord Archer was about to speak when the Halfling suddenly lifted his head, sharp green eyes filled with fear.

"I'm not here to hurt you," Lord Archer said softly, raising his hands. "If you can help us free my daughter and her friend, we'll gladly release you too."

The Halfling squinted at Lord Archer, suspicion and fear in his gaze. "Helping your kind is what got me here in the first place. If I help again, I'll be an outcast."

"You're the Night Elf from the woods who spared Ella's life," Lord Archer replied, recognising him now. "Let me repay you by setting you free."

At the mention of Ella's name, the Halfling's interest lifted. "Ella? Is she one of the twins everyone is talking about?"

"She is," Lord Archer confirmed. "And if we don't free her brother soon," he turned and pointed to Kal, "we could be facing a war that will destroy all our Realms—both above and below."

The Halfling moved closer to the bars, speaking quietly. "To unlock the cages, you'll need a Painite crystal. It's kept on the Night Prince at all times."

Lord Archer smiled and pulled back the sleeve of his cloak, revealing a Painite crystal embedded in his cuff. The Halfling watched in awe as Lord Archer pressed the crystal against the underside of each cage, where the locks were located. One by one, the cages clicked open, releasing Kal, Alana, and finally their new companion.

Once the cages were opened, Lord Archer turned and walked over to the Halfling, placing a firm but gentle hand on his shoulder. "Thank you," he said sincerely. "You've done more than you realise. What is your name?"

"Zelphar," the Halfling said quietly. "I don't know where I belong anymore. I'll be seen as a traitor by both sides—by the Night Elves for helping you, and by the Light Elves for trying to join the Night. Perhaps I deserve what's coming."

Orek joined them, shaking his head. "You're comin' with us, boy. You've helped us, and we'll return the favour. Besides, we need your help to find Ella."

At the mention of Ella's name, a slight spark lit up Zelphar's eyes, which Lord Archer didn't miss. "There's a reason you didn't shoot Ella in the woods, isn't there? You sensed she was special, didn't you?"

Kal, protective of his sister, stepped forward. "How do we know we can trust him? He said himself he's a traitor. He could be trying to win back the Night Prince's trust."

The silence that followed was thick with tension. All eyes locked onto Zelphar, awaiting his response. He knew he was at a crossroads, and the decision he made would change everything for him. After a moment of hesitation, he bowed his head.

"I pledge my loyalty to you," Zelphar said quietly. "I'll fight with you, even if it means to my death."

Sensing Kal's discomfort, Alana gently squeezed his hand. Kal started, then looked down, surprised to see her hand holding his. His heart thudded as he met Alana's kind, reassuring gaze.

"They know what they're doing," she whispered, her voice soothing. "Trust them. Trust me."

Kal swallowed, struggling to keep his voice steady. "I trust you," he replied softly, trying to sound strong. "So, I guess I'll trust them too."

Just as the tension began to ease, a deafening horn blast shattered the silence, so loud that everyone instinctively clamped their hands over their ears in pain. Zelphar was the first to lower his hands, his expression tense.

"We have to move—now! That's the Night King's horn. There's a ceremony starting soon," he said urgently.

Kal's heart spiked with panic, and without thinking, he surged forward. "Ella!" he shouted, bolting toward the nearest tunnel. But a firm hand caught his shoulder, stopping him in his tracks.

Lord Archer spun him around, his eyes stern. "We can't just rush in blindly. We need a plan, or none of us will make it out alive."

Feeling foolish, Kal nodded, trying to contain his emotions. Zelphar's calm voice cut through the tense silence. "The halls will soon fill with Night Elves heading to the Stone Ring for the ceremony. If we wait just a bit, the tunnels will clear out, and we can get through unnoticed."

Lord Archer nodded, his gaze sharpening as he formulated a plan. "We have to assume Ella's sword has been taken."

Kal scoffed, recalling his failed attempt to even lift Ella's sword. "How could anyone take her sword? I thought no one but us could use our weapons."

"You're right," Lord Archer replied gravely. "But you can never be too cautious when it comes to Night Elves. They have ways of manipulating even the strongest magic."

Kal's brief amusement faded, the weight of the situation settling heavily on him once again. Time was slipping through their fingers, and the urgency pressed on them all.

"Her sword will be close by," Zelphar added thoughtfully, his gaze fixed on a distant tunnel. "The Night King would want to harness its power through Ella. The sword is likely part of his ritual preparations."

Zelphar moved forward, motioning for silence as he listened carefully to the distant sounds echoing down the tunnels. The group held their breath, straining to stay as quiet as possible.

"We can go now," he whispered, his voice barely audible, "but we must be swift and silent. More guards will be coming soon. Kal," he said with a pointed look, "I suspect the Night King plans to use you as well. This ceremony isn't just for show."

Kal's face paled, and he nodded, gripping Alana's hand tighter. Together, they crept through the dank, grimy tunnels, the air thick with the musty scent of old stone and earth. Every step was calculated, each sound carefully suppressed to avoid disturbing the oppressive silence around them.

After what felt like an age of navigating twisting passages, they finally reached a set of worn stone steps leading upward, out of the shadows and into brightly lit halls. Zelphar had been right—the halls were empty, the usual guards and attendants absent as they had all gathered at the Stone Ring for the ceremony.

Taking advantage of the deserted corridors, they slipped through the palace. Kal's heart hammered as they headed toward the ceremonial site, a secluded clearing deep within the woods. The air felt charged with dark magic, and he could sense the malevolent energy gathering in the distance.

As they approached, Zelphar raised a hand, signalling them to slow their steps. His voice was low but firm. "From here, every movement counts. The Night King will have guards positioned all around. One misstep, and we'll be facing more than just a few guards."

Lord Archer's sharp eyes flicked across the darkened forest, his expression steely. "We stick to the shadows," he instructed. "Kal, stay close, and keep your focus. We're going to get Ella and stop this ceremony—whatever it takes. But you need to stay calm."

Kal nodded, swallowing hard. Fear churned in his stomach, but it blended with a fierce resolve. Ella was in danger, and there was no way he was leaving without her. He gripped Alana's hand briefly, her steady presence grounding him, before they moved forward. The sense of unity among them gave him strength as they crept silently through the forest, the ominous Stone Ring drawing closer with each step.

The atmosphere grew heavier as the trees thickened, their twisted branches clawing at the sky. The air became dense, filled with a pungent, metallic tang that made it hard to breathe. The ground beneath them was uneven and treacherous, large black tree roots coiling together like serpents desperate to escape the decaying earth below. Each step felt like a test, as if the forest itself were trying to impede their progress.

Zelphar halted suddenly, crouching low and pointing ahead. "There," he whispered, his voice barely audible. Through the dense foliage, they could see the edge of the clearing. A faint, eerie glow emanated from the Stone Ring, casting long, jagged shadows into the trees. The oppressive energy of dark magic pulsed through the air, making it difficult to think, let alone breathe.

They crept carefully around the perimeter, their movements as silent as shadows. Kal's heart pounded as they reached a vantage point. The clearing opened up before them, revealing the Stone Ring and two mounds of rock either side of the upright ring.

"They're incredible, aren't they?" Alana whispered, her voice filled with awe. "I've only ever read about them, but I've always wanted to see them in person. If you're wondering about their age, they date back to before humans even walked the Earth. They were created by the High Priestess of the Elves and were the first Jumping Holes in our realm. These stones hold immense magnetic healing powers. The Green Man grew these woods around them when humans discovered the stones and began using them for their own rituals—to cure diseases and protect against evil."

Kal tilted his head slightly and whispered back, "But I thought humans couldn't get to our Realm Below. How did they use the stones?"

Alana frowned for a moment, then her expression softened into a small smile. "We're not in the Realm Below right now. We're above ground. These woods are protected by Elvish magic, making it nearly impossible for a human to step inside."

"*Nearly* impossible?" Kal's anxiety spiked as he considered the implications. "So, it's still possible?" The thought of humans accidentally stumbling into the dangerous situation unfolding here sent a chill down his spine.

Alana raised her eyebrows, her expression cryptic. She offered no further explanation, leaving Kal with more questions than answers. He opened his mouth to press her further, but before he could speak, a chilling presence silenced his thoughts.

From the darkness, a low, rhythmic hum began to resonate, sending shivers down their spines. The sound grew louder, a guttural chant in a language Kal didn't recognise but instinctively feared. The shadows around the clearing shifted unnaturally, as though something unseen was moving within them.

Zelphar's whispered, calm yet urgent. "Hold your positions. Let them begin—we need to see where Ella is before we act."

Kal clenched his fists, his patience tested to its limit. But he trusted Zelphar's judgment and stayed still, his eyes scanning the clearing for any sign of his sister. He felt Alana's hand on his arm, grounding him again, and he exhaled slowly, trying to steady his racing heart.

The Night Prince stepped into the clearing, dragging Ella behind him. Her hands were bound tightly, and her head hung low, her movements sluggish as though the magic in the air were draining her strength. Kal's breath hitched, his entire body tensing as rage surged through him. He was ready to charge forward, but Alana grabbed his arm, holding him back with a firm grip and a sharp look that warned him not to act rashly.

Ella's chains were secured to a thick metal hoop at the top of the Stone Ring. With a cruel smirk, the Night Prince unclipped Ella's sword belt from her waist, letting it fall to the ground with a loud, echoing thud. The sound rang out across the clearing, silencing even the faint rustle of the wind. A chilling stillness settled over the gathered Elves, as though the very woods themselves were holding their breath, waiting for the ritual to begin.

Kal's gaze darted to Ella willing her to look at him, her face was pale but determined. Even bound and weakened, there was a flicker of defiance in her eyes as she glanced at him briefly, a silent plea for him to stay hidden, to wait for the right moment. Kal's grip tightened around his bow, his resolve hardening. No matter what the Night Prince had planned, he wouldn't let this ceremony reach its end.

Beside him, Alana shifted slightly, her sharp eyes scanning the clearing. "Patience," she whispered, almost to herself, her voice barely audible. "We only get one shot at this."

Kal nodded reluctantly, forcing himself to stay still as the air around them thickened further, charged with the ominous anticipation of dark magic.

CHAPTER NINETEEN

Shadows at the far edge of the clearing began to writhe, pooling together like ink. Out of the swirling darkness, a tall figure emerged, towering over the gathered Night Elves. His form was cloaked in a black that seemed to absorb all light, casting no reflection, not even in the moonlight. His crown, shaped like twisted tree roots, giving him an appearance both regal and terrifying. Every step he took was deliberate and graceful, yet his presence carried an unsettling stillness.

His hair, long and silver like molten moonlight, cascaded down his back in stark contrast to his coal skin. His eyes were voids of pure darkness— There was no white in them, only an infinite abyss.

As the Night King approached the Stone Ring, the very ground trembled beneath him. The moss at his feet shrivelled and died with every floating step, leaving only decay in his wake.

He stopped just before Ella, towering over her, his gaze

locked onto her, and for a moment, it felt as if time itself had stopped, as if the very air around her had frozen.

"You are one of the twins," the Night King's voice was deep and resonant, vibrating through the stone beneath Ella's feet. It was a voice that spoke not just to her ears but seemed to penetrate her very bones. "I wasn't expecting you to be quite so... unremarkable." His words dripped with condescension, though his cold smile betrayed a hunger, a sinister anticipation of what was to come.

Kal clenched his fists tightly, struggling to keep himself from intervening. Every instinct screamed at him to act, but Alana's firm grip on his shoulder kept him grounded. "Orek and I are going around the other side of the clearing," she whispered, her voice calm but commanding. "You two stay here and keep watch."

Kal barely registered her words, his focus entirely on Ella, chained and vulnerable in the clearing. His frustration was a storm building within him, making it hard to think clearly.

Meanwhile, Orek and Alana moved swiftly, their movements silent as shadows as they circled to the other side of the clearing. Alana gestured toward Kal and Lord Archer, signalling their position. Lord Archer caught sight of her and nodded in acknowledgment, but Kal, lost in his turmoil, hadn't noticed. Alana frowned as she saw his shoulders tense, the telltale sign of someone about to do something reckless. She tried to get her dad-Lord Archers- attention so he could intervene, but she were too late.

Kal's fingers released the bowstring he'd been gripping tightly without even realising it. The arrow flew through the air, cutting a deadly arc toward the Night King. Time seemed to slow as the King's lips curled into a sinister smile. With a flick of his wrist, he caught the arrow mid-flight, his cold, lifeless eyes locking onto Kal.

"So predictable," the Night King hissed, his voice like ice scraping against stone.

In an instant, the Night Elves swarmed Kal, dragging him into the clearing and binding his hands. Ella's eyes widened as she saw her brother being captured, a mix of relief and anger flashing across her face.

Alana moved to act, but Orek grabbed her arm and held her back. "Not now," he murmured, his voice low and firm. "We need to see what they're plannin. We'll get em back—I promise."

Though Orek's words were meant to reassure, tension was etched into every line of his face. The stakes were higher than ever, and one misstep could cost them everything.

Kal was dragged beside Ella and chained to the Stone Ring. His heart raced with frustration and regret. He hadn't meant to shoot the arrow—it had been a moment of uncontrollable emotion—but now they were both trapped because of him. He avoided Ella's gaze, ashamed, but the Night King had no such reservations. He loomed over the twins, his soulless eyes scanning the clearing as though daring the others to reveal themselves.

"As I thought," the Night King said, his voice resonating with dark authority. "The other twin rushes in foolishly. Your actions were predictable, boy. And if you have escaped your cages, it means you had help and the others are here as well."

His voice rose, reverberating through the clearing, a challenge cloaked in mockery. "Your weapons and hearts, I'm sure, would slay a few, but we would still emerge victorious. You are not welcome here in our sacred space."

As the final word fell from his lips, a shimmering, transparent dome descended over the clearing, sealing Kal, Ella, the Night King, Prince and his Elves inside. The air within the dome grew heavy with an oppressive energy, the magic pulsing faintly with each breath.

Alana, quick to react, dove under the descending dome just before it closed. Her hood concealed her features as she slipped into the crowd of Elves unnoticed. Orek and Lord Archer, moments too late, were left outside the barrier. Their frustration was evident, but it was mixed with a glimmer of relief as they realised what Alana had done.

Inside the dome, Alana crouched low, moving carefully through the throng of Elves. Her sharp eyes scanned the scene, analysing the nearly impossible situation: over a hundred Night Elves, the Night Prince, and the Night King himself, all poised for their dark ceremony.

Kal heard Ella's voice in his head, a soft whisper amidst the chaos. *Kal, I'm so glad you're here. Where are the others?*

Kal looked up at Ella and gave her a reassuring smile, though dread coiled in his stomach. *They aren't far, El. Don't worry. We've got this.*

But deep down, he wasn't sure how they could possibly survive, let alone triumph. His eyes flicked toward the Night King, who moved with an eerie grace toward the stone steps. His long silver hair flowed behind him like ghostly strands, and the very air around him seemed to ripple with malevolent power.

Ella, Kal thought, forcing himself to focus. *I still have my bow, but my hands are tied—I can't reach it.*

Ella didn't reply immediately, her attention caught by the Night Prince, who approached from the side. In his hands was a strange object, shimmering and wrapped in gossamer-like silk. It glowed faintly in the moonlight, exuding an unsettling energy. Carefully, the Night Prince placed the object atop the Stone Ring between the twins.

Kal twisted his fists, the metal of his chains biting into his skin. *We can do this, Ella,* he thought, his resolve hardening despite his fear. *Alana won't leave us. I know she won't.*

Ella nodded faintly, drawing strength from her brother's words. As she scanned the crowd, something caught her eye —a faint glint of green light. A dark hooded figure moved among the Elves, their face obscured, but their glowing eyes locked on Ella with unnerving intensity. A shiver ran down her spine, but she pushed the fear aside, knowing there was no room for hesitation.

The Night King raised his arms, his voice rising into a deep, rhythmic chant. The language was ancient and harsh, one neither Ella nor Kal recognised, but its power was undeniable. The air swelled with the vibration of his words. The glowing object on the Stone Ring pulsed in time with the chant, and the Elves began to move as one, their movements ritualistic and precise.

"Ardaigh as an tine agus tabhair dom do chumhacht."

As the final syllable left his lips, the twins were suddenly pulled tight toward the Stone Ring by an invisible force, like iron to a magnet. They were trapped now, face to face, only a foot apart, their bodies pressed by the rising energy coursing through the ancient stone between them.

Kal's bow, still slung across his back, began to tremble violently. From the end of the bow, a long, ghostly white wisp emerged, snaking around the Stone Ring. Ella's eyes widened as the ethereal trail coiled around them both, and she realised what was happening. Kal's Bonded animal, Sonny, began to take form, his massive wings unfurling and spreading wide until they filled the clearing. Sonny's wings crackled with blue energy, lightning sparking between his feathers.

Kal shouted to Sonny, but his voice was drowned out by the growing roar of the electric current, and Ella's face had gone pale as she watched Sonny's wings pulse with more and more energy.

Alana, who had been hidden in the crowd, stood frozen in shock. All thoughts of rescue disappeared as she witnessed the twins and Sonny engulfed in a swirling mist of red and white energy. She snapped back to reality as a firm hand gripped her shoulder, pulling her into the shadows. Zelphar, the Halfling, was draped in a hooded cloak and whispered in her ear, "We must stay back," his voice low and oddly calming. "There's nothing we can do right now."

"How are we going to help them?" Alana's voice was desperate, her heart torn between rushing in and waiting for the right moment.

Zelphar's green eyes glinted under the cloak's shadow.

"Look across the clearing, in line with us. See the other hooded figure?"

Alana squinted through the throngs of Elves. She nodded, waiting for an explanation.

"There will be a moment," Zelphar said cryptically, "and when it comes, we will act." But his uncertain smile did little to soothe Alana's growing anxiety.

Suddenly, a loud, scraping noise echoed across the clearing. Ella's sword, Art, began to move on its own, dragging across the ground with a haunting screech. The blade rose into the air, as if summoned by an invisible hand. Ella could feel Art struggling, fighting against the dark magic, but the sword was drawn relentlessly toward the shimmering object between her and Kal.

A moment of clarity passed between the twins as their eyes locked. *It's the Fire Element!* Ella's voice echoed in Kal's mind.

Before they could react, a surge of red and green energy exploded from the point of the sword, wrapping around them in a thick, swirling mist. Sonny's light barely pierced through the haze, casting patches of yellow where the electric blue crackled. The mists twisted together, and the twins felt the heat of the Fire Element seeping into their very bones.

Where are they, Kal? Ella's voice, though projected into his mind, was laced with panic and anger. *I thought you said Alana wouldn't leave us here!*

Kal clenched his jaw, staring at the glowing mist swirling around them. *I don't know, El. I thought they'd be here by now. They have to have a plan... They wouldn't leave us.*

As the mist thickened, the Night King began to chant again, his voice low and resonant, each word dripping with power:

"Ardaigh as an tine agus tabharfaidh mé mo chuid fola."

The swirling energy surrounding the twins began to pull toward him, and he spread his arms wide, his chest open to receive the power of the Fire Element.

Kal's mind raced, his eyes darting between the Night King and the sword. Desperately, he willed his bow to free itself, hoping against hope that he could stop the dark monarch from absorbing the Element's energy.

The Night King's black eyes gleamed for the first time as he prepared to take the Fire Element's power. He believed victory was inevitable.

Alana sprang forward, pulling her bow back and aiming for her target. But once again, Zelphar pushed her arm down, urging her to wait.

"I have a clear shot! How can you ask me to wait? This *is* the moment!" Alana's voice was sharp, frustration growing as she began to doubt whose side Zelphar was really on.

Zelphar calmly nodded for her to look. When Alana turned, she saw the black-hooded figure emerge from the crowd. The figure moved with smooth, soundless grace, passing unnoticed, even as they entered the open space at the centre of the gathering. The Night Elves gave no reaction, their focus fixed on their King.

The hooded girl positioned herself between the Stone Ring and the Night King. As the swirling red and green mist approached her, she held her sword aloft. In an instant, a massive surge of energy struck the blade. The sword absorbed the essence of the Fire Element and Artemis, creating a blast so powerful that it knocked everyone—Night Elves, Alana, and Zelphar—off their feet. The Night King, staggered by the force, fell to one knee.

Alana quickly seized the opportunity amidst the chaos as the dome surrounding the clearing began to collapse, and white mist from Sonny enveloped the area. She moved through the fallen Night Elves as though wading through quicksand, skilfully shooting the chains binding Ella and Kal's hands. The thick mist clung to the air, obscuring the twins vision and making it difficult for them to see their rescuer.

Just as Kal struggled to regain his bearings, he felt a heavy thud on his back. Whipping around, he found Alana clinging tightly to him, her grip firm and determined.

"You're late," Kal said, his tone sarcastic but his eyes gleaming with relief.

"I'm so sorry," Alana breathed, still holding on to him. "Zelphar wouldn't let me get to you." She was mere inches from Kal's face, and it was only then she realised just how desperate she had been to get him back.

For a brief moment, Kal was lost in Alana's beautiful, open face, her features soft yet resolute after the battle. But his thoughts snapped back to Ella. Was she okay? Where was she? The urgency clawed at him. Almost jumping out of Alana's arms, Kal hurried to the other side of the Stone Ring. There he found Ella, kneeling on the ground, her wrists raw and bruised where the chains had bitten into her skin.

"El, are you okay?" Kal asked urgently, his voice trembling with concern. He knelt beside her, gently lifting her by her elbows before pulling her into a fierce hug.

Ella met his gaze, her relief reflected in her tear-filled eyes. "I'm okay," she whispered, her voice shaky but steady. Despite her words, Kal could feel the exhaustion radiating off her.

But there was no time to dwell on their reunion. The ground beneath them seemed to tremble as the Night King rose once more. His overwhelming presence rippled through the clearing, making the air feel sharp and suffocating all at once. His voice boomed, shaking the trees surrounding them.

"YOU HAVE NO CLAIM OVER THE FIRE ELEMENT, OR ANY OF THE OTHERS!" he roared, his words dripping with fury. "IT IS ONCE MORE THE TIME OF THE NIGHT ELVES. WE WILL TAKE OUR RIGHTFUL PLACE ABOVE GROUND AS RULERS!"

The already dark forest grew impossibly darker, the shadows bristling with an oppressive, electric energy that made every nerve in Kal's body stand on edge. The air seemed alive, charged with malice and anticipation.

From the corner of his vision, Kal saw the hooded girl standing alone, shrouded in shadow. She turned to face the Night King, her movements deliberate and unflinching despite the suffocating weight of his presence. Her blade gleamed as she drew it, her stance unwavering. With a swift, determined motion, she slashed at him.

Red and green energy erupted from her sword, cascading through the air in brilliant arcs. The magic rippled through the Night King's frame, forming a shimmering barrier that kept him from advancing. The clash of their powers sent shockwaves ripping through the clearing, forcing Kal and Ella to shield their faces.

The Night King snarled low, a guttural sound that seemed to seep into the marrow of their bones. His glowing eyes burned with fury as he hissed, his voice venomous. "This is not over, little girl. You cannot hide behind the Fire Element forever."

And with that, his form dissolved into black, writhing tendrils of shadow. They twisted and coiled into the air before vanishing into the void, leaving behind an eerie silence that blanketed the clearing. The oppressive energy lingered, heavy and thick, as if the forest itself was holding its breath.

Kal, his breathing finally steadying, nodded toward the hooded girl still standing where the Night King had been. Her sword hung at her side, and her shoulders rose and fell as though she had spent every ounce of her strength.

"Who is she?" Kal asked, his voice low and wary.

"I don't know," Alana replied, her tone tense. Her eyes stayed locked on the girl, her body poised to act if necessary. "Keep your eyes on her. I'm not sure if she's a friend of our Clan... or something else."

Ella, drained and overwhelmed, turned her attention back to the Stone Ring. Slowly, she reached up to dislodge her sword from the top of the ancient structure. The familiar weight in her hands brought no comfort. Instead, the absence of Artemis hit her like a punch to the chest. Her fingers trembled as she clutched the blade, her knuckles white.

"She's gone," Ella whispered, her voice so quiet it was almost lost in the stillness of the clearing.

She took a deep, shaky breath, forcing herself to steady her racing heart. Sheathed her sword with deliberate care, she clasped her trembling hands together, trying to focus. Her attention drifted back to the hooded figure, whose shoulders still heaved from exertion. Something about the figure's presence seemed both powerful and fragile, as though she were holding herself together by sheer will.

The girl turned slowly, and as her hood fell back, her face was illuminated by the faint glow of the magic still lingering in the air. A look of pure hatred burned in her eyes, her expression twisted by rage and something deeper—pain.

Ella's throat tightened, her breath catching as recognition struck her like a blow. Her knees felt weak, and she struggled to form words.

Standing before her, unmistakable despite the subtle changes, was Rhi.

Ella could barely speak, barely breathe. "Rhi?" she finally whispered, her voice trembling with a mixture of shock and heartbreak.

The figure's lips curled into a bitter smile, her eyes cold and unyielding. "Hello, Ella," Rhi said, her tone sharp and cutting, like a blade sliding into old wounds.

Ella looked back at Kal, her expression pleading for help, her eyes glistening with unshed tears as her heart fractured under the weight of betrayal and heartbreak. She needed him to see her, to anchor her to something solid amidst the chaos. But Kal's gaze remained locked on Rhi, his mind spinning as he tried to piece together what he had just witnessed. His face was etched with confusion and disbelief, as though staring at a puzzle he couldn't solve.

Ella's silent plea was met with nothing. Kal was too consumed by his own inner storm to notice the way her shoulders sagged, the way her breath hitched as if she were trying to hold herself together. The sight of Rhi—her best friend, her sister in all but blood—standing there with nothing but venom in her gaze, was too much to bear.

CHAPTER TWENTY

The world around Ella seemed to blur, the edges of her vision fading into a hazy swirl. She knew Rhi was a faerie too—her parents had told her—but she hadn't prepared for the possibility of meeting her again in such a charged and hostile moment. All Ella wanted was to run to her best friend, throw her arms around her, and reconnect with the person she had trusted most. But the look on Rhi's face froze her in place. It was clear that such a gesture wouldn't be met with kindness—only contempt.

Kal finally turned to his sister, his voice hesitant. "Ella, it's..."

But he didn't need to finish. Ella's expression already told him that she knew.

Alana nudged Kal sharply, snapping him out of his stunned daze. "Kal, who is that?" she whispered, her tone urgent. The nudge startled him, but he quickly answered.

"That's Rhi—Ella's best friend. Well... she *was*, until Rhi found out she was also a faerie. And being the Byrnes' daughter, she's… our sworn enemy, apparently." Kal's voice faltered as the weight of the situation hit him, leaving him unsure of what to do. He felt rooted to the spot, his mind reeling.

Alana's sharp gaze locked onto Rhi, studying her intently. "So this is the famous Byrne daughter…" she muttered under her breath, her tone a mixture of curiosity and caution. It was hard to look away from someone so significant, both to the conflict and to Ella's heart.

Ella's attention shifted as movement caught her eye. Lord Archer and Orek were pushing through the rising crowd of Night Elves. Some were sprawled on the ground, groaning, while others stumbled to their feet, shaking off the force of the earlier blast. Without hesitation, Ella sprinted toward Rhi, her emotions surging in a chaotic mix of hope and desperation. She grabbed Rhi's arm, pulling her back toward the Stone Ring, her voice trembling as she spoke.

"Are you okay? It's so good to see you…"

But Rhi's icy glare cut through Ella like a blade. Her cold, hateful expression made Ella's chest tighten, and her eyes filled with tears. Without a word, Rhi yanked her arm free and turned away, her face unyielding. She ignored Kal completely, but her eyes briefly locked with Alana's. Alana's stare was sharp and unflinching, filled with venom. The silent confrontation lasted only a moment before Rhi tore her gaze away, her head held high. Then, in a blink, she disappeared into the shadows, leaving nothing but a chilling silence in her wake.

Ella stood frozen, her breathing shallow. She turned back

to Kal and Alana, her voice trembling as she tried to hold herself together. "I can't go through this again with Rhi. She really hates me."

Kal opened his mouth to respond, but before he could speak, the air was pierced by the sharp clanging of metal and the distant sound of shouting. The noise grew louder, chaos unmistakably brewing nearby.

Alana's head whipped around, her eyes narrowing as she spotted the source of the commotion: a battlefield unfolding before them. Lord Archer and Orek were in the thick of it, their weapons flashing as they fought fiercely against a horde of Night Elves. The dark forms of the Elves moved like shadows, their blades and arrows gleaming as they closed in on the two warriors.

With a sharp, determined smile, Alana drew her bow and nocked an arrow in one fluid motion. Her eyes gleamed with adrenaline as she glanced back at Kal and Ella. "You guys ready to put your training into practice?" she asked, her voice steady but laced with a challenge.

Kal straightened, his resolve hardening as he gripped his weapon. "Ready as I'll ever be," he replied, his voice firm despite the storm of emotions raging within him.

Ella wiped at her eyes, forcing herself to focus. Her fingers wrapped tightly around her sword hilt as she nodded. "Let's finish this," she said quietly, her voice steadying, she had no time to think of Rhi now as the three of them stepped forward, ready to face whatever lay ahead, their bonds unspoken but unbreakable.

Kal exchanged a glance with Ella, his jaw tightening. Whatever doubts or hurt lingered had to be shoved aside—

there was no time for hesitation. The fight had come to them, and they couldn't afford to falter.

Both Ella and Kal had reached their limit. They were tired of being victims, tired of being on the defensive. Without a word, they charged into the chaos, heads held high. Kal flicked his wrist, summoning Sonny from his bow, at the same time as Alana called out Flare. The massive birds of prey screeched as they joined the battle, diving toward the fray. Sonny began picking off Night Elves, tossing them into the trees like rag-dolls. Some landed gracefully in the branches, only to leap back down and rejoin the fight, while others vanished into the darkened woods, never to return.

Ella ducked under the swing of a Night Elf wielding what appeared to be nothing more than a long stick. She hesitated for a moment—was it really fair for him to only have a stick? But as she caught the sneer stretching across his coal-black face, she realised this was no ordinary weapon. The elf spun it with terrifying speed, striking the back of Ella's legs with precise, punishing blows. Pain exploded through her body with each hit, and her knees buckled slightly, making it impossible for her to get close enough to use her sword.

Across the clearing, Kal, dodging arrows with practiced precision, caught sight of Ella struggling. His heart dropped. Without hesitation, he let out a sharp, low whistle.

Sonny, mid-dive, shifted his attention to Kal's signal and followed his gaze toward Ella. The giant eagle swooped in, its massive shadow spreading wide across the ground where Ella fought. The Night Elf glanced upward at the approaching bird, the momentary distraction was all Ella needed.

With a quick, decisive strike, she found the elf's weak spots, disarming him and driving her sword through his chest before he even realised what had happened.

As her blade sank deep, Ella's face came so close to his that she could see intricate, markings etched into his skin, symbols that pulsed faintly with a sinister energy. His expression held no fear, only cold malice. Black blood sputtered from his mouth, splattering onto Ella's face. Her eyes widened, adrenaline coursing through her veins, sharpening her instincts into a primal edge: kill or be killed.

The elf's body slumped to the ground, her sword still lodged in his chest. Breathing hard, Ella shoved him aside with her foot and yanked her now-blackened blade free. She stared at it for half a second, the weight of her actions beginning to press against her, but there was no time to dwell on what she had done. More Night Elves were swarming toward her, their weapons gleaming in the eerie light.

For a fleeting moment, she wished desperately for Artemis to be by her side, the comforting presence of her Bond a steadying force. But she quickly pushed the thought away. She couldn't rely on Artemis anymore. She had to survive on her own. Tightening her grip on her sword, she turned to face the next wave of attackers.

Two elves dropped in front of her, arrows protruding from their backs. Ella glanced up to see Kal firing arrows with such precision and speed it seemed he'd been training for years.

The air grew heavier, the battlefield becoming a chaotic blur of movement and sound. Fallen Night Elves piled up across the clearing. Kal paused to assess the situation, his chest tightening. The Night Elves' numbers weren't dwindling—if anything, they were growing. His gaze flicked toward the tree line and his stomach turned. More Night Elves were emerging from the shadows, their dark forms blending with the forest.

"LORD ARCHER!" Kal shouted. "THEY'RE COMING FROM THE TREES!"

Lord Archer turned at Kal's cry, but in that split second, an arrow pierced his sword arm. He dropped his weapon with a sharp gasp, the pain driving him to his knees.

Kal felt like he'd been struck too. Seeing such a giant of a man fall was unbearable. Across the battlefield, Ella saw him fall as well and sprinted toward him, cutting her way through the throng of Night Elves, slashing and punching without hesitation. Sliding to the ground beside Lord Archer, who was next to the Stone Ring, she glanced up as Sonny swooped overhead, picking off attackers before they could close in.

"What do I do?" Ella asked, panic clear in her voice.

"I need to release *Laoch*, but I can't hold my sword," Lord Archer gritted out, the pain twisting his features.

"Help me roll onto my side—I'll use my other hand," he instructed. His face contorted as Ella tried to shift him, the pressure on his injured arm drawing a howl of pain. She quickly stopped, realising he couldn't take more.

They sat there, wide-eyed and panicked, when a strange vibration began to build in Ella's chest. The sensation was so intense she thought she might be sick, but before she could question it, Warren tumbled through the Stone Ring, rolling straight into the fight. More Fae followed, their numbers pouring into the battlefield. Griffin entered cautiously but didn't hesitate to kill a charging Night Elf with a single, lethal strike.

Seizing the opportunity, Ella grabbed Lord Archer and began dragging him toward the Stone Ring. She glanced back for Kal but couldn't see him amidst the chaos. Summoning every ounce of strength, she pulled Lord Archer through the Ring.

Focusing on her mother, Ella found herself half-pinned beneath Lord Archer, lying on a cold floor bathed in bright light. It took her a moment to adjust, but when she did, she screamed for her mum.

Diana burst from a side room, her eyes locking onto her bloodied daughter trapped under the giant warrior. Panic flooded her face as her gaze darted around, searching for Kal.

"Ella! Oh, my darling, are you—where's Kal? We've been so worried about you both!" Her voice cracked as her eyes returned to Ella, desperate for answers.

"He's okay! He was, last I saw him," Ella reassured quickly. But urgency overtook her voice as she gestured to Lord Archer. "Mum, we don't have time! Lord Archer was shot by a Night Elf's arrow. Can you help him?"

Diana's expression changed instantly, shifting from a mother's concern to a Healers focus. She touched a brooch on her jacket, and within seconds, a team of healing personnel arrived. They carefully moved Lord Archer off Ella and onto a stretcher, rushing him into a pure white room. Before following them, Diana paused, looking back at her daughter with tears in her eyes.

"I am so very, very proud of you," she whispered before disappearing into the room.

Ella lay motionless on the cool floor, breathing in the fresh air. After a few moments, she forced herself up, using energy she didn't think she had left, and walked over to the room where they had taken Lord Archer. She was shocked to see through the glass wall—everything was visible. She had never been in a hospital, apart from when Kal had an X-ray on his knee after a school PE injury, and she thought patients were always shielded from view. But here, nothing was hidden.

Lord Archer was lying flat on his back, gasping for air, his body convulsing as he vomited. It looked like he was drowning in his own lungs. A nurse passed Diana a small green bottle, and she carefully rubbed a tiny amount of the liquid onto his lips. Almost immediately, he sank into a deep, pain-free sleep.

Diana and her team carefully removed Lord Archer's armour and shirts. As they worked, Diana prepared various green glass bottles, lining them up on the counter. When she returned to her patient, she slipped on gloves and opened the wound, gently extracting the arrowhead that had lodged deep within his arm.

One of the healers examined the arrowhead under thick glasses, swabbing it and running the sample under a liquid from one of the green bottles. A blue mist rose from the swab, and it was passed back to Diana, who mixed it into a dish filled with other ingredients. The scene reminded Ella of *George's Marvellous Medicine,* as her mother seemingly measured nothing.

With precision, Diana applied the mixture to the wound, and a nurse, wearing heavy-duty gloves, began cleaning the surrounding area with the same liquid. Ella couldn't imagine what was in the mixture, but it was clear it was no ordinary medicine.

Diana glanced over and saw Ella watching. She beckoned her daughter inside and wrapped an arm around her as they stood by Lord Archer.

"Is he going to be okay?" Ella asked, her voice trembling with worry.

Diana smiled, proud of her daughter. She placed a reassuring hand on her shoulder.

"He will be, thanks to you. He wouldn't have lasted much longer with that amount of Hemlock in him. Night Elves are notorious for dipping their arrows in poisonous plants—it's usually Hemlock, Wolfsbane, or Deadly Nightshade. Any of those can cause horrible and deadly side effects if not treated quickly and correctly."

Ella felt like she was seeing the complete version of her mother for the first time, not just the person she *had* to be while living in the human Realm. It all started making sense now—the plant remedies Diana was always preparing, the books on herbalism and ancient traditions.

"Mum, what did you give him?" But before Diana could answer, Fae warriors began Jumping into the healing rooms. Some were being held up by others, while a few looked like they might be dead. Ella's heart leapt into her throat as she rushed out, frantically searching for Kal. *Please don't be hurt, please don't be hurt,* she repeated in her head, and then, just like a miracle, she heard the response she had hoped for.

"You ducked out a bit early there, didn't you?"

Ella turned and lunged toward her brother, who was standing just a few feet away. She threw her arms around him.

"I'm so glad you're okay! Have you seen Orek?" she asked, pulling back and noticing that Kal had also been worried about her sudden disappearance.

"I saw him just before we Jumped, so I'm sure he's here somewhere. Have you seen Mum?" Kal's voice was laced with exhaustion, but the relief of seeing his sister was palpable. Together, they headed back to the room where Lord Archer was being treated.

The door opened, and Diana turned to see both her children, battered and bruised but alive. A wave of relief spread across her face. She gently embraced Kal, pressing her forehead to his and whispering, "I'm so proud of you."

Diana guided Kal to another table in the room and began cleaning his cuts and scrapes. Just as she finished, a flashing red light came from her brooch, and she immediately shifted back into Healer mode.

"I have to go. It's probably going to be busy here for a while. Stay as long as you need, and I'll come find you later," she said, giving them both a kiss before rushing out the door.

Neither of the twins needed to say anything—they both agreed to stay. They wanted to find Orek and keep watch over Lord Archer until he woke up.

As they wandered through the hallways, peering into the treatment rooms that Kal thought resembled space pods, they couldn't find any sign of Orek.

"He has to be here. I saw him right before I Jumped, and there weren't any Night Elves around who could have hit him—at least I don't think there were!"

Then, from a pod further down the hall, they heard a gruff voice grumbling in indignation. They exchanged knowing glances, chuckling to themselves, recognising the voice instantly. As they rounded the corner, they saw two nurses trying to remove Orek's armour to inspect him for injuries. His face turned from annoyance to relief when he saw the twins.

"Ahh, I'm glad you're both well and not bein' TREATED LIKE AN ANIMAL!" Orek shouted, shrugging off the nurses who were just trying to help.

"Where's Archie? Did ya get 'im back okay, Ella?" he asked.

"He's being treated by Mum," Ella replied. "But we're not sure how he is. Mum mentioned Hemlock poisoning."

Orek's face darkened, showing just how dangerous Hemlock could be.

"Take me to 'im. He needs to know what's goin' on."

Without hesitation, the twins led Orek back to the room where his cousin lay resting, eyes still closed. Orek sat down next to his cousin and stayed silent for quite some time.

Kal nudged Ella. "Should we say something?" he whispered.

Ella shook her head. "I think they're talking—in their heads, like we can." Kal took a moment to realise that Orek and Lord Archer were communicating telepathically. After another ten minutes of silence, Orek finally turned to the twins.

"I've got somethin' to show ya. Come 'ere," Orek said, beckoning them over. The twins joined him next to Lord Archer. From under his armour, Orek pulled out the Fire Element's vessel. It was blackened with dust and lacked the glow it once had.

Ella picked it up and examined it closely. Kal, itching to get a better look, waited just long enough not to seem rude before taking it from her hands.

Ella looked hopeful as she asked, "I thought Rhi took the Element?"

"She did. This is just the vessel. The Element can only be contained within somethin' powerful, and there ain't much in any Realm that can do that," Orek explained.

Kal was mesmerised by the intricate design of the vessel. His fingers traced the delicate hide and crystals embedded within the ornate metal carvings. Orek noticed the look in Kal's eyes and knew what he was thinking.

"It's dragon hide if you were wonderin'. It's the only thing that can withstand the heat. Those crystals—you've seen them before too, on Ella and Archie's armour," Orek explained.

Kal's eyes flashed and head whipped around at the mention of dragon hide, this was the first time he'd heard anything about dragons, but he wasn't given the chance to ask questions.

Ella touched the jagged, blood-red crystals embedded in her armour. Suddenly, she felt a surge of power, like she'd been hit hard by something. In front of her stood Artemis, her Bond, and though she couldn't tell where they were, she could feel the strength emanating from Artemis, bringing her a wave of relief.

Kal was about to shake Ella out of her trance, but Orek stopped him.

"Look," Orek whispered, nodding toward his cousin. "They're connecting."

Lord Archer's, eyes still closed, clutched his chest where a crystal lay on a piece of cord, his eyelids flickering like he was in the middle of a dream.

Ella turned instinctively, sensing someone behind her. There, in a strange place she didn't recognise, stood Lord Archer. She had no idea how he was able to see what she was seeing.

I don't understand. How are you here, and where is here? Ella found herself communicating through telepathy without intending to.

We've connected through our Painite crystals and are somehow being shown where Artemis is, Lord Archer replied, his eyes widening at what he saw behind Ella. Hefe Byrne, Rhi's father, stood there alongside Rhi. Ella took a step back, fearful they might be seen.

They won't see us, nor hear our thoughts, but we can listen to theirs, Lord Archer reassured her, stepping forward alongside Ella.

"I'm sorry, Father, I didn't bring the vessel back with me. I won't fail you next time," Rhi said, her voice low and filled with self disappointment.

Ella felt the familiar icy grip around her throat. Part of

her had hoped Rhi was being coerced into all of this, but now she wasn't so sure. Rhi's expression reflected anger, not defiance.

"You did well, considering the circumstances. You brought back the most important part of the Fire Element— its Essence." Hefe Byrne strolled around the room, cold and emotionless.

How could she feel anything from him? Ella thought, confused. *I don't understand how she could be so loyal to someone who never cared for her.*

Lord Archer's voice interrupted her thoughts, solemn and heavy. *Heartbreak can be a powerful fuel for hatred. Don't underestimate Rhiannon. She may have been your best friend once, but that girl is gone now.*

Before Ella could respond, Hefe Byrne motioned his daughter to join him at a table, where a large book lay open. Ella and Lord Archer moved closer, but the pages were blurred, even though Rhi and her father seemed to have no trouble reading them.

"Rhiannon," Hefe continued, "take a small team and search the forests, pools, and waterfalls. We need the Water Element next, and it will likely be with the Merrow or Niskai, though we can't rule out the Tree Nymphs, or even the Kelpies. Do this discreetly, and if you encounter any Fae who aren't aligned with us... you know what to do."

Rhi bowed her head and disappeared from view, followed closely by Artemis' essence.

Ella and Lord Archer opened their eyes at the same moment, finding themselves back in the treatment room with Orek and Kal. Lord Archer winced, clutching his injured arm as he slowly sat up.

Just then, Diana entered the room, Alana trailing behind her.

"Look who I found hunting for a certain young man," Diana said with a teasing smile, her words making Alana blush as her eyes met Kal's, but her expression quickly turned to concern when her gaze fell on her father, Lord Archer.

"Are you okay? What happened?" Alana asked, her voice trembling slightly as she took her father's hand. Worry clouded her eyes as she searched his face, noting his dazed demeanour.

"He was shot with a Hemlock arrow in his sword arm, but he's recovering... right, Mum?" Ella said, her voice tinged with a mixture of hope and apprehension. She glanced at Diana, silently pleading for reassurance that she hadn't given Alana false hope.

"He's doing much better, especially considering how much Hemlock was in his system, anyone smaller would have died within minutes," Diana replied calmly, though her brow furrowed in thought. She pulled out a small piece of white paper and approached her patient. "Let me check something."

Placing the paper on Lord Archer's tongue, Diana watched intently as it changed colour—first from white to light green, then to a deep black. She frowned slightly.

"There's still some poison left," she murmured, almost to herself, "but he's healing remarkably well."

She straightened up and addressed Lord Archer directly.

"You still need rest—Healer's orders. Everyone out for the evening. I'll let you know if there's any change. Now go, get some rest yourselves."

Ella lingered for a moment as everyone began moving toward the door, her gaze fixed on the huge warrior who lay on a bed not made for someone of his size. The weight of the knowledge she now carried about the Byrnes' plan made her hesitate, unsure of what to do next.

Noticing her uncertainty, Lord Archer gave her a reassuring nod and whispered warmly, "We'll talk tomorrow, Ella. But don't speak to anyone else about it before then— not even Kal."

Ella nodded reluctantly, her lips pressed together in silent agreement. Diana moved toward the door, gently guiding everyone out. She kissed Ella and Kal on their heads as they passed. "Goodnight, my darlings," she said softly before shutting the door behind them, leaving Lord Archer to rest in peace.

Outside the treatment rooms, the group stood in heavy silence, each reflecting on the whirlwind of events over the past few days. The weight of their shared experiences hung between them, unspoken but palpable. Finally, Orek broke the quiet.

"I shall return to the mines and speak to our council," he announced, his deep voice steady. "I'll be back tomorrow to see how the big fella's holdin' up."

Alana stepped forward, wrapping her arms around her uncle in a warm hug and planting a kiss on his cheek. "Thanks, Uncle Orek," she said softly.

Orek gave her a small, comforting smile before turning

to leave. His heavy footsteps echoed down the hallway, fading into the distance as he disappeared around the corner.

Ella watched him go and suddenly felt out of place, unsure of what to do with herself now that the chaos had settled into an uneasy quiet. "I think I'm going to head to the house to see if Dad's there," she said finally, her voice hesitant. "Then I'm going straight to bed, and I don't plan on getting up for as long as possible."

Kal smirked, his expression sheepish but clearly relieved that the tension hadn't turned awkward. "Night, sis. If Dad's there, let him know I'm fine and I'll be back later."

Ella gave him a small smile before focusing on her Holed Stone and Jumping out of the hospital.

The familiar sight of what now felt like home brought an unexpected wave of comfort. Ella slumped onto the living room sofa, her body heavy with exhaustion. She began shedding her armour piece by piece, letting each one clatter to the floor. With every piece removed, she felt a small weight lift from her shoulders, bringing her closer to the promise of sleep.

From upstairs, a familiar voice called out, cutting through the quiet.

"Diana, is that you?" Rowan's voice carried down the hall. Moments later, his footsteps descended the staircase, and when he saw Ella, his worn features softened. His tired eyes lit up with relief, and he walked toward her slowly, arms outstretched. Pulling her into a tight embrace, he held her close, as though afraid she might vanish if he let go. Despite everything she had faced recently, nowhere felt as safe as her father's arms. She melted into him, allowing the stress and fear of the past days to drain away.

"We are so proud of you, Ella," Rowan said, his voice thick with emotion. He held her just a little tighter, as though his words alone couldn't fully convey how he felt.

"It's so good to be home, Dad," Ella replied, her voice warm but heavy with weariness. A small smile crept onto her face as she added, "Kal says he'll be home later. He's out with Alana." She raised her eyebrows playfully, teasing him.

Rowan pulled back slightly, studying her face with a chuckle. "Well, I suppose I'll be hearing more about that later," he said, amusement flickering in his tired eyes. "Why don't you head upstairs and get some sleep? You've earned it."

Ella nodded, not needing to be told twice. She shuffled toward the stairs, her limbs aching with fatigue. As she reached the middle of the staircase, she paused and turned back, her voice soft but heartfelt. "Night, Dad. Love you."

"Night, Ella. Rest well," Rowan replied, his voice gentle but brimming with warmth. He couldn't stop smiling as he watched her retreat up the stairs, the relief radiating from him as if her return had brought light back into the house.

Ella climbed the rest of the way to her room, her steps slow but steady. As she entered, the strange familiarity of her surroundings wrapped around her like a warm blanket. For the first time in days, she allowed herself to feel the safety of home, however fleeting it might be. With a deep sigh, she sank onto her bed, letting exhaustion finally take her.

CHAPTER TWENTY-ONE

Kal and Alana Jumped back to the training dome. They changed quickly into their regular clothes, the weight of battle replaced by a fleeting moment of normalcy. As Kal adjusted the sleeves of his top, Alana took his hand with a relaxed smile.

"Come," she said, her voice soft but excited. "Let me show you something. Follow my Jump."

Kal barely had time to process her words before she disappeared. He focused on her, willing himself to follow. Moments later, he opened his eyes to find her standing just inches away, her face lit with anticipation.

Not wanting to seem relieved that he'd managed to follow her successfully, Kal straightened and turned to take in his surroundings. His breath caught in his throat as the sight before him unfolded. A soft cough escaped him, the sound echoing through a vast, breathtaking cave.

"This is my favourite place within our Realm," Alana said, her voice beautifully calm as she gazed out over a tranquil, glistening pool. "I bring books down here from the library and read all day sometimes."

Kal's eyes followed hers to the pool, which was about ten feet wide and perfectly round. Its symmetry seemed impossibly precise, as if shaped by the hands of a master craftsman, yet its organic beauty was unmistakably natural. Rich, dark moss surrounded the pool, forming lush cushions that seemed tailor-made for sitting. The water shimmered in shades of crystal-clear green, reflecting the jagged rocks above. The cavern stretched upward toward a misty grey sky visible through an opening at the top of the rocky walls.

"The Seer comes here to do her scrying when it's a Blood Moon," Alana explained, her voice quiet, as if not to disturb the peace. "No one is allowed near this place on those nights, but I like to come the day after. The smell of burnt sage that she uses is so comforting."

She crouched down and picked up a half-burnt bundle of sage tied with a delicate green stem. Bringing it to her nose, she inhaled deeply, a smile spreading across her face. The gesture seemed almost sacred, as though she were momentarily connected to something much older and wiser.

"Here," she said, offering the sage to Kal. "Go on, have a smell."

Kal hesitated for a second looking at the sage, unsure how to respond to the almost ritualistic moment. As he took the bundle from her and brought it to his nose, he caught the earthy, smoky aroma. He glances at Alana, a big smile spreading across his face. Alana caught the smile and immediately frowned in mock annoyance

Kal chuckled and stepped closer to Alana. With a gentle motion, he reached out, wiping away a smudge of black charcoal from her nose left behind by the sage.

Alana spat out a laugh, her cheeks reddening as she quickly covered her nose in embarrassment. "It'll come off," Kal said with a teasing smile. "Just a splash of water, and you'd never know it was there."

He walked toward the pool, bending down to scoop up some water. But before his hand could touch the shimmering surface, Alana's scream pierced the air, echoing through the cavern.

"KAL, NO!"

He froze, turning to see the alarm etched across her face. "What is it? What's wrong?"

Alana's hands trembled slightly as she stepped closer. "I should have told you earlier," she said, her voice unsteady. "This water is sacred. It has immense healing properties, but only when harvested correctly. There are many names for it in human folklore, but 'The Elixir of Life' is the most common. If you drink from it or even touch it without performing the proper ritual, it can kill you—or worse."

Kal felt a shiver run down his spine as her words sank, and not wanting to know what '…or worse' could mean. He glanced back at the pool, its serene beauty now tinged with an eerie, untouchable danger. "Thank you," he said softly, his voice sincere.

Alana's expression softened as she gave a small nod. "It's what friends are for," she replied. Her words were light, but the depth of her gaze told him just how relieved she was.

Kal smiled back, the tension between them easing. They

sat quietly for a moment, the silence no longer heavy, as the soft glow of the pool reflected the dim light filtering in from the misty sky above.

Kal leaned back against the moss-covered rocks, a content smile tugging at his lips. He glanced at Alana and said playfully, "I thought your nose looks kind of cute with the smudge on it anyway."

Alana rolled her emerald green eyes, though a grin spread across her face. "Charming as always, Kal," she said, nudging him lightly with her elbow.

Kal let out a small laugh and shifted to sit more comfortably, feeling a sense of peace he hadn't experienced in what felt like forever. Alana gazed up at the jagged opening above the rocks, her thoughts seemingly distant, before turning back to him.

"You did really well with the Night Elves," she said, her tone warm and genuine. "It was like you'd been fighting for years. How do you feel about it... everything that happened?"

Kal grew quiet, his gaze fixed on the shimmering pool as he searched for the right words. After a moment, he finally spoke. "This might sound strange, but it felt... right. Natural, almost. Like I was supposed to be there, doing what I did."

Alana laughed softly, shaking her head. "Well, you certainly are a natural. And so is Ella. You two are stronger than you realise." She paused, her expression growing more thoughtful. "Ella's going to really need you, you know. It must've been so hard for her, seeing her best friend like that —and losing Artemis on top of it."

Kal's chest tightened at the mention of Ella. "Yeah," he said quietly. "I know. She's putting on a brave face, but I can tell it's tearing her apart. Rhi, Artemis... it's a lot."

Alana reached out, placing a reassuring hand on his arm. "She's lucky to have you, Kal."

Kal's expression darkened as his thoughts shifted to his sister. He felt a heavy weight settle over his heart. "Rhi was part of our family for years, and then she just dropped Ella like she was nothing. I don't know if I could ever forgive her for that, no matter what the reasons were."

Alana stayed quiet, carefully considering Kal's words. She didn't want to push too hard. "I understand why Rhi's parents wouldn't want her to be close to the enemy's daughter," Alana said thoughtfully, "but if they were such close friends, you'd think they would've at least talked about it. How can Rhi be so angry at Ella just for being born? It doesn't make sense."

Kal wanted to change the subject. Thinking about everything that had happened only dragged his mood further down, and he desperately needed a distraction.

"So," Kal began, his tone shifting to something slightly cheeky, "Lord Archer's your dad, huh? Is that why Barrett thinks so highly of you?" He smirked, watching Alana for her reaction. Truth be told, he hadn't guessed they were related at first and only knew because she had called him 'Dad' a few times.

Alana smiled, understanding the dig but choosing to take it in her stride. "He is, yes," she said, her tone light. "I didn't ever live in the World Above. I was born down here and started training to be a warrior when I was ten."

Kal nodded, the pieces falling into place. It made sense now, how she was so far ahead in her training compared to everyone else their age. "Why didn't you live Above?" he asked, his voice gentle. He didn't want to pry if it was something she didn't want to talk about.

Alana looked up, her gaze drifting to the darkening sky above them, the faint light of the stars just beginning to shimmer. "Dad is half dwarf," she explained. "And dwarves live most of their lives in the mines, so he didn't really have a choice. Not that he ever minded, I think. He became one of the most feared warriors to ever live, and I guess growing up down here had a lot to do with that."

Kal raised an eyebrow, intrigued. "Do you ever wish you'd lived Above? You know, had a life without the constant worry of war and training to kill?"

Alana was quiet for a moment, her eyes still on the sky. "Sometimes," she admitted, her voice soft but steady. "When I've been Above and seen the sun rise and set... that's pretty magical. There's a beauty up there that's hard to describe, and I can see why Faeries choose to live Above before their child turns sixteen. But my heart has always been here, in this realm."

Her words carried a quiet certainty, her face calm and at peace. There wasn't a hint of regret in her expression, and that struck Kal more deeply than he expected. He wondered, briefly, what sort of teenagers they might have been if they'd never experienced life as humans. What would it have been like to grow up knowing who they were from the start? Would they be as strong and determined as Alana seemed, or would they have taken their lives for granted, never knowing the dangers lurking beneath?

"You seem so... sure about it," Kal said finally, his voice filled with a mix of admiration and curiosity. "It doesn't bother you at all?"

Alana shrugged lightly, glancing at him with a small smile. "What's the point in wishing for something you can't change? I've made my peace with it. The World Below is my home, and the life I've had here—it's shaped me into who I am. I wouldn't trade that."

Kal couldn't help but admire her perspective. It wasn't that she ignored the hardships or pretended they didn't exist—she simply accepted them, embraced them even. Compared to his own constant anxiety and lingering doubts about his place in this strange new world, Alana's unwavering certainty was like a steady flame in the darkness.

"Fair enough," Kal said with a grin, though he couldn't resist adding, "But you've got to admit, the sunsets Above are hard to beat."

Alana laughed softly, the sound warm and genuine. "They are," she agreed. "But so is the way the crystals down here catch the light, or the way the air feels alive with magic. There's beauty in both worlds, Kal. You just have to know where to look."

Kal was about to respond to Alana when a sharp, burning sensation shot through his head. It wasn't just a headache—it felt like his mind was being seared. He pressed his hands over his eyes, trying to dull the pain. He didn't want to admit something was wrong, and he definitely didn't want to leave. But then his thoughts were drawn urgently to Ella, and a deep sense of worry settled over him like a heavy weight.

"Alana, I'm really sorry," Kal said, his voice tight with concern. "But I just have this feeling that Ella might need me. Could we maybe continue this another time?"

Alana nodded, her expression softening with understanding. "Of course. Go to Ella. I'll hold you to coming back here, though."

Kal gave her a quick, grateful nod and reached for his Holed Stone. *This had better be good, El,* he thought as he focused on his sister and Jumped.

He landed in the living room and immediately called out, "Ella, Ella!" A shout from upstairs cut through the silence—it was his dad.

"Kal, is that you? Quick, get up here!"

Kal raced up the stairs, taking them three at a time. He burst into Ella's room, his chest heaving, to find his dad holding his sister down on the bed. Ella was thrashing and twisting, her eyes tightly shut, as though trapped in a nightmare.

"Dad! What are you doing? What's going on?" Kal's voice was sharp, laced with panic.

Rowan, clearly distressed, kept his grip firm. "I heard her shouting for you, so I came up and found her like this. She won't wake up."

Kal knelt beside his sister, placing a hand on her arm. "Dad, go get Mum—I'll stay here."

Rowan hesitated, his worry etched deeply into his face, but then he nodded and Jumped out of the room. Left alone with his sister, Kal focused on her, speaking softly through their mental bond. *Ella, I'm here. What's happening? Why can't you wake up?*

For a moment, there was nothing but the sound of Ella's shallow breathing and the frantic pounding of his own heart. Then, faintly, he heard it—a desperate voice in his mind. The words were unclear, fragmented, but the urgency behind them sent a chill down his spine.

Kal instinctively leaned in closer, as if proximity might help him understand. His pulse quickened, his body taut with tension. Just then, their parents Jumped back into the room. Diana rushed to Ella's side, her Healer's instincts taking over as she checked her pupils and felt her temperature.

Kal grasped Ella's hand, hoping his touch might anchor her somehow, might pull her back from wherever she was trapped. Suddenly, a force unlike anything he'd ever felt yanked him inward, dragging him into a vortex of red fire and violent winds.

The searing heat whipped painfully against his skin, and the ground seemed to vanish beneath him. Kal spun wildly, searching for Ella in the chaos. Finally, he saw her—standing perfectly still in the eye of the storm, untouched by the flames swirling around her.

"Ella!" Kal called, reaching out to her. But she was just out of his grasp, her form wavering like a mirage.

Before he could move closer, something struck him from behind with the force of a sledgehammer. The impact sent him hurtling into darkness, the world around him going silent and still. For a moment, he thought he might be dead. But slowly, consciousness returned.

When he blinked his eyes open, he found Ella kneeling beside him, her face filled with relief.

"What just hit me?" Kal gasped, still disoriented.

His answer came not in words but in a series of enthusiastic, slobbery licks. Blinking in confusion, Kal realised it was Artemis. The sight of the massive beast brought a strained laugh from his chest, the sound shaky but genuine.

"Well, if that's how you show love, I'm in for some trouble!" Kal said, chuckling as he reached out to rub Artemis's enormous face. He glanced at Ella, the shadow of a smile breaking through her otherwise weary expression.

"Sorry, Kal, Art was the only way I could get you through the storm and in here with me. I've been trapped in here."

Kal stood, brushing himself off as he took in their surroundings. They were in the centre of an enormous firestorm, the swirling flames forming a barrier around them. Yet, there was an almost eerie calm where they stood.

"Where are we?" he asked, his voice low with awe and confusion.

"I don't know for sure but I think we could be inside the Fire Element," Ella replied, uncertainty flickering in her tone. "Art came to me in what felt like a dream, but it wasn't, I think she's pulling the Fire Element back to us through our Bond."

Kal stared at her, the weight of her words settling heavily in his chest. Before he could respond, the calm they were standing in began to shrink, the fiery winds closing in around them with alarming speed. The flames roared louder, their searing heat growing more intense with every passing moment.

Instinctively, Kal and Ella reached for each other's hands, their fingers locking tightly as they braced themselves. Artemis shifted, placing herself firmly between them and the encroaching fire. Her fiery eyes glowed brighter, fierce and unyielding as she let out a powerful cry, the sound reverberating through the storm like a challenge to the flames themselves.

The heat reached a blistering peak, the flames licking at their skin with an intensity that felt unbearable. For a moment, Kal was certain they would be consumed entirely, their bodies reduced to ash. But then, just as the firestorm seemed ready to engulf them, a massive pulse of red electricity erupted outward.

The surge of energy jolted through them, searing and electrifying all at once. It felt as though fire and lightning had fused into one, coursing through their bodies in a raw, primal force. Kal clenched his teeth against the overwhelming power, his vision blurring as the world around him faded into darkness.

When Kal's eyes snapped open again, he was lying on Ella's bed, the cool air of her room a stark contrast to the suffocating heat of the firestorm. His chest heaved as he gulped in air, his body drenched in sweat. His clothes clung to him uncomfortably, and his limbs felt heavy, as though he'd run a marathon.

Ella was beside him, equally drenched and struggling to catch her breath. Her wide eyes stared at the ceiling for a moment before she turned to look at him. Above them, their parents' worried faces hovered, their expressions a mixture of fear and immense relief.

"We're okay, Mum," Kal managed to say, his voice weak but laced with reassurance. He wasn't entirely sure he believed his own words, but for now, they were alive—and together.

Diana let out a shaky breath, her hand resting gently on Ella's forehead. "What happened?" she asked, her voice soft but edged with urgency.

Kal glanced at Ella, who met his gaze. For a moment, neither of them spoke, the memory of the firestorm and the raw energy still fresh in their minds. Finally, Ella found her voice.

"I think we were inside the Fire Element," she said quietly. "But it was also inside us, I don't know how to explain it, all I know is that Artemis brought it back somehow."

Rowan stepped closer, his brow furrowed with concern. " It sounds like you're saying you Bonded with the Fire Element, but how is this even possible?"

Ella shrugged but found herself nodding slowly, realising she was agreeing with her dad, "I think so. But it wasn't just me. Kal and I... we were both there. It's like it knew we needed each other to survive."

Kal swallowed hard, the weight of her words sinking in. Whatever had happened in that firestorm, it had changed something within them. He could feel it—a deep, pulsing energy that hadn't been there before. It wasn't just the Fire Element they'd encountered. It was something bigger, something that tied them together in ways he was only beginning to understand.

For now, though, he pushed the thoughts aside. "We're

okay," he repeated, his voice steadier this time. "That's what matters."

Diana and Rowan exchanged a glance, their worry not entirely dispelled but tempered by the sight of their children alive and safe. Diana leaned forward, brushing a damp strand of hair from Ella's face. "You need to rest," she said gently. "Both of you. Get changed into some dry clothes. We'll talk more in the morning."

Kal and Ella nodded, their exhaustion too great to argue. As their parents left the room, Kal turned to his sister. "You did good, El," he said softly. "We did good."

Ella smiled faintly, her eyelids growing heavy. "Yeah," she murmured, her voice barely audible. "We did."

And as sleep claimed them both, the faint hum of the Fire Element's energy seemed to linger in the room, a quiet reminder of the storm they had faced—and survived—together.

A soft knock at Ella's door stirred them both from their dreamless sleep.

"Ella, Kal, are you awake?" Diana's voice called softly through the door before it gently creaked open. Seeing them both stirring, she entered with a warm smile. "I've made a pot of tea downstairs. It'll give you some energy and freshen you up. Then I suggest you both take a shower because this room..." She wrinkled her nose playfully. "...Well, it smells. I'm Jumping to work soon, so if you want to come by and check on Lord Archer, I'll be there."

Kal exchanged a glance with Ella and rolled his eyes, earning a suppressed laugh from his sister. Diana left the door wide open as she headed downstairs, leaving the twins alone.

Kal stood up, stretching his arms overhead with an exaggerated groan. "I'll see you downstairs after a shower. By the way, you *really* do smell bad," he teased, dashing out before Ella could retaliate with a pillow.

After freshening up, they met downstairs for a pot of ginseng tea and breakfast. Kal made a point of teasing Ella about how long she took in the shower, which she brushed off with a sarcastic remark. Their energy renewed, they prepared to visit Lord Archer and discuss the events of the night before.

The twins Jumped to their mother's workplace and approached Lord Archer's room. Ella suddenly hesitated, her hand tightening on Kal's arm just as he reached for the door.

"Wait... what if he's not okay?" she whispered, her voice trembling with doubt. Her feet felt rooted to the floor.

Kal turned to her, his expression reassuring. "El, don't overthink it. Mum would've let us know if something was wrong. Come on, it'll be fine." Without giving her a chance to retreat further, Kal pushed open the door and stepped inside.

Inside, the soothing murmur of conversation greeted them, along with a familiar voice.

"Kalan, it's good to see you. Is your sister not here?" Lord Archer's voice carried warmth and concern. He peered around Kal, his brow furrowing until a nurse bustled in and practically nudged Ella into the room.

"Lord Archer, you're not supposed to be moving!" the

nurse scolded, her tone stern as she adjusted his bandages. "How's the charcoal poultice meant to work if you won't keep still?"

Lord Archer muttered an apology, clearly more amused than chastised, and waited until the nurse left the room. He turned his attention back to the twins, his expression softening as he addressed Ella. "There you are. I didn't get a chance to thank you both yesterday for getting me back safely. You fought bravely—both of you."

Ella and Kal exchanged an uneasy look, unsure of how to start. Kal opened his mouth to speak but fumbled over his words, his usual confidence faltering. Lord Archer immediately picked up on their hesitation.

"Is something troubling you?" he asked, his tone calm but edged with curiosity.

Ella took a deep breath and stepped forward. Once she began, the entire story spilled out—about the dream that wasn't a dream, Kal joining her in the vortex, Artemis's intervention, and their belief that the Fire Element's essence had somehow split between them.

Lord Archer's eyes widened as the weight of their revelation settled in. He gestured for Kal to close the door, then motioned for them to sit beside his bed.

"Who else have you told?" Lord Archer asked, his voice laced with urgency and concern.

"No one," Kal replied quickly. "Not even our parents. We wanted to speak to you first. What do we do now?"

Lord Archer leaned back slightly, his expression turning serious. He paused, as if weighing his words carefully. "This must remain between the three of us—for now. We cannot be certain who is truly on our side. It's crucial that this information stays secret, especially from Alana and Orek. Do you understand?"

Ella frowned, her unease clear. "But Lord Archer, they're your family. How can you not trust them? Is there something you're not telling us?"

His face became unreadable, his reply curt. "Nothing."

The blunt response left a heavy silence hanging in the room. Kal glanced at Ella, his thoughts brushing against hers through their Bond. *El, this is where everything counts. We have to stay strong and use who we are to fight for our people—both Fae and human.*

Ella closed her eyes, taking a moment to absorb his words. She drew a steadying breath, feeling a flicker of resolve rise within her. When she opened her eyes again, Kal noticed the faint red shimmer glowing within them—a subtle but undeniable sign of the Fire Element's lingering power.

The twins shared a quiet, determined understanding. Whatever lay ahead, their journey was far from over, and the weight of their new reality pressed heavily on their shoulders. But together, they knew they could face what was to come.

ACKNOWLEDGMENTS

Firstly, I want to acknowledge the two incredible humans who inspired me to write this book—my own Twins of Fire, Pixie and Bertie. I'm so incredibly proud to be your mum.

For a girl who once felt too anxious to write a book, my husband Paul has been my unwavering champion, giving me the space and support to bring my story to life. I couldn't have done it without you.

To my late dad, who always believed there was nothing we couldn't achieve—thank you for instilling that belief in me. And to my mum, my rock, thank you for keeping me going with your love and zero judgment. Your support has meant everything.

To my brother Angus, who unknowingly helped inspire certain character traits in this book, I love you—even if you have "s*$t for brains!" (family joke!). To Emma and my niece and nephew thank you for the constant family love.

A special thank you to my beautiful cousin Tatiana for helping me edit and for giving me the honest feedback I so desperately needed.

And to my very special friends—Pixie, Min, Emily, Wadsworth, and Hilin—you've each been a source of strength and positivity in my life, and I'm forever grateful for your presence.

ABOUT THE AUTHOR

Katie is an emerging author, and *Twins of Fire* marks her debut novel. Growing up amidst the picturesque landscapes of Devon, in southwest England, Katie developed a deep love for nature and a lifelong fascination with the mystical. She often felt as if she were just a step away from glimpsing into the realm of the Fae. Her passion for Celtic mythology was ignited by stories of her Scottish grandfather, who, although he passed before her birth, became a cherished symbol of her connection to ancient tales.

Katie's love for English and Drama during her school years hinted at her creative potential. However, dyslexia initially made the path to storytelling and theatre feel challenging. Years later, she embraced the unique perspective her dyslexia provided, transforming it into a strength. By channeling her creativity into writing, Katie celebrates the power of her imagination in this captivating first venture into fiction.

instagram.com/katiebutterworthbooks
tiktok.com/@kbutterworthbooks

Printed in Dunstable, United Kingdom

68816162R00180